MIND READER

Victoria Cole

Published by Silhouette Books New York

America's Publisher of Contemporary Romance

SILHOUETTE BOOKS
300 East 42nd St., New York, N.Y. 10017

MIND READER

ISBN: 0-373-07510-3

First Silhouette Books printing July 1993

Printed in the U.S.A.

Chapter 1

It was about to happen again.

She knew it. Sensed it. Smelled it as distinctly as she smelled the freshly brewed coffee in her kitchen.

And there was nothing she could do to stop it.

The images forming in her mind were as vivid and real as the chips in the porcelain tabletop in front of her. As real as the steam rising from her coffee cup. And because they were real, dread and cold fear clawed at her stomach. She *knew* what would come next, and yet she was powerless to stop it.

Rain pelted against the window of her apartment. Caron stared at the flattened drops beading on the pane, wishing she could force the image away.

Then it was too late for wishing. The image was there. The image of a little girl, eight, maybe nine, with shoulder-length brown hair and wide green eyes that were almost black with fear—more fear than any human being should ever know.

Caron swallowed hard. Where was the girl now? The lighting was dim, everything was blurry. Focusing all her energy and concentration on the girl and her surroundings, Caron tried to sharpen the image. But a sense of betrayal grew strong, then stronger and stronger, until Caron couldn't get past it to pick up on anything else. Acid churned in her stomach. She began to shake, then to shudder. It was happening again—just as it had with Sarah!

Caron clenched her muscles, fighting the resentment she felt at her life once more turning topsy-turvy, spinning out of control—and fighting the guilt that came with the resentment. From the time she was seven, she had considered the images confusing, a curse, because even then she hadn't seen ordinary people. She had seen victims.

And Sarah James's case had proven Caron right; she was cursed. That case, a year ago, was the last she'd helped Sandy with, and after it, everything had changed. After nineteen years, the images suddenly had stopped.

Now they were back.

Why did she have to go through this again? *Why?*

The need to hear someone's voice—anyone's voice—hit her hard. Caron sent the phone a desperate look. She could call Dr. Zilinger, her analyst, or her aunt Grace—anyone but her mother. Her mother never had understood why Caron didn't just "ignore" the images, and all the explanations in the world hadn't convinced her mother that Caron could no more ignore them than her mother could have ignored the pain of childbirth.

A sense of urgency seeped through Caron's chest. Sandy. She had to talk to Sandy. She grabbed the phone and dialed.

It seemed to ring forever, but he finally answered, "Yeah, Sanders here," he said.

His familiar gruff voice helped ease the lump from her throat, but the tightness in her chest remained. "Sandy." Why, after all this time, was talking to him so difficult? "I'm on my way to your office. We have to talk."

"Caron?" He sounded surprised.

She supposed he *was* surprised. It had been nearly a year since her last call. "Yes, it's me."

"What's wrong?"

His wary tone held fear, a fear she'd felt before and had hoped she'd never feel again. But now she was. The receiver in her hand grew sweat-slick. The words choked her.

"It's happening all over again." Her voice cracked. She slumped against the counter and held on.

"I'll come to you. Where are you?"

"No." She was scared stiff, but she couldn't lean on him, or on anyone other than herself. If nothing else, she'd learned that. Her temples were pounding. Rubbing circles on the left one, she forced her eyes open. "No, I'll come to you."

She slid the receiver back onto the hook, her hand shaking. She should have been stronger and not deluded herself into believing that the images would never come back. But she hadn't. Now she would have to fight this battle the same way she'd fought all the others—alone.

Caron grabbed her purse and headed for the door.

Outside, she dipped her head against the rain and ran, dodging murky puddles and dark patches of soft, squishy mud. Water gushed along the curb to the drain and splashed down with a hollow *thunk* somewhere beneath the street. She took a giant step over the water and climbed into her Chevy. Then while the engine warmed, she tissued the raindrops from her face.

The images were back. When they'd stopped, she'd felt naked without them. The way a man must feel when he discovered he was going bald—at the mercy of his body, helpless.

She tossed the soaked tissue onto the floor mat. Seeing the images *was* like that. She was helpless to stop them. No matter how much she wanted just to teach her students, just to be normal, she was reduced to suffering the empathy pains and the emotional upheaval of the victims, and to wondering, *Why me?*

A crash of thunder shook the car. A bare-limbed oak tree to her right became the image of a dark-haired man with a stubbly chin and wicked green eyes. He belched, and the smell of beer nearly gagged Caron. Lightning flashed, a little sizzle rent the air, and then, as quickly as it had come, the image disappeared. Shaking, Caron rolled down the window an inch. Rain and fresh air rushed into the car on a chilly gust. The wind whistled and whipped at the craggy oaks lining the scrap of lawn in front of the apartments.

The limbs looked like sneering gargoyles, twisted, grotesque and menacing.

"God help me," Caron whispered. "I'm suffering a landslide."

A horn sounded in a long, steady blast from in front of the corner store across the street. Her stomach muscles clenched. Seeking solace in common, ordinary things, she gripped the steering wheel hard and watched the wipers sweep the windshield, click at the base, then sweep back again. The store's illuminated yellow sign flickered as the power fluctuated. It read "2 Litre Cokes $1.29." A car sped past, kicking up a spray of water, and a kid hung out the window yelling at a second guy who was getting into his car. "Hey, Bobby, come on, man!"

She didn't know either boy, but at that moment she knew their thoughts and feelings. Knew them physically. Bobby was late for the basketball game. David, the one hanging out the window, was ticked that he was missing the tip-off.

There was no solace.

The little girl's image snapped back into focus. Caron felt the child's fear, the grisly sense of betrayal, and cringed. She couldn't ignore the images. Not now. Not ever. She had to accept the inevitable. The images had come again, and she was doomed to suffer them.

Every self-preserving instinct in her body screamed for her to run. Yet she couldn't. Whoever she was, this child was hurt and confused and afraid, and she was *not* going to face whatever happened alone.

Caron straightened, slammed the gearshift into Drive, and pulled out into traffic, hoping her bravado would outlast the time it took her to drive to police headquarters.

"Anytime today would be just fine, ma'am."

Caron jerked and looked back. A drop-dead-gorgeous guy in a flashy black Porsche waved an impatient hand for her to vacate the parking slot.

"I'm coming, not going," Caron said, sliding the man a withering look and easing the Chevy alongside the curb. Not even his looks could excuse his sarcasm.

The man nodded, then drove on.

"Charming," she muttered, tugging her keys from the ignition. She snatched up her purse, then went inside.

Detective Hershel Sanders was in his same dismal office. Surrounded by gray metal cabinets and awful green walls, and so cramped he couldn't turn around without bumping his little paunch, Sandy sat buried behind the mountain of files on his desk, an unlit cigar stub clamped between his teeth.

According to Dr. Zilinger, Sandy hadn't lit up since Jim Garrison dragged New Orleans into national focus, claiming Kennedy's assassination was a political conspiracy. The district attorney had lost his job, and because Sandy had agreed with him, he'd been demoted and left to swelter in this hole ever since, punching the clock and waiting for retirement.

Caron plastered a smile to her lips, folded her arms across her chest and leaned against the doorframe. "Still hiding behind the clutter, Detective?"

Sandy looked up. His gaze, seen through his black-framed, half-moon glasses, hadn't yet focused. A shock of blond hair sprung out from his head. He'd been forking his fingers through it again. He should let it grow and ditch the glasses and the stubby cigar. It'd take ten years off of him.

For a second, his jaw hung loose. Then he whipped off his glasses and slapped his palm down on his desk blotter. "Where've you been, kid?"

To the fiftyish Sandy, the twenty-six-year-old Caron would always be the seven-year-old she'd been when they first worked together. "Oh, nowhere special," she said.

She knew she was being evasive, but she didn't want to share her "normal" life with him. She wanted to hoard every moment of that time to herself. A normal life was all she'd ever wanted, and she'd had a taste of it. Now that the images were back, her memories of normalcy were even more precious, and more private.

She walked in—and saw that he wasn't alone. A man pushing thirty sat scrunched up in a chair, his shoulders wedged between two file cabinets. *Big, brawny, beautiful*—all those words came to mind. His hands were fisted inside the pockets of his black leather bomber jacket. And the look on his face made his feelings clear. He didn't like her.

That set her back on her heels. When the surprise settled, she nodded in his direction. "Sorry I interrupted. I thought Sandy was alone." Then she recognized him. He was the one who'd been driving the flashy Porsche downstairs. Remembering his sarcasm, she frowned, not much liking him, either. "I don't believe we've met."

He let his gaze slide down her length and linger on her breasts before returning to her face. "I'm a friend of Sandy's," he said, in a tone that told her he wasn't impressed with what he saw. "A private investigator."

"I see." She flushed heatedly. Whether because of the intimacy in that look, or in anger because he'd so brazenly perused her, she wasn't sure. Probably a bit of both. If they'd been alone, she'd have found out. But they weren't. Sandy was watching—avidly. She forced herself to be civil and extended her hand. "I'm Caron Chalmers."

He seemed reluctant, but clasped it. His hand swallowed hers; it was as huge as the rest of him.

"Yes, I know." His grasp was firm, strong, and he didn't flinch, slump or look away. "Parker Simms."

The man was gorgeous, one any woman could appreciate, but the emotions seeping from him were alien to her. No one ever had looked at her with such raw animosity. But why? A parking slot didn't warrant this kind of emotion, not even for a guy driving a Porsche.

They hadn't met before; she was certain of that. A woman wouldn't forget meeting a man who looked like him—and she'd *never* forget being looked at in the way he was looking at her. Feeling crowded, uncomfortable, she stepped back.

Sandy cleared his throat. "I thought Parker should be involved in this."

She darted a look at Sandy. He refused to meet her gaze. Her insides started rumbling, but she forced herself to calm down. "You told him about me." She tried not to let it, but resentment and accusation edged into her voice.

"I had to, Caron." Sandy's eyes held an apology. "For both our sakes."

Her purse strap slipped off her shoulder. She shoved it back. Why did every man in her life have to betray her? Was there an invisible bull's-eye drawn between her shoulder blades, a sign that read Men, Stab Here?

"I'm worried," Sandy said with a lift of his hand.

He *was* worried; she could see it in his expression. But she wasn't sure whether his concern appeased her or not. Her phoning earlier had cued Sandy that she'd imaged a victim. His calling in his detective friend could mean he doubted that there was a case. It could also mean that he thought she needed a keeper. And a keeper she would not tolerate. "I work alone."

"So do I." Parker's voice was as cold as his chilly look.

She didn't know what to make of his remark. "If you feel that way, then why are you here?"

Before he could reply, the phone rang. Sandy didn't answer it. His faded blue eyes flickered an uncertainty that the smile he'd carved around the cigar couldn't hide. "I asked Parker. I thought he could listen in and maybe help."

Sandy was still ducking his phone calls—and he was darned nervous, busying himself ruffling through an inch-thick stack of pink phone messages on his desk. He'd known that she wouldn't like Parker Simms being here, and he hadn't been at all sure how civil she'd be about it. Somehow that doubt made his having violated her trust easier to take. Still, she was feeling darned bitter.

Explaining her gift in the past had netted two effects. One was her being used; the other, her being ridiculed. She didn't care for an encore to either.

Working alone was easiest, best. Yet after what happened to Sarah, could Caron afford to turn down reliable help?

Emotionally torn, she nodded toward the mystery man.

Parker Simms nodded back, but his expression didn't soften. What was with him? Her having interrupted his meeting with Sandy couldn't raise this much hostility, any more than the parking slot could, especially considering that Sandy had brought Simms here to hear what she had to say. So what had she done to irk him?

She focused, trying to pick up on his emotions. Though they were strong and turbulent, she couldn't peg them—or the source of his animosity.

That surprised her. She cocked her head. But then, she wasn't able to read everyone. With Sandy, the minute he looked into her eyes, it was as if some magic shield slid into place and hid his thoughts. She didn't probe. It'd taken years of working with him, but she'd come to trust him. With Parker Simms, it was more complex than that, though she couldn't have said exactly how or why... not yet.

Sandy stuffed the cigar into an overflowing ashtray he kept on his desk for appearances, then stood, curled a beefy arm around her shoulder, and squeezed reassuringly. "Dr. Zilinger didn't tell me you were back in town."

"I haven't called her yet." Caron hugged him back, feeling self-conscious. Parker Simms had the most intense gaze she'd ever seen. And the most sinfully gorgeous gray eyes. Long, thick lashes and black-winged brows.

"Ah, then I was wrong." Looking relieved, Sandy sat down again, retrieved the cigar and lazily sprawled back. The chair springs creaked. "This is a social call."

She wished Simms weren't here, wished she could talk freely to Sandy and openly explain the situation. Outsiders just didn't understand. For the most part, she supposed, her gift frightened them—though she had a hard time imagining Parker Simms being afraid of anything. The man seemed more likely to inspire fear than to suffer from it.

"I wish this was a social call, Sandy. Until three days ago, it would have been." She let him see the truth in her eyes. "But not anymore."

"What happened?" He rocked forward, picked up a pen and held it poised over his blotter.

She looked at the scrawls in the margin, unable to watch him during the telling, or at Simms during the objecting. "Can we speak privately?"

Simms didn't move. She hadn't figured he would.

Sandy rubbed his jaw. "Parker's here for a purpose, Caron. I haven't forgotten what happened last time. He can help... if you'll let him."

He couldn't help. For some reason, the man strongly disapproved of her, and he made no bones about letting her know it. His body language was as expressive as a chalked blackboard. "I work alone," she reminded Sandy.

"I'm staying, Ms. Chalmers." Parker glanced at his watch. "Accept it, and let's get on with this."

"Ease up, Parker." Sandy frowned, then motioned to a chair and softened his voice. "Come on, Caron. Talk to me."

Caron stayed where she was. She hadn't asked for Parker Simms's help. His hostility, whatever the reason for it, wasn't her problem, and she slid him a hard glare to let him know it.

He didn't so much as blink. Disappointed, she focused on Sandy. "Three days ago, the sensations started coming back."

"Sensations?" This from Simms, complete with a frown in his voice.

"The feeling of being on the brink," she explained. "Of something big about to happen."

"What?" Curiosity replaced the frown.

"I didn't know, I just had the feeling." She forced herself to be patient, looked up at him, and immediately wished she hadn't. His grimace could stunt growth.

"But you found out," Sandy said.

She nodded, then leaned back against the wall, lifted her chin and stared at a water spot on the ceiling. "That afternoon. I was checking out at the grocery store. I handed the cashier a fistful of coupons. 'Customers and their damn coupons,' she said."

"I don't get it." Sandy shrugged. "That's rude, but not odd."

Caron slumped, dreading Parker's reaction to this. She deliberately refused to look at him so that she wouldn't see it. "The woman hadn't said a word."

Understanding dawned in Sandy's eyes. "Are you sure?"

"I'm sure." Caron rubbed her temple. "She was cracking her gum, and I was looking at her lips. They hadn't moved."

"You heard her thoughts," he said softly, sliding the cigar into the ashtray.

Hearing Parker's sigh, she winced inwardly. "Yes," she answered Sandy, knowing they both knew exactly what her hearing the woman's thoughts meant. Caron's time without imaging, her time of freedom and peace, was over.

The "gift" was back.

"What did you do?" His voice had an odd catch in it.

She let out a self-deprecating laugh. "Flatly denied that it was happening again. Refused to accept it." She'd cried all the way home, too, mourning the loss of her normal life in Midtown, and her students, who deserved a teacher who wasn't distracted by visions. She didn't want the gift. She'd been blessed enough.

Sandy leaned forward. "Could you?"

"What?"

"Refuse to accept the images?" Parker said, interrupting them. Muttering his impatience, he propped his elbows on his knees.

"I tried." She had. But by the time she'd stored the chicken noodle soup on the pantry shelf, she'd known she had to help. That was when she'd first "seen" the little girl . . . and when all hell had broken loose inside her.

Sandy frowned, clearly perplexed. "So you *can* refuse them, then?"

He was hoping for a way out . . . for her. But, though she appreciated his concern, there wasn't one. Not one she could live with, anyway. "No, Sandy. I can't refuse them."

"That would be too convenient." Parker's voice held a condescending smirk that she thoroughly resented.

Sandy rubbed his jaw, then his nape, studying her for a long minute. He put down the pen and laced his hands across his desk. "I'm going to be blunt here, Caron."

"Okay." Hadn't he always been?

"Can you handle this?"

Though it stung, it was a fair question. One she had been asking herself since her first inkling that the images were returning. She'd agonized, rationalized, but no matter what path her thoughts had taken, all roads led back to one. "I don't have any choice."

"Of course you don't." Parker grunted, making it clear that he'd meant the exact opposite of what he'd said.

That was the one. The proverbial back-breaking straw. Who did this guy think he was? She frowned at him and held it so that he wouldn't miss it. "I'm sorry you don't approve, Mr. Simms. But I haven't asked for your approval, or for your help, so could you can the sarcasm?" She slid her gaze to Sandy. "This is hard enough without a stranger's censure."

Simms lifted his brows, but said nothing.

His hostility had her angry and nervous inside. She needed a minute to get herself glued back together. She pushed away from the wall and peeked out between the dusty venetian blinds. "Can you believe this rain? It should be snow."

"You know New Orleans doesn't get much snow," Sandy said, "not even this close to Christmas. And you don't seem fine. Maybe you ought to give Dr. Z. a call."

"Later." Hearing the steady rap of his pen against his blotter, she turned back toward Sandy. "When there's time."

His faded eyes lit with compassion. As if knowing she wouldn't welcome it, he shifted his gaze. "Look, I know that last case was hard on you," he said, avoiding speaking Sarah's name. "Finding her like—like that. Well, I know it was rough."

Caron stiffened and tried hard not to recoil. Parker, too, had tensed. Just the indirect mention of Sarah had Caron remembering what had happened—and reliving it.

Images flooded Caron's mind. Images of Sarah's battered body, unnaturally twisted, lifeless and cold. Images of flames sweeping up the walls, engulfing the building where Sarah had suffered and died. And images of the empathy pains, so staggeringly severe that she nearly had died with Sarah.

Her stomach folded over on itself, and Caron shuttered her thoughts. Still, her hands shook, and her knees were weaker than her aunt Grace's tea.

Afraid she'd fall if she didn't sit, Caron plopped down in an old chair wedged between Sandy's desk and the wall.

Parker looked at her from around the corner of the file cabinet. "What's wrong?"

"Nothing," Caron assured him. "I'm fine."

He lifted a brow and spoke to Sandy. "She looks a little green around the gills."

If she'd had the strength, she would've slapped him. The man didn't have a compassionate bone in his body.

Sandy held his silence and rocked back, rubbing his chin. The split leather cushion swooshed under his weight and creaked when he rolled closer to his desk to reach for his glasses. He draped them over the bridge of his nose and propped his elbows on his desk pad. "What do we have this time?"

This time.

Would there be more times? Or was this one a fluke? Swallowing hard, Caron dropped her shoulder bag onto the floor. Again she wished that Parker Simms were anywhere in the world *except* Sandy's office. After this, the man would add "flaky" to his list of her sins.

Resentment churning her stomach, she looked at Sandy and began disclosing the facts. "A nine-year-old girl. Brown hair. Green eyes. Frail."

"Caron?" Sandy asked, stiffening, his voice tinged with reluctance.

He was afraid for her. Afraid she couldn't handle the pressure or the empathy pains. So was she. But she *had* to take whatever came—for the little girl. Caron schooled her voice, but it was still faint. "Her hands are . . . bound."

"Oh, God."

Caron looked up and met Sandy's gaze. It was all there for her to see. Fear for her. Raw terror for another victim—a younger Sarah.

"Do you have any proof?" An angry white line circled Parker's lips.

"Let her tell the story, Simms." Sandy's tone carried a warning, one Simms would be wise to heed.

The men locked gazes.

Parker didn't back down.

Sandy blinked rapidly three times, then turned his chair toward the computer on the stand beside his desk and positioned his fingers on the keys.

She heard him swallow. "Bound with what?"

His tone told her that Sandy, the man, had buried his emotions. Sandy, the cop, had stepped in. Caron took comfort in that. "Rope." She squeezed her fingers around the cold metal arms of the chair. "A greasy rope." Her wrists twinged. She looked down, half expecting to see black grease marks. But, of course, there were none.

Sandy began to type. "Paint me a picture."

It was as hard as the telling itself, but Caron forced herself to look Parker Simms right in the eye. It was obvious that he didn't believe her. But that was his problem, not hers. "She's huddled in the corner of an old wooden shed— the wood's slick, weathered. Sunlight's slanting in, between the slats. Inside it's maybe eight by ten—no larger."

"What's inside?" Sandy's voice was hoarse.

Caron couldn't concentrate. Parker's gaze had gone black. It was disturbing, seemingly reaching into her soul.

She closed her eyes and blocked him out. The images grew sharp. A spider crawled up the far wall, then onto a shovel caked with dry mud that hung there from a shiny nail. "Lawn tools," she said. "Rusty cans of paint and insecticide are on a shelf above the little girl. There's a big bag of—" the writing was faded, and Caron strained to make out the letters "—Blood Meal." That was it. "It's on the floor, propped against the far wall. That's where she's huddling."

The steady clicking of the keys stopped. Sandy gulped down a swig of coffee. "What's she wearing?"

From his grimace, the coffee was cold. "Blue jeans," Caron said. "The color of Mr. Simms's. They're ripped over her left knee." She paused and felt her own knee through her white linen slacks. No pain. No burning from a scrape. The frayed fabric was worn, not ripped. The girl's knee was fine. "And a yellow T-shirt."

"Anything written on the shirt?"

"There's an emblem, but I can't see it. Her hands are curled to her chest." Cold? No, she wasn't cold. Caron scanned the image, then closed her eyes to heighten her perception. "Black sneakers—muddy. And yellow socks."

He keyed the last of what Caron told him into the computer. "What about height, weight, distinguishing marks?"

"She's sitting down and curled, but about four feet, and maybe sixty-five pounds. She's fragile-looking, small-boned." Caron pushed herself to sense the girl's emotions, her physical condition, opening her mind to the images. Her stomach churned. Pain flooded it. Fevered and flushed, she felt dizzy. The smell of mud and chemicals grew stronger and stronger, until she couldn't breathe. She snapped her eyes open and gasped.

Sandy jumped up and touched her shoulder. "Hey, take it easy, Caron."

"I'm okay." She took in great gulps of cleansing air. The expression on Sandy's face warned her that the second she left his office he'd be calling Dr. Z. to express his concern that Caron was still suffering from trauma-induced psychic burnout. "She's sick, Sandy. Very sick."

"Was she beaten, bruised—anything else?" Parker asked.

How could Simms sound so calm and unaffected? Again Caron sensed his disbelief, his hostility toward her. "No." Her head was clearing. "Just sick."

She dabbed sweat from her forehead. "I don't know about the man."

"What man? Now there's a man?" Parker grunted. "What next? Flying saucers?"

"Damn it, Simms, knock it off." Sandy looked back at Caron and gentled his voice. "Tell me about the man."

She closed her eyes and again saw his face, his piercing eyes. They were green, and as ice-cold as Parker Simms's.

She blinked and focused on Sandy. Her voice rattled. "I imaged him on the way over here. He might not even be connected. I'm not sure yet."

Then it hit her. The little girl had dimples. So did the man. "No, they're connected. He's her . . . father." That didn't feel quite right. Not at all sure she was interpreting properly, she hedged. "Maybe. There *is* a connection."

Sandy moved back and watched the computer screen. "We're coming up empty. Ready to look at some pictures?"

Caron nodded and picked up her purse. From under her lashes, she stole a glance at Parker. He'd pulled his chair away from the wall. And, sitting sprawled with his elbow propped on the armrest and his chin cupped in his hand, he looked bored and irritated. He hadn't bought a word she'd said.

Caron sighed inwardly. She'd met his kind before—one too many times. "No photos of runaways," she told Sandy. "The girl's not a runaway. She was abducted." She could feel herself breaking out in a cold sweat.

Abducted. Just like Sarah James.

Sandy had been tapping his pen, and he abruptly stopped. "Any idea of where from?"

Caron knew exactly. "A store on the west bank. The corner of Belle Chase Highway and Twenty-first Street. There's a shopping center there, a reddish brick building. She was behind it on her bicycle. It's lavender."

"They're coming fast, aren't they?"

She nodded, resigned. The images were coming very fast. And Simms's expression had turned to stone.

Sandy added the latest info to the rest in the computer. "Do you have a name?"

She paused, waited, but nothing came. It hadn't with Sarah, either, not until later. "No."

"We're still dry here." He nodded toward the monitor.

"Nothing?" Caron frowned. "The child was abducted. How could there be nothing in the data bank? Her parents—somebody—had to notice her missing!"

"There's nothing here." He raked his hair with a burn-scarred hand—another legacy of the James case.

"Maybe she wasn't abducted." Parker let his hand drop to the armrest. "Maybe none of this is real. Maybe you're—"

"I wish the images weren't real. You have no idea how often I've wished it." Caron leveled him her best hostile look. How could any man so gorgeous be such a narrow-minded thorn in the side? "But they are."

Compassion flitted over his face. He clamped his jaw and squelched it. "At the risk of sounding sarcastic, let me ask my trivial question again. Do you have any proof?"

She flushed heatedly again. For a second she'd thought he might come around, but he hadn't. He was no different from the others. She lifted her chin. "Nothing you can touch, see, smell or feel, Mr. Simms. Only the images."

Parker looked at Sandy. "And there's no missing-person report?"

Grim-faced, Sandy shook his head. An uneasy shiver rattled along Caron's spine. Before now, there always had been a report. That there wasn't one now had her feeling grim, too. Grim and uncertain.

Parker stood up. "As far as I'm concerned, that covers it."

Caron tried hard to keep her temper in check. Not only was the man insulting and rude—he might as well have called her a liar straight out—his negative feelings were unjustified. That infuriated her. "Look, Mr. Simms—"

"No, you look, Miss Chalmers," he cut in, his voice cold and steady. "It's a simple matter of logic. If your child were missing, would you file a report?"

"Yes, I would, but—"

"Well, there you have it. Right from the psychic's mouth." He leaned against a file cabinet and cast her an acid look that she would have thoroughly enjoyed knocking off his face. "No report, no abduction. And no case." With an annoying little shrug, he straightened. "Now, if you'll excuse me, I have real work to do." Refusing them so much as a nod, he walked out of Sandy's office.

Caron glared at his retreating back. "You're wrong, Parker Simms. Dead wrong!"

He didn't stop, or turn around.

"Parker has a point, Caron." Sandy said on a sigh. "Are you sure about this?"

After all their years together, Sandy doubted her. That hurt. "Yes, I'm sure," she snapped. "Do you think I *want* to see this child dragged through hell? Do you think I'm looking forward to being dragged through hell with her?"

"I didn't mean to offend you. It's just that..." His face tinged pink. "You and I both know you had a really close call with—with the James case." A desperate edge crept into his voice. "You nearly died, Caron."

He looked down at his desk pad, his eyes unfocused. "It's been a year today."

A year ago today, they'd found Sarah James. Dead. A surge of bitter tears threatened. "I know." How could she not know? She'd never forget. Sarah's killer being in prison didn't help at all.

"Could you be getting your wires crossed because of it?"

His question was valid. Caron *had* nearly died. During the week-long investigation, she'd followed up on the leads she'd imaged, and her health had deteriorated quickly. The more deeply engrossed in the case she'd become, the more acutely she'd suffered every atrocity that Sarah James had suffered at the hands of her captor. And Sarah James had been tortured.

Following the grain in her padded chair with her fingers, Caron looked at Sandy, knowing her regret was shining in her eyes. "This isn't confusion. I wish it was. I wish the child wasn't in danger. But she is, Sandy. I swear, she is."

He pinched the bridge of his nose above his half-moon glasses. A smudge on the lens caught in the light.

When it became clear he wasn't going to respond, Caron turned the subject. "Why did you bring in Parker Simms?"

Sandy looked away. "I told you. I think he can help."

"Help?" She guffawed. "He's the most hostile man I've ever met."

Indecision creased Sandy's brow, and he stuffed his hand in his pocket. "He's got his reasons. I agree that Parker's in a black mood most of the time these days, and he's damn rough around the edges. But he's the best at what he does."

Sandy knew more than he was saying, and her expression must have told him that she knew it. He gave her an uneasy smile. "Come on, you can handle Simms. Just don't take it personally. When the man dies, he'll probably ask God for his ID."

"And God'll give it to him," she said with a hint of a grin. There was no sense in alienating Sandy. She'd get Parker Simms's measure...eventually.

"He probably will." Sandy gave her shoulder a firm pat. "Let's look at those pictures, hmm? Maybe we'll get lucky."

Nodding, Caron went into the outer office and got busy.

Parker sat in the Porsche outside Sanders's office and stared up at the rain-speckled window. She was still in there, filling Sanders's head with bull.

His hand shook on the wheel. God, if he'd blown this... No, he hadn't blown it. He'd been rough on her—not that she didn't deserve worse—but she had no idea who he was, that he'd been tailing her, or that he'd gathered a year's worth of proof that his ex-partner, Harlan, had been right. She was no more psychic than he was.

For prosecution purposes, it was circumstantial evidence, true. But it was strong enough to convince Parker. A year of teaching second-graders sixty miles away in Midtown, and the lady couldn't hack playing it straight. So she'd come back and picked up where she'd left off with Sanders.

Parker had figured that it would take an out-and-out threat to get any information on her from Sanders. All he'd managed for the past year was Sanders's admission that he and Chalmers were friends. But things had taken an odd turn.

This morning, Sanders had called and seemed almost relieved to spill his guts and tell Parker she was coming down to headquarters. And then Sanders had done something even odder. He'd asked him to *help* Chalmers.

That request had knocked Parker for a loop. Sanders was genuinely worried about her; there was no doubt about that. Parker had seen Sanders's look in his own mother's eyes too often not to recognize it. And that worry made Sanders Chalmers's victim, too. Not the same kind of victim Harlan had been, but still her victim.

Parker's stomach lurched, and the lump in his chest turned stone-cold. He grimaced, doubly resolved. Harlan was right. Caron Chalmers was a fraud. And, by God, he meant to stop her—before she caused anyone else's death.

After an hour of staring at photos and coming up as empty as the computer's data bank, Caron stood up at the long table and stretched, then looked back over her shoulder. Through the half-open glass door, she saw that Sandy was alone, but talking quietly into the telephone.

From the intimate tone of his voice, she knew the call was personal. Caron lifted a brow. It was hard to imagine Sandy loving, or as a lover. What kind of woman would be attracted to him?

Sandy hung up. Caron tossed her foam coffee cup into the overflowing trash can and tapped on his door. When he looked up, she leaned her head against the doorframe. "You guys should use paper cups or real mugs."

He glanced up from an open file. "What?"

His eyes looked a little glazed. Must have been one hot call. Parker Simms and his broad shoulders flashed through her mind. She blinked the disturbing image away. "Foam doesn't break down. You know, save the planet."

"Oh." Sandy set the file down and, elbow bent, propped his chin with his hand. "I'll mention it."

He wouldn't. Typical Sandy. "There's nothing in the photos. I'm going to ride over to Gretna and see what happens."

"Be careful."

Caron nodded. "I'll give you a call."

"You want company? I guess Simms skated out on us, but I could tag along."

Sandy was worried about her, but that wasn't all of it. She couldn't blame him. After Sarah's case, how could he not be worried? Caron herself was worried—and tempted to take him up on his offer.

Before she could give in to the fear, she replied. "No, but thanks. I have to get my feet back."

She hiked up her shoulder bag to hide her own misgivings. How well *would* she cope this time? Okay, so she was scared stiff. She had honest concerns about her abilities, and about the empathy pains that always accompanied the images. How much could she physically withstand? She hadn't been tested since the images had come back, either. How accurate were her perceptions?

As much as she hated to admit it, hostile or not, Parker Simms *had* made a valid point. For the first time ever in a case, she didn't have a missing-persons report, or any other hard evidence. But she did have the images. After what had happened to Sarah, trusting them was as hard as trusting outsiders. Yet the stakes were too high for her not to; more than for herself, she was terrified of what was happening to the little girl. Of what *could* happen to her—if she found her too late.

She squeezed the strap on her purse until it bit into her palm, and pushed away from the door casing. The white paint was chipped and peeling away in splinters. So was she . . . inside.

She didn't want to, but she had to warn Sandy. Not that there was anything he could do about it without a report. But maybe it was herself she had to warn—out loud—just in case this little girl ended up like Sarah. "She's sick, Sandy. She could get sicker."

"I understand."

Their gazes linked and held. He did understand. They both did. And whether or not Parker Simms believed her, Caron knew the truth. The little girl *had* been abducted. She was in serious danger. And unless Caron interpreted her images dead-center, the girl could die.

Chapter 2

The pavement was nearly steaming. It was beyond hot; it was sultry and close and still overcast. Lousy weather for the Christmas shoppers. The shower earlier had the humidity hovering near the hundred-percent mark, which made breathing a major obstacle ... especially for a child locked in a leaky shed with a damp, dirt-crusted floor and a bag of insecticide.

Getting into her old Caprice, Caron saw another image. The girl at a park, with a second man. He was pushing her swing. He was tall and lanky, homely, but expensively dressed. And when the girl laughed, the man laughed. The skin at the corners of his eyes crinkled, and love shone in them. The warmth in the sound and the sight spread through Caron like syrup over a snow cone, slowly soaking in.

The sharp contrast between the two men she'd seen surprised her. Then, suddenly, it made perfect sense. This man and the little girl's abductor were adversaries. But in what? How did the little girl connect them?

And why hadn't Sandy found anything on her in the data bank? It incorporated all the outlying areas and suburbs.

Having no answers, Caron cranked the engine and glimpsed into her rearview mirror. A flashy black car was about three lengths behind her. She twisted to look back.

"Simms," she muttered. Her courage took a nosedive, and her heart slammed against her ribs. It was him, all right; she'd have recognized those shoulders anywhere. He'd left Sandy's office eons ago. Why was he just now leaving headquarters?

He couldn't be following her. The man thought she was a mental patient; he hadn't believed anything she'd said. So why was he there?

No sooner had she asked herself the question than Simms peeled off, turning right at the corner. Maybe he'd been working on another case?

A trickle of disappointment that he wasn't following her seeped through her chest. Peeved at herself, Caron shifted on the seat. She had enough problems without adding Parker Simms to them. The man could make her dizzy with just a look. He could also make her want to strangle him. With the case tapping her emotions—and sure to drain them—she didn't have any to spare. Especially not for a man who thought she was a flake. The distraction could be lethal.

Traffic on the Greater New Orleans Bridge heading to the west bank was bumper-to-bumper, and moving about as fast as a pregnant snail. She glanced from the Superdome's marquee, which was flashing a red Happy Holidays, to her watch, and she groaned. Four-fifteen. Rush hour for downtown commuters. And she had skipped lunch again. Stomach growling, she grabbed a Butterfinger candy bar from her purse and ripped it open.

She was two-thirds through with the candy before traffic thinned out. She crossed the Mississippi River, then exited and hooked a left onto Belle Chase Highway. Several blocks ahead, she could see the reddish brick buildings, long before she could read the street sign. But she didn't need the sign. This was definitely the place. Meyer's Properties, a real estate office, was there on the corner, right next to the grocery store, exactly as she'd imaged it.

The shopping center had been around a while, too; the concrete of the parking lot was cracked, and as full of potholes as the street. She steered around an orange sawhorse straddling a hole big enough to hold her Chevy, drove on to the back of the building, then stopped. Stuffing the candy wrapper into her purse, she closed her eyes and let the images come.

When they had, she drove the path they'd shown her, certain that she following the same route the little girl had taken. Down two blocks. Then three more. A right turn, and...

At the corner, Caron hit the brakes hard and stared at a sagging green house. Two trucks—both up on blocks— were in the front yard. A shiny new Lincoln, looking totally out of place, was parked beside one of the trucks. The lawn needed mowing; the grass and weeds stood half a foot tall. Two huge evergreens stood sentry over an unwelcoming front door. Long scratches dug deep into the wood on the bottom half of it. A mean-looking Doberman, running ruts into the ground along a length of hurricane fence, explained the scratches and warned Caron that she was far from welcome.

The girl didn't belong here. Caron knew that as well as she knew her own name. But she had been here, or she was here—Caron couldn't tell which. And, needing to determine that, she called out from the car. "Hello!"

No answer. Just the Doberman barking, snarling, showing her his vicious teeth, his ears lying back flat. She locked the car door. Totally irrational—the dog could hardly open it—but it made Caron feel better.

Then the front door opened, and the first man she'd imaged walked out, waving a can of Budweiser.

Beer sloshed onto his T-shirt. Once, it might have been white, but that hadn't been lately. It was stained by perspiration, dirt, and now beer. Only God knew what else.

"Whaddaya want?"

He was drunk, potently reminding Caron of Sarah's abductor. The dog went wild, as if to prove to his master he was earning his keep. Shaking from head to toe, she cranked down the window all the way, cleared her throat and yelled out, "I'm looking for someone. Maybe you can help—"

"Shut up, Killer!" he shouted at the dog. Then, at her: "I can't hear ya."

The dog stopped barking, but didn't stop growling. "I'm looking for Parker Simms," she said, tossing out the first name that came to mind. "I thought this was his house."

"It ain't."

"Do you know which house is his?"

"No." He let out a healthy belch and rubbed his belly.

"Have you ever heard of him?"

The man didn't answer. He slid her a narrow-eyed glare, walked back inside, then slammed the door. Given no choice but to come back later, Caron pulled away from the curb.

Two blocks down the street, a blinding pain streaked through her stomach. Caron bent double over the steering wheel and groaned. When she could move, she veered to the side of the street and braked to a stop.

The pain was so strong! Appendicitis? What? What illness had struck the little girl?

A long shadow fell across her window and stayed there. "Caron?"

Parker Simms. Oh, God, not now. He was the last thing she needed right now. Holding her stomach, she again lowered the glass.

"Are you all right?"

Her stomach hurt like hell, and she was in a cold sweat. "I'm fine." She forced herself to glance over at him. *Big, brawny, beautiful*—all those words came to mind...again. "What do you want, Mr. Simms?"

"Parker." He crouched down and looked in through the window. "You sure you're okay? You look half-dead."

She felt worse. "I'm fine." The pain lessened to a dull ache. She grabbed a tissue from the box on the dash and wiped the beads of sweat from above her lip and at her temple. "What are you doing here?"

"I want to help."

Caron dropped the tissue box. "You walked out on me once. I don't have time to play revolving-door games. This girl's in trouble—and I don't need a keeper."

"Look, I wasn't ready to hear what I heard. This psychic stuff is pretty hard to swallow. So cut me a little slack, okay?" He gripped the top of the car door and leaned closer. "And just for the record, *I* never thought you needed a keeper."

She didn't miss the strong insinuation that Sandy did think so. A sharp pain seared her left side, and she winced.

The man's eyes softened to the gentle gray of a molting mallard. "Are you sick?"

"No." She shuddered out a steadying breath. "Just empathy pains." Why had she told him that?

He shifted, and something hard flashed in his eyes. "Can we go somewhere to talk?"

Feeling human again, she gave him a second look. Charming smile. A perplexed black brow and soft gray eyes that were questioning. Nothing threatening there. His hair was a riot of close-cropped curls that teased his ears and the collar of his black leather bomber jacket. His shoulders seemed to spread out forever, and no man that she'd ever seen could better fill out a pair of jeans. Lean hips.

Moneyed, but not flashy—except for the car. Her third impression mimicked her first and second. He *was* big and brawny... and beautiful.

"I think we should confer on the case." His eyes twinkled a what-you-see-is-what-you-get promise.

It wasn't at all convincing. Why the turnaround? He'd been a third-degree pain at Sandy's office. What had him soft-soaping her now? He smiled, as if knowing she'd been summing him up and still wasn't sure she was on solid ground. "Why should we confer, Parker?"

He shrugged. "To help the girl."

Caron didn't see it, but she sensed he was a man on a mission. And that mission had nothing to do with benevolence.

"Look," he said, as though sensing her uncertainty. "My father and Sandy were friends for a long time. Occasionally he asks for my help. When he does, I give it."

"You work on cases you don't believe exist?"

"When asked to by family friends. Haven't you ever been put on the spot by family friends wanting favors?"

She had, and some of those favors had cost her dearly. But how did Parker know? He couldn't know about her father; she'd never breathed a word about him to anyone.

Understanding settled in Parker's eyes. Was it genuine? She couldn't tell that, either. In fact, she couldn't read Parker Simms any better than she could Sandy. And that oddity had a fair shiver racing across her shoulders.

"Hey, I'm not going to stand in the street and beg you to let me help you. If you want me, I'm available, okay?" He reached into the inner pocket of his jacket and flipped out his card. "Just give me a call."

She studied him for a long moment. He seemed sincere, and not at all hostile. Maybe he could help, after all. Sandy had said Parker was the best, and she knew from experience that Sandy was darn hard to please. She'd be a fool not to accept Parker's offer. She couldn't let the little girl end up like Sarah. If she worked alone and failed, wondering if Parker could have saved the girl would torment her the rest of her days.

"All right, Parker Simms," she said, sounding a lot more confident than she felt. "We'll confer."

"Great. There's a Shoney's up on the corner. Meet you there." He walked away, toward the shiny black Porsche.

Caron frowned and called out, "Hey! Why are you really doing this?"

"You're the psychic." He slid her a wicked smile chock-full of challenge, and waggled his brows. "Figure it out."

Figure it out?

The tiny hairs on her neck lifted. She'd dragged the man's name through every muddy pothole between New Orleans and Gretna for being antagonistic, and now he was teasing her?

No, Caron shivered. He wasn't teasing. He meant exactly what he'd said . . . and, once again, she inexplicably thought of Sarah James.

Parker whipped into Shoney's parking lot and killed the engine. Had he lost his mind? He'd practically demanded that Chalmers nose around until she found out why he was going in on this case!

He'd figured that if he pushed, she'd do the opposite. For as long as he could remember, it had worked with his mother and his younger sister, Megan. But Caron Chalmers wasn't like them. Maybe he'd screwed up. Maybe he shouldn't have pushed so hard. He wanted her curious, but if she got too curious and started checking up on him. . . .

Hell, done was done. He'd just have to hope she didn't, and press on as planned. He shoved his keys into his pocket; they jangled, clashing with loose coins.

Chalmers pulled in and parked. Relief soaked through him, and he let out a breath he hadn't realized he was holding. She'd come. He hadn't blown it—this time.

In the future, he'd be more careful. He'd ruffled her feathers pretty good at Sandy's, and he'd forgotten a snippet of advice he'd learned on his mother's knee. Remembering it could save him a lot of heartburn in dealing with Caron Chalmers. *"You win more flies with honey than with vinegar."*

When she'd seen him, Chalmers *had* done a double take. Her pupils had dilated, and her lips had parted just enough to let him know she was interested. At least she had been, until she'd recognized him from the parking slot incident.

He shouldn't have done that, at least not the way he had. But he hadn't been sure how he'd react to getting his first up-close glimpse of her. He'd had to test himself while he was alone to minimize his risks; she wasn't a slow woman.

As it worked out, it was good that he had tested himself privately. Caron Chalmers was more than just not slow; she was damn fast on the uptake.

The stunt had cost him. After she'd recognized him, she'd become distant, and from there, things had zoomed downhill.

Finally she got out of her car, locked the door and started toward the restaurant. The wind caught her hair and blew it back from her face. Harlan had been right; Caron Chalmers was a knockout...and she was a fraud. A missing child, and no report? Get real.

Harlan had failed. But Parker would take care of it.

The woman was going down.

From the corner of her eye, Caron saw the Porsche parked under the streetlamp. She pretended not to, and went on inside Shoney's. Before she talked with Parker Simms again—his unexplained turnaround still gave her the willies—she had to talk to Sandy.

In a hallway near the rest rooms, she saw a phone, and she fished a quarter from her purse.

Sandy surprised her by answering right away; he hated phones. But he probably thought it was his "hot caller" phoning back. Parker flitted through her mind and, annoyed, she said, "I'm miffed with you. You promised not to tell anyone about me. So why did you tell Parker Simms?"

"We've been through this."

Calm and reasonable. How could he twist a knife through her heart and still sound that way? "I trusted you. I knew better than to do it, but I trusted you anyway, and look what—"

"I'm sorry, honey. I know people have made it hard for you. But considering the circumstances, I thought—"

"Sandy, please." She didn't want to hear it again. She didn't want him to remind her that she'd blown a case. And she didn't want to visualize Sarah lying there dead. Not again.

Watching a doodlebug inch across the carpet, Caron forced herself to calm down. The damage was done, and no amount of complaining could undo it. "Parker met me on the street over here. He's offering to help on the case."

"I'm not sure we have a case. I've been watching the reports filed all afternoon, and I've checked with Gretna, Marrero, Westwego—all of the surrounding cities. There's nothing on a kidnapping in any of them."

So now his doubt was out in the open. It hurt her more than him telling Parker about her gift. And it angered her. Sandy knew how many cases she'd successfully solved.

She kicked the paneling with the toe of her sneaker. "The girl has been abducted, Sandy. That's not the issue. Parker Simms is the issue."

Sandy hesitated.

Caron prodded. "Well?"

"Let him help."

Sandy didn't just doubt her, he thought she'd lost it and gone off the deep end. Though she knew she shouldn't, she felt even angrier and more betrayed. He was trying to protect her, but she didn't want his protection. She wanted his faith. "You know I work alone. I always have." She should have to explain why to him, of all people.

"What I know is that Simms is sharp and he has connections." Sandy dropped his voice. "If there is a case, he might give you an edge."

There *was* a case! Caron squeezed her eyes shut. A year ago today, she'd thought she didn't need help. She'd been wrong, and Sarah had paid the ultimate price for Caron's mistake. "So you'll vouch for him?"

Again Sandy hesitated. "Yeah. Yeah, I'll vouch for him. I walked the beat with his father for twenty years, Caron. Charley Simms never crossed anybody. And no son of his could be a demon from hell out to get you. Parker's one of the good guys. Give him a break."

"Give *him* a break? *He* doesn't believe *me*." Because she wished he did, she again kicked the paneling with her toe.

"Most people don't believe you," Sandy argued. "That's never slowed you down before. Why is Simms any different?"

Parker Simms *was* different—though she didn't want to ask herself why. Sandy was half-right, though; most people's doubts hadn't slowed her down. But they had bothered her. Like everyone else, she wanted acceptance and approval.

She glanced down the hallway to make sure she was still alone. It was empty. "Okay, Sandy. I'll give Parker the benefit of doubt. But if he's a lousy partner, I'm ditching him. I can't afford the distraction."

"No, you can't."

Caron didn't like Sandy's tone. Something hid there, but she couldn't put her finger on exactly what it was. Still, if Sandy was willing to vouch for Simms... Well, the least she could do was to talk to him. "I've got to go."

"Keep in touch." He sounded anxious.

Caron quirked a brow at the phone. "31224," she said, repeated the code number that let her access his answering machine for messages. That was how they'd always kept tabs on each other during a case.

"Right."

After hanging up, Caron ducked into the bathroom, splashed cold water on her cheeks and wrists, then went out to the dining room.

Parker stood up at a secluded booth and waved her over. When she'd been in the car, she hadn't realized just how big he was. But standing next to him, it was obvious. At least six-three, and as broad-shouldered as a linebacker.

"Well, did Sandy give you the green light on me?"

Direct. She liked that. But she didn't like the gleam in his eyes. He could be a charmer when he wanted to, and she had no use for charmers. "Sandy vouched for you, yes."

"Good." Parker laced his hands together on the scratched tabletop.

A waitress stepped up. He smiled at her, and the woman darn near drooled. The female in Caron fully understood that; he was a dynamite-looking man. A curl teased his left ear. She wanted to brush it back.

"Caron?" he asked, in a tone that told her he'd asked before.

"Sorry." What was she doing having fantasies about touching the man? She didn't even like him. Her face flushed hot. "Excuse me?"

"What will you have?" the waitress asked.

"Coffee."

"Cream and sugar?"

"No. Black." She saw the corner of Simms's mouth turn down, and asked the waitress, "Do you have candy bars? Butterfingers?"

"No." She pointed with the tip of her pencil through the window. "Seven-Eleven does. Right across the street."

"Thanks."

"Sir?" The waitress shifted toward Parker, her expression softening.

"Coffee, black," he said with a smile that could undoubtedly twist an unsuspecting woman right around his pinky.

"Yes, sir."

Caron wasn't unsuspecting. Her leg stung like fire. She grimaced and slapped at it. Nothing was there, but the sting didn't ease. The little girl? Caron wondered.

The waitress returned with the cups. Chilled, Caron wrapped her hands around hers to warm them. "So, Parker Simms, tell me. Why do you want to work with me when you don't believe there's been an abduction?"

His cup stopped in midair. He took his time sipping, then answered. "I don't."

Was he intentionally being ambiguous? "You don't want to work with me, or you don't believe there's been an abduction? Which do you mean?"

"Both," he said, without a trace of remorse.

His ease made her edgy. "So why waste your time?"

"I prefer working alone." Steam from his coffee had him squinting. "But I'm not willing to risk being wrong about this."

That, she completely understood. But he was still fencing with words. Direct, but cagey. She had the feeling they were discussing two different topics, and she was only privy to one. She was certain he hadn't disclosed his real reasons for getting involved. So maybe it was time to stop being defensive and take the offensive.

"Why are you putting your backside on the line in a case you don't believe exists? And, please, don't tell me it's for your father."

Parker set the cup down and gave her a look free of guile. It did more to arouse her awareness of him as a man than all the devil's smiles in the world heaped together.

"If you're wrong, all I've lost is time. But if you're right, the girl's in trouble. I have a special interest in abduction cases, Caron. If I can, I have to help."

Have to, not *want* to help. Someone he loved had been abducted. The flash of certainty stayed with her and strengthened. She bit her lip to keep from asking who. It wasn't any of her business; she had no right to pry. But Parker still wasn't playing it totally straight with her. And dishonesty rankled her more than any other vice known to man.

She gave him a steady look. "I *have* imaged the girl."

"So you've said." His gaze was just as steady.

He wasn't pulling his punches. He wasn't convinced, but he wasn't positive that she was wrong, either. It appeared they had stepped onto common ground. They were granting each other the benefit of doubt.

He again drank from his cup, then motioned to the waitress for a refill.

The woman nearly knocked herself out getting over to Parker fast enough with the coffeepot. Parker held up his cup and thanked the waitress with another drop-dead smile. Her healthy chest heaved with her indrawn breath. Simms had a definite effect on women. Caron had to give him that.

He watched the waitress leave. "Is the guy you were talking to at the house your kidnapper?"

Caron sputtered, nearly spraying out coffee. She'd thought she was alone outside the sagging house; she hadn't sensed Parker there. "What man?"

"Forty-five or so. Five-ten or eleven. Black hair, going gray. A slob." Rubbing the sugar dispenser with his thumb, Parker lifted a black brow. "Shall I go on?"

"No." Caron gripped the vinyl seat beneath her and tried to regroup. It was hard to accept that she hadn't known it, but Parker had been there, all right. He'd described the guy at the sagging house, the first man Caron had imaged, perfectly.

"I think, for the girl's sake, we should try to work together, Caron. Two heads are better than one—especially when a third head is at stake."

A third head was at stake. A helpless child's. Caron flinched. She didn't trust Parker Simms. But she didn't trust herself to go it alone, either. She couldn't afford any mistakes. It was the child who would suffer. Caron had to take every precaution to ensure that the little girl didn't end up like Sarah. Simms was a pro. The best, Sandy had said. One of the good guys. Could she afford to refuse? Could the little girl afford for Caron to refuse?

"So, do we give it a shot?" His gaze grew intense. "At least see if two loners can work together?"

Once again, fate had intervened. The risks were too high; she had no choice. And she hoped she'd have no regrets. "We give it a shot."

Relieved, Parker slid down in the booth. For the first time since Caron Chalmers had walked over to him, the tension knotting his insides had loosened.

The woman had slam-dunked him at Sandy's office, and he still hadn't recovered. He'd had her under surveillance for a year, but until today he'd never seen her up close. She was tiny, maybe five-seven, and delicate-boned. There was something about her, too, that got under his skin, and he couldn't shake it loose. She seemed vulnerable, and pain hid in the shadows in her eyes. He hadn't expected any of that.

What had he expected? Cold and calculating? Brazen and coming on to him? He knew better than that, too. In the year he'd watched her, she'd been the model of decorum, a prim and proper schoolteacher who played leapfrog with her students and coached the math club. Oh, she'd had dates, but only a few, and never twice with the same guy. Smart, considering her sideline. She couldn't risk letting anyone get too close. They might see her for what she was.

He sighed and lifted his cup. "Where do you want to start?"

"The house." Caron again rubbed her leg. "Either the girl is still there, or she was there."

"Oh?" Had he missed some sign at the house that she'd picked up on?

She held his gaze. "I saw it."

"Saw it?"

"*Saw* it." She smoothed back her hair and pointed to her temple. "Psychic, remember?"

She didn't back down. And she didn't flaunt her "gift," either. That confused Parker. Human nature would have made it natural for her to capitalize on her gift. Yet she was damn near broke. Half of everything she made she sent to that biddy of a mother of hers over in Mississippi, who lived with Caron's only aunt, Grace Collins. That, too, bothered Parker. It had ever since Harlan had first mentioned Caron Chalmers. If she was gifted, why didn't she use the gift to help herself? Financially, the woman was still struggling.

The answer was easy, of course. She wasn't gifted. The fact that Harlan was six feet under now proved that.

Edgy, Parker straightened in the booth. Their knees bumped under the table, and Caron's hand slid from her calf to his thigh. Their gazes clashed across the table. His throat went dry. No way, he told himself, looking into her lavender eyes. No way would he allow himself to feel attracted to this woman.

She jerked her hand back. It thudded against the underside of the table. Clearly she felt the sexual tension between them, too. And, just as clearly, she didn't like it. For some reason, that annoyed Parker. And because it did, he cursed himself as a fool. "What's wrong with your leg?"

"Excuse me?"

Wide-eyed innocence. He wasn't buying it. Megan had worn out that particular feminine wile years ago. "Your leg. You keep rubbing it."

Caron looked away. "It's nothing."

"Then why are you rubbing it again now?"

Snapping a cold glance his way, she gripped the edge of the table. "I said, it's fine."

Her overreaction bothered him. It was defensive, not evasive. A woman who'd masqueraded for years should be more in control of her responses.

She gazed up and dropped her shoulders. "Look, Parker, there's something you'd better understand right up front."

He leaned forward. His hands were close enough to feel the heat radiating from hers. He didn't like that, either. A cold woman should feel cold, and look cold. Chalmers didn't. "What's that?"

She licked her lips. "When I'm working a case, I tune in to the victim. I don't know why. It just happens. I feel what they feel, when they feel it."

Her response had been controlled, after all. She was mixing her signals to knock him off guard. He tested the theory. "Is that what was wrong earlier in the car?" She'd say it was, of course. But it was more likely that she'd scarfed down one Butterfinger too many and been riding out the crash from a sugar high.

She nodded.

Naturally. More confident now that he had a fix on her, he feigned concern, and denied he was feeling any. "And now it's your leg?"

"It stings."

He narrowed his brows. "Have you checked it?"

"There's so sign of anything wrong. It just stings."

"So what you're telling me then, is that it's the girl. Something's wrong with her leg." Chalmers had to be half-nuts if she thought he was going to swallow this.

"That's exactly what I'm telling you." She swept a long lock of hair back over her shoulder and reached for her cup.

He watched for signs of nervousness, of lying, but she'd looked him straight in the eye and her hand hadn't trembled—and it still wasn't trembling. She hadn't shifted in the booth, or done anything else typical of a liar's body language. Either Caron Chalmers was telling the truth, or she was well practiced at lying. His money was on the latter.

He cleared his throat. "I'll check out the tags on the two trucks and call my secretary to get things rolling. We'll watch the house."

"Wait." Caron blinked, then blinked again. "You're moving too fast."

"If the girl's been abducted and now something's wrong with her leg, I think we should move fast."

"Fast, yes." Caron's eyes clouded. "But with caution."

She was afraid. He didn't like it. And he liked even less that he didn't know why she was afraid. Was she worried about being exposed as a fraud, or about making a mistake?

Outside the window, thunder rolled. A cloud split open and dumped a downpour. Heavy drops of rain slashed against the window. Caron watched them for a long minute, then turned that cool, competent gaze back to him.

"I have to move slower, Parker. I can't afford to make a mistake. If I fail, the child could die."

A shiver shot up Parker's backbone. Not from what she'd said; a good con could tear your heart right out of your chest. But because he could see the genuine effort that saying it had taken Caron. She was good. The best he'd ever seen. He'd go along—for now. "So how do you want to handle this?"

"First, I think we should set up a watch on the house."

"Sounds reasonable." Hadn't he just suggested that a moment ago and met with a brick wall?

"Good. You do that. I'll find out who occupies it, then meet you there in thirty minutes."

"That's pretty quick. Are you forgetting the guys at the station move slower than slugs?"

"No, I haven't forgotten. But I don't need them." She dropped two bills onto the table, then scooted out of the booth. "Sandy says you're resourceful." She treated Parker to a rare smile. "In a pinch, so am I."

Caron greeted the woman at Meyer's Properties with an open smile. "Sorry I'm dripping on your rug."

"It's hard not to with all this rain." The petite brunette's high heels clicked on the tile at the end of the rug. "I'm Meriam Meyer."

"Caron Chalmers." She stretched out a hand.

The woman took it. "Are you looking for a house here?"

"Yes," Caron said, glad that it wasn't true. The neighborhood looked tired, as weary as her own. "I'd like some information on the neighborhood."

"Have a seat, please. I'll be with you in a moment."

The front door opened, and a chime went off somewhere in the back of the office. Caron felt the cold draft on her back. She didn't have to turn around to know it was Parker. Right on schedule.

Meriam's attention shifted to the door. A spark of interest twinkled in her eye. "Hi."

Parker walked forward, toward Meriam's desk, and gave the realtor one of his knock-you-to-your-knees smiles. "Hi."

"Be with you in just a second." Meriam looked from Parker to Caron, and her eyes lost a bit of their sparkle.

"Do you have a rest room?"

"Sure." Meriam swiveled her chair and stood. "Be right back," she told Parker.

The phone rang, and she paused to answer it.

Caron waited until Meriam was deep in conversation, then turned to Parker and dropped her voice to a whisper. "You distract her, I'll get the street index."

"I'll handle her," Parker whispered.

Caron resisted a frown. He'd handle Meriam, all right—and Caron had no doubts as to how he'd do it. He'd charm the woman right out of her panty hose.

Meriam hung up the phone. "This way," she told Caron, then quickly moved down the hall.

They passed two private offices—both empty—then a cluttered copier room. Caron slowed her step. A fax machine was on a long table near the far wall. A pile of maps was stacked on the other end, and there was a row of books in between. Scanning the titles, Caron saw the street index.

"Here you are." Outside the rest room, Meriam paused and waited for Caron to catch up. She nodded toward the front office. "Isn't he gorgeous?"

"Yeah, gorgeous." Caron resisted the urge to sigh.

"I dated a guy like that once." Meriam sank her teeth into her lower lip. "It was three months of sheer heaven." On a wistful sigh, she returned to the front office.

Summarily dismissed and surely forgotten, Caron doubled back to the copier room and grabbed the index. She looked around, saw no one, then tucked the book under her raincoat. Visions of herself being arrested and carted off to jail ran through her mind, and guilt had her face nearly steaming.

Stealing didn't sit well on her shoulders; it went hand in hand with dishonesty in her inbred guilty-conscience package. But she needed the information now. A child's life was at stake. When this was all over, she'd return the book.

Back in the hallway, she heard Meriam's desk chair squeak, and heard her offer Parker a seat. Caron peeked around the corner just as he took one—on the corner of Meriam's desk.

Caron huffed under her breath. Simms sure didn't mind using *his* gifts. He had more slinky moves than a big cat . . . and more sex appeal than the law should allow.

Meriam's husky laughter grated on Caron's ears.

She slid a covert glance at Parker, and wasn't surprised to find him watching Meriam. That was what irked her about him, Caron realized. When Parker Simms looked at a woman, he really looked at her. One hundred percent focus, total concentration. That attention from such a hunk was flattering. And Meriam was working hard at not letting that flattery go to her head—but she was losing.

Caron shouldn't be watching this. She had the book; she should just leave. But, curious about him, she didn't move.

Parker reached over and brushed at a speck Caron felt certain didn't exist from Meriam's cheek. The woman let out a breathless little groan that had Caron gritting her teeth.

He winked at her. He knew she'd been watching!

Caron hiked her chin, positively refusing to feel awkward about getting caught. She *should* observe the way he worked; they were partners, weren't they? Reluctant partners, but partners nonetheless.

She narrowed her eyes. Parker shrugged, and that corner of his mouth tilted up. She was quickly coming to hate that tilt. He knew his effect on women. Who was he trying to kid with that innocent what-did-I-do look?

Caron slid him a glare that said she knew exactly what he was up to, then sniffed to let him know she thought it was rotten.

That darn tilt grew to a full-fledged smile.

It nearly left her breathless. She looked away, out the front window. A dynamite man could do serious damage to a woman's dignity, and, though she'd have liked to be, Caron wasn't immune to Parker's charm. Worse, he knew it.

Meriam was jotting down some information Parker was feeding her. Caron snickered. Probably his phone number, or the address of someplace they could meet. He dipped his shoulder and whispered something that had Meriam giggling like an idiot. Couldn't the woman see what he was doing?

Irritated, Caron looked down at the clutter on the desk. Parker's throaty chuckle had her working to keep a grimace from her face. What difference did it make to her if Parker was coming on to Meriam? Caron barely knew the man. But she knew he was dishonest. He'd lied to her about why he was getting involved, and right now she was watching him lie to another woman. Different circumstances, but the same actions.

She'd seen enough. Caron didn't interrupt the quiet conversation, just crossed the room to the door. She kept a death grip on the book, scared to death it'd fall out from under her raincoat and she'd be caught red-handed in a nasty spot.

A glance through the glass told her that it was still pouring. She shivered, then wondered if it wasn't the girl who was cold. "Since you're busy, I'll come back later," Caron said to Meriam.

"Sure." She didn't even bother to look Caron's way.

Caron tucked her chin and avoided looking at Parker; he'd follow, if only to gloat. She couldn't wait to give him a piece of her mind; after watching him operate, though, she needed time to decide how big a piece. What, if anything, should she tell him as the case unfolded?

He had his reasons for getting involved. And until she knew what they were she didn't dare risk being completely open with him.

The warm, intimate sounds of him and Meriam laughing shredded Caron's raw nerves. She stepped out into the rain, and the door swung shut behind her.

Once again she was alone with her fears and worries. Isolated. From the dark sidewalk, she glanced longingly back into the illuminated office. Parker *would* follow, wouldn't he?

Parker met Caron outside. "Well, did you get it?"

"Right here." She patted her stomach. The spine of the book bumped against her ribs. "We need a phone."

"There's one in my car." He pointed left. "Over here."

Caron slid into the Porsche. The smell of leather lingered in the air. So did Parker's spicy after-shave. Feeling her stomach flutter, she cracked open the window, then the book.

By the time Parker got in beside her, Caron had her notebook out and had found a Butch Decker listed as the occupant of the sagging house. But there was no phone number in the index. Caron copied the name down, then went on to copy the names and phone numbers of his neighbors.

Parker draped an arm over the steering wheel. "Well?"

Backed against the wall, she motioned toward the phone clipped to the dashboard. "Butch Decker."

Parker passed her the handset, an odd look in his eyes.

Caron dialed Sandy. That he answered surprised and pleased her. "Hi, it's me. Caron."

"You okay?"

Worry. "Sure." Caron lightened her tone, hoping Parker wouldn't pick up on it. If he didn't know that Sandy, too, had doubts about the case, she didn't want to be the one to tell him. "Can you run a check on a Butch Decker for me?" She gave Sandy Decker's address.

"Hang on."

Through the phone, Caron heard Sandy's computer keys clicking. Parker was watching her nonstop, with that same focus he'd used on Meriam. She hated feeling like a specimen under a microscope—especially in a car that seemed to have shrunk the minute he'd gotten into it—but her pride wouldn't let her ask him to stop staring.

Sandy came back onto the line. "That's D-e-c-k-e-r, right?"

Caron verified the spelling. "Yes."

"We've got nothing on him. Not even a parking ticket."

"Thanks. I'll check in later." Caron hit the hook button.

"Nothing on the man, right?"

Boy, did she wish she could say no. "Don't look so smug, Parker. It's early yet."

Thoughtful, she studied her list of Decker's neighbors. Ina Erickson. A good feeling suffused Caron. If the numbers ran as they should, Ina lived directly behind Decker, on Twenty-second Street. Caron dialed the number.

An older woman answered. "Hello."

"Ina Erickson?" Caron sensed the woman's uneasiness. She didn't receive many calls after dark. And the storm had her edgy.

"Who is this?"

"We haven't met, Mrs. Erickson. My name is Caron Chalmers." Caron closed her eyes and saw a crucifix on Ina's wall. Though the rest of the modest furniture was dusty, the crucifix was polished to a high gloss, not a speck of dust anywhere on it. Ina could be trusted. "My partner and I need to talk with you about something very important. It concerns your neighbor, Butch Decker. I wouldn't ask like this, Mrs. Erickson, but it's very important. If possible, my partner, Parker Simms, a private investigator, and I would like to come over right away."

"Parker Simms?" Ina asked. "Is he related to Charley Simms, the cop?"

Caron looked at Parker. "His son."

Ina's tone lifted a notch. "Why, I knew Charley for better than twenty years. 'Course, I'm retired now, but in my younger days, I worked at a laundry. A young crackerjack robbed me one night, and the police sent Charley over. After that, he dropped by once in a while to check up." She paused to grab a breath. "Pretty much kept his thoughts to himself, but he was a fine man. A body could tell. I was sure sorry to read in the paper that he'd died. Getting shot like that. I sure did hate it."

A lump settled in Caron's throat. Parker had masked his expression. Had Charley been abducted? Was he the reason Parker had gotten involved?

"You and Parker come on over now, you hear? I'll put on a pot of coffee. It's a bad night to be out, what with the storm and all."

"Thanks, Mrs. Erickson. We'll be right there."

Caron handed Parker the phone. "She knew your father."

"A lot of people did." Parker clipped the phone back to the dash. "He was a cop here for a long time."

She knew she shouldn't ask, but something inside made her do it. "Parker?"

He didn't answer. His hand was on his thigh. She covered it with her hand. "Was Charley abducted?"

"No." He moved his hand and cranked the ignition, then turned on the radio.

Parker obviously didn't want to talk about it. She turned down the volume almost before she realized she'd moved. "If we're going to work together, you've got to stop clamming up every time I touch on a subject that's not comfortable."

No answer.

"Maybe I should explain."

"That would be refreshing."

Back to sarcasm. Though sorry to see it, she didn't let it deter her. Talking about Charley had Parker veering close to the emotional bone, and snapping at her to hide it. "I know someone you care about was abducted. I sensed it when we were talking at the restaurant. When Ina mentioned your father's death, I thought it might have been him."

Still no answer.

"Okay, you win." She leaned back against the seat and closed her eyes. She couldn't force the man to confide in her. He didn't like or trust her, so why *should* he confide in her? His attitude didn't bode well for their working relationship, but what more could she do? She'd reached out her hand, and drawn back a stump. The next move was his.

Ina answered the door wearing a dusk-blue bathrobe and a white shower cap. Raw-boned and wrinkled, she was close to seventy.

"Hi, Mrs. Erickson. We called a few minutes ago. Caron and Parker."

"Do you have any ID?"

Pleased that the woman was cautious, Caron reached into her purse and pulled out her driver's license. Parker passed a card and stepped into the light on the porch.

"My word, you look just like your daddy."

Parker gave Ina a smile that warmed Caron's heart. "Lots of people say I do."

"Well, they're right. You're a cop, too—like your father."

"No, I'm not." Resentment flashed through his eyes, then disappeared. "I'm a private investigator. But I'm helping the police. So is Caron. That's why we're here."

"Well, come on inside." Ina stepped back to let them pass. "Don't look like the rain's ever gonna quit." She bustled around them. "Hot coffee's in the kitchen. Come on back and take off the chill."

Soon they were seated at Ina's kitchen table with hot cups of coffee and large wedges of homemade cinnamon rolls.

Parker bit into one, gave Ina a dreamy-eyed look, then chewed and swallowed. "Wonderful, Mrs. Erickson."

"Thank you. And call me Ina." Ina preened and refilled Parker's coffee cup. "Now what can I do for you children?"

Caron looked at Parker. He motioned, giving her the honor of explaining. "I have a gift, Ina." Nervous, she let out a little laugh. Opening herself up for ridicule was something she normally avoided like the plague.

"That's good. A woman needs grit today. Things were a lot simpler back when I was a girl. Why, I recollect once—"

Caron touched her hand to Ina's forearm. "Not *grit*, Ina. *Gift.*"

"Speak up, child. My ears ain't what they used to be."

"I said, I have a gift."

Ina stilled her fork. "What kind of gift?"

Caron took the plunge, left herself vulnerable. "I'm psychic—I see things."

"Things?"

"People," Caron amended, strumming her fingertip against the coffee cup. "People in trouble. A little girl was abducted, and no one believes me, including my partner." She glanced at Parker. Not so much as a muscle twitched. "I have to find proof to find her, Ina."

"Uh-huh." The old woman's voice grew stronger. "All right. What can I do? And what does Decker have to do with this?"

Caron cocked a brow. "You believe me?"

Ina nodded. "Yes, I do."

Parker groaned, and Ina must have heard it. She gave him a wrinkled frown. "You're just like your daddy, Parker Simms. Charley wouldn't believe nothing he didn't see for himself, either. There's something you ought to be remembering, boy, that your daddy never did. A body ain't apt to strut around saying they're different if they ain't. People are mean to 'em for it. So them telling they're different don't make much sense, now does it?"

Parker looked properly chastised, but it was as put-on as those tilted smiles of his. Still, Caron appreciated Ina's support, and there was a mean streak in her that thoroughly enjoyed seeing Parker Simms on the receiving end of a pointed finger for a change.

"Thanks, Ina." Caron swallowed a bite of the roll and shoved a raisin around in her mouth with her tongue.

"For what?" The woman looked genuinely surprised. "At my age, it don't take a genius to figure out there's more that goes on in this world than I understand." She laced her fingers on the table. "Now, what's this all about?"

"You can't tell anyone what I'm about to tell you," Caron warned the raw-boned woman. "It could hurt the girl."

"I know how to clamp my jaws, child." Impatience wove into Ina's voice. "I see everything that goes on around here, and I don't say anything to anyone about it. Can't abide gossip. Just can't abide it, and never could."

Even with Ina's assurance, Caron knew the telling was risky. Ina did keep a lot to herself, and Caron could sense that the woman could be trusted, but this was different. Trying to help, she might blab everything Caron told her throughout the neighborhood. Word could get back to Decker. Caron might become his new target—or, worse, he might panic and hurt the child.

A quick glance confirmed that Parker was still entertaining doubts. Caron hated to see that. Why was he so distrustful? "Swear on the cross, Ina. Total secrecy."

"Not until I hear what you've got to say. I didn't crawl out of the swamp yesterday, child. And I don't swear to my Maker till I know for a fact exactly what it is I'm swearing. If you want my help, you'll have to trust me."

Caron propped her elbows on the table. She'd trusted, and been burned. Instinct told her that Ina was a good woman, that it was safe. But her instincts had been wrong before. She couldn't—the girl couldn't—afford for her to be wrong again.

"Butch Decker—" she heard Parker begin.

Ina interrupted without hesitating. "Scum."

Caron frowned, then dared to ask, "Have you seen anything unusual going on with him in the last few days?"

"Unusual?"

"Anything odd—for Decker," Parker clarified.

Ina clicked her tongue. "Tuesday night, I did. Struck me more than odd, I don't mind saying."

Caron tensed. "What?"

"Well, I was sound asleep on the sofa. Dozed off watching the Tonight Show—after the monologue. It just ain't the same without Johnny. Anyway, I heard a cat mewing. More like screeching, truth to tell. It woke me up. The Kleins, across the street, have a Persian, Fluffy. I figured she'd gotten stuck in Decker's yard again. Fluffy and Killer don't exactly get along. He trees her on the shed roof pretty often. Anyway, I looked out my living room window, and I saw Decker outside. He was getting something out of the trunk of his car."

Parker leaned forward, over the table. "What was it?"

"Well, it didn't make sense then, and it don't now. Decker don't have a wife or kids, just Linda—his sister who lives in town—but he was getting a lavender bicycle out of that trunk."

Caron's stomach sank to her knees. Tuesday was the day she'd first imaged the little girl being abducted—off a lavender bike.

Parker poured hot coffee over the cold in his cup and reached for a second roll. "Could the bike belong to one of Linda's kids?"

"Shoot, Linda don't have any children, boy. She wouldn't ruin her figure. Married herself a highfalutin man from downtown." Ina dropped her voice to a conspiratorial whisper. "They say he's richer than that young Trump fellow, but I can't say that for sure. Don't see him much. Linda comes around every Tuesday, though, regular as clockwork and dressed up fancy."

"Was Linda there this past Tuesday?" Caron gave Parker an I-told-you-so glare that clearly annoyed him.

"Sure was," Ina said. "I was out working in my flower bed, getting it ready for planting, when she drove up. Smiled and talked real friendly, like usual. But when she left, she sure wasn't smiling. She was fighting mad, and yelling at Decker that he must have lost his mind."

"About what?" Parker asked. "Do you know?"

"No, I didn't hear it. But Lily Mae—she lives on the other side of Decker—says she bets it's got something to do with Linda's husband. Lily Mae's seldom wrong about things like that. She's got this friend, Mary Beth, who works down at the diner near the man's office. We drop by for lunch sometimes, and from what I've overheard, he'd make a fine snake-oil salesman." She winked and dipped her chin to confirm what she'd said. "Slick tongue."

Caron passed the woman a second card. "Here's my phone number, Ina. If you think of anything else, or see anything odd, will you call?"

"Sure will. As long as you don't tell Decker. I don't need any more trouble with him. Last time we had a run-in, he stomped my irises. Ain't much of a man who stomps a woman's irises, if you ask me."

Caron agreed.

Parker smiled, and when Ina escorted them out, then shut the door, he said, "I think Ina Erickson can hold her own."

Caron would've answered. But she couldn't get her voice to work. She'd never seen Parker relaxed and at ease. His smile touched his eyes, and the accusing gray glints had softened to soft gray glimmers.

"Caron?"

His amused tone had her snapping to; he was holding the door open. She avoided his eyes and slid into the car, flatly refusing to accept what was happening. She *couldn't* be attracted to him. Not to Parker Simms. The man was insulting and rude—and he didn't even think there was a case!

He folded himself into the car, and the smell of his cologne and rain mingled with the scent of leather. Her throat felt thick. Parker Simms was guilty on all counts. But he was also the first man in a long time who had her hormones humming louder than a swarm of droning bees.

She didn't care for the feeling; actually, she hated it. But only a fool would deny it. And only a fool would fail to accept that under the circumstances being sexually attracted to Parker Simms was stupid *and* crazy.

Knowing that, she must have misjudged her reactions to him. Checking to make sure, she gave him another look. The flutters came back to her stomach, and that little tingle of anticipation danced along her nerves. He smiled, and her hormones zipped into overdrive. There was no mistake; she was attracted.

And stupid and crazy.

Chapter 3

Caron shivered.

Sitting in her parked Chevy about three houses down from Decker's, she pulled her raincoat closer around her and looked up at the streetlight. Through the rain, it glowed hazy. The lights inside the houses did, too. But the street itself was eerily dark between the amber lamps, and quiet.

Caron locked the car door with her elbow, then reached for the box of tissues. Her breath had the window fogging, blocking her view. The temperature must have dropped ten degrees since dark.

A tap sounded on her window. Caron gasped.

"Hey, it's me."

"Parker." She relaxed. He'd gone to get them something to eat. She reached over and unlatched the passenger door. "Go around."

He did. Caron watched him through the smeared windshield. He was holding a paper bag.

Parker cracked the door open, mashed the button to keep the dome light off, then slid in. "It's really coming down."

Rain slicked his hair and ran in rivulets down his face to his throat and disappeared inside his jacket. Watching it,

Caron felt her throat muscles tighten and heard her stomach growl.

"Good." Parker slid her a grin. "You *are* hungry." He dug inside a crackling sack, then held out something wrapped in white paper. "Hamburger."

Caron's mouth watered. She could smell the still-sizzling meat, the mustard and dill pickles. She loved dill pickles. "Thanks."

"You're welcome." He pulled a cup from the bag and passed it, too. "Coffee. Black coffee."

"Observant." Caron set the cup on the dash and lifted the top. Steam rose from it and fogged the windshield again. She unwrapped the crinkling white paper from the burger and took a bite. Mmm, it was good. Hot and juicy, just the way she liked. The Butterfinger she'd had for lunch had worn off a long time ago, and it was already after 9:00 p.m.

Parker pulled a carton from the sack. "Egg fu young," he said. "I wasn't sure if you'd like it. So I got you the burger."

He'd made the right decision; she wouldn't have liked it. "I hate vegetables."

She took another bite. It didn't want to go down. There was something too intimate about sharing a meal in a dark car on a rainy night with Parker Simms.

Parker opened the carton and stabbed his fork into his egg fu young. He splashed brown gravy onto his finger and licked it off.

Great hands. Long, competent fingers. Sexy. She stopped eating long enough to sip the coffee. It warmed her throat, and she stopped shivering. But the overall temperature seemed to have spiked fifty degrees, and, she admitted, it had nothing to do with the coffee or with Mother Nature's whims. Caron gave Parker a wary look. "You're a health food nut, then? Only vegetables?" It fit. He was a big man, powerfully built.

"Not really. I just don't dump chocolate into my body twenty-four hours a day." He shifted and pulled a candy wrapper from the seat beneath him. "Do you ever eat anything besides Butterfingers?"

"Not if I can help it." Despite an explicit decision not to, she smiled. Inwardly groaning at her weakness, she swung her gaze to Decker's front door, determined to keep it there and her mind off Parker Simms's attack on her senses.

"I guess I owe you an apology, don't I?"

Caron turned back to Parker. "An apology?"

"I'm sorry I clammed up about Charley."

She waited, but he didn't say any more. "And I'm sorry you lost your dad, Parker." Maybe his pain was worse than her own. He had a lifetime of memories of his father to recall. She had only seven years.

"He was a good man. I admired him."

She wanted to say something, but feared that if she did Parker would stop talking.

"He was shot," Parker said softly. "You asked how he died."

"That must have been hard. No time for goodbyes."

Parker frowned, his gaze on his food. "My mother had a really hard time accepting it. So did my sister, Megan."

So had he. Caron brushed a raindrop off his neck. "How old were you?"

"Twenty. Megan was fifteen."

There was bitterness here, deep-rooted and blinding. "What happened?"

Parker's shrug brushed their shoulders. "Megan had just started dating. Her first boyfriend came around to pick her up. They were going to the movies."

He paused for a second. Caron didn't push.

"Charley recognized the guy and refused to let Megan go. He was a hood, Caron. Charley wouldn't have interfered if he'd been a decent guy."

"He was protecting his daughter."

"Yes." Parker put the carton on the dash. "Megan was angry and upset. Charley tried to calm her down. So did Mom. But she wasn't ready to be calmed."

"At fifteen, a girl holds a lot of righteous indignation when people get into her love life."

"Exactly," he said, sounding relieved. "Anyway, when Charley left for work, Megan still wasn't speaking to him.

And about four the next morning, the officers came to tell us that Charley had been shot."

Caron could only imagine the horrible shock and pain of that visit. She reached out and touched Parker's sleeve. "It was Megan's date, wasn't it? He shot Charley."

Parker nodded, and for an instant she saw pain flash in his eyes. It was gone so quickly, at first she thought she'd imagined it. But she felt him tremble under her hand and she knew that she hadn't. Parker had been very close to his father, and she would have bet her life that he hadn't shared his grief or loss with many others.

She'd been wrong about him, thinking he was cold and lacked compassion. He wasn't. He was one of those men who lived close to the bone, kept things that mattered private.

A porch light across the street from Decker's flicked on. Parker grunted. "That's the third time."

"I haven't seen it."

"You've been watching me and not seeing anything else. Tunnel vision."

Caron wished that weren't true. Then she wouldn't have glimpsed inside Parker Simms and become even more attracted to him. But she had. "Not guilty," she lied. "I've been fixed on Decker's."

"Right."

Knowing she'd never swallow another bite after telling that whopper and having it disputed, she wrapped the uneaten half of the burger and put it on the dash. "What have I missed?"

"Two doors back, left side of the street. There's a couple in the car, arguing."

Caron looked back. The car was parked directly under the streetlamp, and she could see the outlines of two people inside.

"That dog," Parker went on, pointing half a block up the street, "is making hash of somebody's garbage. He's strewing it all over the place."

"What dog?"

Parker leaned closer. "That one."

His body heat flowed to her, seeping deep inside her. She moved away. "Okay, so I've been fixed on Decker's," she said defensively, and not honestly. "But that's why we're here."

Parker gave her a look she couldn't see well in the dim light, though she sure could feel it. "You've got to learn to expand, Caron. Not to fixate on one thing at a time."

"I have to focus," she said, gripping the steering wheel. "Otherwise, I might miss something important."

The porch light flickered on a fourth time, and a woman peeked out through a curtained window. "She's noticed us."

"Yes." Parker dumped his empty carton into the sack, crunched it, and set it on the floorboard. "Her husband will be out in a minute."

As if on cue, the front door opened and a man stepped out onto the porch, wearing a yellow slicker and mud boots. The woman stood behind him, watching. He walked down the steps and headed toward them.

Parker waited until the guy passed the end of the box hedge and turned onto the sidewalk. Then he pulled Caron into his arms and dipped his head to kiss her. Near her mouth, he paused and brushed her lips with his fingertip. Her eyes stretched wide. Very pretty, that. "Mustard," he whispered, then covered her mouth with his.

She let out a little gasp and pushed against his chest.

"Shh, kiss me, Caron," he said, and as if she understood his motives then, she stilled her hands and let them just rest against his chest. Beneath her fingers, he felt his heart pound. God, but her lips were soft. And she smelled so good. So warm and sweet. He'd wanted to kiss her at least a hundred times today.

Her fingers began moving, rubbing tiny strokes against his jacket. She flattened her hand against it, as if the creamy leather were seducing her palm. She wanted to touch him. Parker groaned and thrust his tongue deep into her mouth. She tried pulling back, but he buried his hands in her hair and held her firmly to him, crushing his lips down on hers.

"Parker," she gritted out between sweeps of his tongue. "Knock it off."

"Shh." He pulled back far enough to talk, but his voice was as shaky as an old woman's. "Make it look good, or have your answers ready."

From the corner of her eye, Caron saw the man near the front of the car, and again fused her mouth with Parker's. His lips were gentle, soft and heated, and he tasted faintly of shrimp and brown gravy. She loved shrimp and smooth, hot brown gravy. He smelled wonderful, too. Like fresh air, rain, and some heavenly cologne she'd didn't recognize. Very masculine. Very inviting. Very, very tempting.

He caught her lower lip and tugged, then plunged his tongue deep into her mouth. White heat washed through her body, and Caron nearly melted into the seat. His throaty groan told her he had noticed her reaction, too. And, determined that he not make a one-sided issue of the matter later, she wound her arms around his neck, her fingers into the silky curls at his nape. Never in her life had she felt anything so sensual as that silky curl wrapping around her finger while the back of her hand caressingly brushed against warm male skin.

There was a tapping on the window, and it was growing insistent. Parker cranked down the glass without breaking their kiss, then looked over at the man. "Yes?"

"What are you two doing out here?"

Parker thought that was obvious. Every window in the car was steamed up. Caron tried to move away. He should let her—their kiss had served its purpose and more. But he held her to him. "We had a little disagreement," he told the man in an unsteady voice. "But everything's fine now."

The man gave Parker a totally male look. "Well, find a motel. My old lady's breaking her neck watching you two."

Parker rolled the glass back up, then glanced at Caron. Her hand rested in a fist against his chest. She kept her gaze fixed on his neck, but even in the dim light he could see that she was blushing.

"Don't you ever do that again," she said from between gritted teeth. She pulled away, shifted over on the seat, and gripped the steering wheel so hard her knuckles stood raised like knobs. "Not ever."

"It wasn't that bad." Parker ignored the daggers she was sending his way. "I'll admit you could use a little practice. But you don't kiss that bad." If she'd been any better, he'd have been making love with her on the front seat. That lack of control over his own body infuriated him. Of all the women in the world, this one he *didn't* want. The trouble was, his body did want her. And it wanted her badly.

"Shut up, Simms."

"What did I do?" He knew exactly, of course. Her breathing hadn't yet steadied, either. The aroused male in him loved that; he knew from watching her that she didn't often come unglued in a man's arms. But she'd come unglued in his.

"Would you just shut up?" She grabbed a tissue and began swiping at the windows.

She didn't look vulnerable now. She looked ready to scratch his eyes out. Knowing she'd been just as affected as he took away some of the sting. His body had betrayed him. But hers had betrayed her, too. Lust was tough on the ego, and on the conscience. It demanded tackling before it could be dismissed. So, Parker told himself, he'd tackle. "What did you think?"

"About what?"

If she kept rubbing that same spot as hard as she was, she'd wear a hole in the windshield. He covered her hand with his and held it still. "About the kiss, Caron."

She drew in a sharp breath, then let it out slowly. She didn't fight him, didn't try to free her hand. It felt small, nearly fitting into his palm. And warm. So warm.

"I didn't like it."

Her breath warmed his face. He smiled into her eyes. Passion still lurked there. She'd liked it...too much. "Good. I didn't like it, either."

That frosted her voice. "You don't make sense. Has anyone ever told you that? You kiss like an inferno, then claim you're an iceberg. Are you always like this?"

He brushed her hair back over her shoulder. Her flesh quivered under his hand. "Look, honey, let's cut to the chase."

"I'm not your honey."

"No, you aren't. But for some reason neither one of us can figure, our bodies have been whispering sweet nothings to each other all day and half the night. No, don't deny it. I'm not dull, and neither are you."

"Okay, I won't. I can be honest about my feelings," she said, strongly implying that he couldn't. "You're a gorgeous hunk. What woman wouldn't react to that? But I don't like you, Parker. And I hate myself for knowing that and yet still finding you appealing. Inside, you're as phony as they come."

"Phony?" He frowned, genuinely surprised. "Me?"

"You," she insisted. "You weren't any more attracted to Meriam Meyer than you are to me, yet you were able to cozy up to her as though she was irresistible."

His jaw hung loose. Where did she come off, saying *he* was a phony? "In case you didn't notice, Snow White, it was our plan for me to keep Meriam occupied so you could have some privacy to steal the book."

"Oh, I noticed. You were all over the woman."

"I wasn't." Was she jealous? Impossible... Maybe...

Caron reached over and made an exaggerated show of tenderly brushing an invisible speck from his cheek, then gave him a smile that turned his mind to mush and his body into a furnace. "What's that action called, then?"

Parker gritted his teeth. "It's called, getting an ink smear off a woman's face."

"Right."

"That *is* right." He had half a mind to kiss her again, to let her feel every drop of his heat. Instead, he shifted his body weight to lean against the door. "With your 'gift,' you should've known that."

"My gift only works on important matters. And that certainly doesn't include you."

If that was true, then why was she so ticked? "So you can't tell what I'm thinking." He'd been worried about that, in case there was a grain of truth to her psychic claims.

She slumped her shoulders and rubbed her temple. "No."

"Why not?" He was surprised she'd admitted it.

"I just told you."

Because he wasn't important? That didn't wash. She expected him to believe she saw images of complete strangers. "But you can read other people's thoughts."

"Some of the time."

Parker softened his voice. "So why not mine?"

"I don't know." She slumped forward over the steering wheel, clearly exasperated.

She did know. But he was pushing her too hard. There was a strain in her now that hadn't been there earlier. She was a phony who needed exposing, but she was a human being, too, a woman. And women required finesse, not bullying. "Would it help if I apologized?"

She rolled her cheek against the wheel and looked at him. Her voice sounded hopeful. "Would you mean it?"

He hadn't done anything to apologize for. Kissing a beautiful woman with shadows in her eyes wasn't a crime— just stupid, considering the woman he'd kissed was Caron Chalmers. But to find out what he wanted to know... "Yes."

"Yes, then. It would help."

"Okay." He leaned over, covered her hand on the wheel, and felt her tremble. "I'm sorry, Caron."

"Fine."

If her voice got any tighter, she'd squeak, but she didn't move her hand. The top of hers nestled under his palm. Warm. Tiny. Fragile. When he knew what she was, what she'd done, how could she strike him in that way? How could she make him want to prove her innocent? How could she touch him emotionally?

They lapsed into silence. Rain pattered against the windows and the hood of the car, steady, rhythmic, relaxing. The silence wasn't heavy, Caron decided, just indicative of both of them being tied up in their own thoughts. She watched the drops hit, bead into balls and glisten in the glow from the streetlamp. Rubbing her leg with her free hand, she wondered why Parker was still holding her other hand. Why didn't he move it? Why didn't *she?* Did not being alone in this situation feel *that* good?

"Where do you come from?" Parker asked.

"Here." She rubbed harder, grazing her shin. Her leg felt swollen, but it wasn't.

"Me, too." He sighed. "You are single, aren't you?"

"What?"

"Single," he repeated. "As in no husband to hunt me down for being alone with you in a dark car."

"I wish I was married. You could use a little adjustment. But, no, I'm not."

She studied the feel of her leg, wishing she'd worn a skirt instead of slacks so that she could better isolate the pain. The girl must be injured. Caron sensed swelling.

"Do you have family here?"

"They're in Mississippi." She glanced at him. "You?"

"My mother and Megan." He let his head loll back against the seat. "You remind me of her."

"Who?"

"My mother."

Caron grimaced. "Just what a girl wants to hear."

That remark earned her a grin that was more lethal than his smile. "Yeah, well . . . She's a special woman."

"Most mothers are."

"Do I detect an 'except mine' somewhere in there?"

"No." Caron fiddled with the keys dangling from the ignition. "Including mine."

"Hmm . . ." Her words said one thing, her tone something else. Her relationship with her mother was strained; he'd have bet his license on it. "What about your dad?"

She stiffened. "I haven't seen him for a long time."

Pain etched her voice, and Parker just couldn't make himself push her. He rubbed her thumb with his.

After a long moment, he looked over at her. The strain was still there, around her eyes, but she was in control again. "You haven't told me what Sandy said about Decker."

Caron paused, then decided that if he was to be of any use to her, Parker had to know what was going on.

She wished for the hundredth time that she could read his thoughts. She couldn't read Sandy, because she refused to probe. That wasn't the problem with Parker. But she was positive she'd figured it out. It was so basic, so simple that

she couldn't believe it had stumped her. Physical awareness dulls psychic awareness. The moment she'd looked
into his eyes, her awareness of Parker Simms had tossed her
into a total psychic shutdown. "Sandy didn't find anything on Decker. Not even a traffic violation."

"And?"

Caron held off a sigh. So Parker knew there was more.
Sandy had said Parker was sharp; that, at least, had been
the truth. "And there's still no report of any abduction."

"So we still have no hard evidence."

"Ina saw Decker getting a girl's bike out of his car trunk.
It was lavender . . . just like the bike I imaged."

"Mmm." Parker stretched out, rested his arm on the
back of the seat. "We need more."

They did. But at least he wasn't disputing her images.
That was progress. Only then did it occur to her just how
much she wanted him to believe her.

Her stomach rumbled.

"Didn't you get enough to eat?" he asked.

Her hand felt cold without his covering it. She buried it
in her lap. "Too much."

"Why's your stomach still growling?"

His fingertip brushed her nape. Caron looked down to
his chest. "I'm not hungry."

"You sound hungry to me." One finger became four and
a thumb, kneading the knots from her muscles. "And
you're tense."

She was tense. The images coming back. Worrying about
the little girl. Parker touching her. How could she not be
tense? But he was wrong about the rest. "I'm not hungry." She gave him a flat look. "The girl is."

He clamped his jaw shut and moved his hand. "Don't
you think it's time to play straight with me instead of
pawning off this—"

"Caron interrupted him, squeezing his jean-clad thigh.
"Decker's leaving."

He swung his gaze to the front door, but then saw Decker
backing out of the garage in a raggedy Plymouth.

"You follow him in your car," Caron said. "I'll check the house."

"What about the Doberman? He'll swallow you whole."

Caron grabbed the leftover burger from the dash and predicted, "He'll welcome me with open arms."

"No. What if someone else is there? You don't know what you might be walking into here."

"I'm hoping I'll walk in on the girl." Caron swept her hair back from her face. "I feel her here, Parker. I have to go in."

He hesitated for a long moment. It would be better if he went up against Decker. Still, Parker hated the idea of her entering that house alone. "All right." He dropped his voice. "But be careful."

When Decker was busy closing the garage door, Parker cracked the door open and slid out, then leaned down to look back at her. "You will be here when I get back?"

"Yes." Caron's heart raced.

Parker shut the door.

Caron waited until Decker drove off and Parker followed him. Then she got out of the car. Killer met her at the gate, growling and raising a ruckus. She broke off a bit of the burger and tossed it to him, wishing she had a muzzle. She'd always been afraid of large dogs. And Killer was monstrously large.

He gobbled up the burger and returned for more. Caron opened the gate and stepped inside. When he didn't lunge for her, she broke off a second piece and dropped it beside him, praising him for not biting her.

A third bite fed got her to the front door. It was unlocked, which surprised her—despite the Doberman—and she left the rest of the burger on the front stoop, then went inside and closed the door behind her.

The living room was a disaster. The television was on and tuned to a Saints-Redskins game. Beer cans littered the coffee table and an end table beside a worn-out recliner. Caron stepped over a misshapen stack of newspapers Decker hadn't bothered to unroll and entered the kitchen.

Half a TV dinner that looked like it had been there for a week was on top of the stove. More beer cans were on the counter. And the only way to get another dish into the double sink would be with a wedge. The tile counter was greasy. So was the torn potato chip bag on it. She noticed some scribbling, and a pen set beside the bag, and looked closer. A phone number had been written there.

She copied the number, then walked through the kitchen to the door. The garage. Dirty and messy, just like the rest of his house. She glimpsed color and swung her gaze. There, in the far corner, she saw the little lavender bike.

Her heart pounding hard, thudding against her chest wall, Caron walked across the oil-stained concrete and looked closer at the bike. A name had been etched into a metal plate at the center of the handlebars. *Misty.*

That was the child. Caron knew it. Tense, she reached over and traced the letters with a trembling fingertip. Betrayal flooded her. Fear joined it. A fear so cold, so chilling, that she had experienced it only once before. The night Sarah James had been murdered.

Whimpering, Caron tried to pull back, but she couldn't move. Her fingers had gone stiff on the handlebars. She felt frozen. Willing herself to calm down, she felt her wrists begin to throb, her leg to burn like fire where before it had only stung.

A car horn honked. Parker, warning her.

She spun around. Decker! Decker was back!

The garage door started to open. Caron ran inside. If she hurried, she could make the front door *before* he made it in through the back one.

She jerked the front door open. Killer growled, showing her every sharp tooth in his head. Caron heard the garage door going down, and slammed the front door. Where could she go? How was she going to get out of here?

The door leading to the kitchen creaked open, then slammed shut. Something heavy thunked down on the tile. Caron rushed down the narrow hall and ducked into the first room. A bathroom? There was nowhere to hide in a bathroom!

Fighting panic, she stepped inside the shower and drew the curtain almost closed. The tub was caked with soap scum. Black mold had taken over the tile grout and caulking. She couldn't die in this pigsty. She couldn't!

The bathroom door groaned open. The shower scene from the movie *Psycho* flashed into her mind. Sweating profusely, her flesh crawling, Caron flattened herself against the back wall of the shower, shaking with fear.

Decker stuck his hand in and cranked the faucet. Caron glued her gaze to his beefy fingers, not daring to breathe. The pipes moaned and hissed, and then ice-cold water streamed out, soaking her from head to toe. She held her breath and didn't move. She wanted to move. She tried to move. But, God help her, she couldn't so much as bat an eyelash.

Chapter 4

The water grew hot and steamy.

Caron stood in the shower beneath the stinging spray, her clothes plastered to her body. Mesmerized, not daring to draw breath, she watched a distorted Decker through the frosted shower curtain. He was a big man, barrel-chested and thick-muscled. Bullish. And she harbored no illusions; to hide his involvement in Misty's kidnapping, Decker would kill her. Pushed, he would kill both her and Misty. The hard-knocks Deckers of this world resented being pushed, and they pushed back—hard.

He unbuttoned his shirt.

Shivering, Caron forced her numb mind to think. When he dropped his pants, she'd push past him, and run. That was her best hope of getting out of here alive, of finding Misty.

Decker unbuckled his razor-thin belt. Through the curtain, it looked like a black snake. A potential weapon. Grabbing one end to pull it from the loops, he stilled, as if listening. Caron strained to hear, but the fear pounding through her veins, the splatter of the water against the fiberglass tub, drowned out all other sounds.

"Damn it," Decker muttered, then left the bathroom.

What was going on? She stuck her head out and heard the doorbell.

Parker! Imaging him pacing outside Decker's front door, she stumbled from the tub, her knees weak with relief.

Dripping water onto the threadbare carpet, she eased her way along the wall to the mouth of the hallway, near the living room. Her shoes hissed out water. She took them off, her adrenaline pumping hard, her heart knocking against her ribs.

A bare-backed Decker stood dead ahead, facing the front door. With as little as a half turn, he would have her in plain sight. Parker's voice rang out, and she caught a glimpse of him over Decker's shoulder. No one ever had looked or sounded so good.

She slipped past Decker and inched to the back door.

On the other side of the screen, Killer was waiting.

Snarling, he hulked down, growled deep and throaty, baring his teeth. In a cold sweat, Caron snapped the screen door back. The dog reared, lost his balance, and toppled. Scrambling to his feet, he barked wildly.

Caron shushed him, but the dog didn't listen. From the front door, Decker bellowed, "Come here, you damn mutt!"

As if she was no longer there, Killer took off through the shrubs and weeds and mud, clipping the corner at the front of the house. Caron hurried out, shut the door behind her, shoved on her shoes and ran straight to the back fence. She hooked the toe of her best taupe flats into the hurricane fencing and hoisted herself over. When she hit the ground, she sank to her ankles in a bed of soft mud.

"Psst!"

Shoving her dripping hair out of her eyes, Caron looked up at the clapboard house, toward the sound. Wearing a faded pink chenille robe and a purple satin turban, Ina was watching through the curtains.

She shoved them back and bent low to the small opening in the window. "What are you doing out there?"

"It's Caron." She rubbed the gooseflesh from her arms.

"I figured that, child. You just stomped my irises."

"I'm sorry." Caron stepped closer to the window. "Decker came home."

Curiosity turned to worry, pitting deep wrinkles around Ina's mouth. "Best you come inside, then."

"I can't." Her heavy breathing fogging the chilly air, Caron looked back over her shoulder. Killer was still barking at the front of the house, and there was no sign of Decker. "Parker will wonder what's happened to me."

"You dry off right away, then, you hear? A body can catch pneumonia just like that—" Ina snapped her fingers "—on a night like this."

"I will." Pneumonia. Was that what was wrong with Misty?

Ina shut the window, then moved away. Caron turned down the shell driveway. Between the lights, shadows sliced thick, dark wedges into the pavement. Concealed by them, she crossed to the opposite sidewalk, made her way around the corner, then down the block to her car.

Nearly giddy with relief, she opened the door and slid bonelessly onto the seat. Even as she swung the door shut behind her, she closed her eyes and began to hum, starting the relaxation exercises Dr. Z. had taught her years ago. A long minute later, her heart had slowed to a mere canter.

"Quit shaking, will you?" The deep voice came from the back seat. "You're slinging water."

Caron gasped and whipped around. A wet clump of hair stung her cheek and clung. "Damn it, Parker, you scared ten years off me!"

"Sorry." He studied her face, frowned, then passed her a crisp white handkerchief. "How did you get wet?"

It smelled like his cologne. Her throat tight, she patted her face dry. "Decker turned on the shower. From the looks of him, I figured that was the one place I'd be safe. I was wrong."

Parker chuckled.

"It's not funny."

"Sure it is."

"It's not, Parker," she said from between her teeth. "He would've—"

"He didn't." Parker's eyes sobered. "Let it go, Caron. You've got no time to waste on what could have happened."

"Give me a minute, okay?" Parker Simms had the compassion of a swamp stump. "I'm cold and wet and my leg hurts like hell."

He slid forward and draped his arms over the seat. "You're scared."

She glared at him. "He scared me. Of course he scared me. I'm not stupid, Parker. If he'd caught me in there, I know what Decker would have done."

Parker swept her hair back from her face. "But he didn't catch you. You're fine. Now get over it."

Sliding to the door, Parker got out of the back seat, then got back into the front beside her. "Let's go."

"Go?" She wadded up the handkerchief and pressed it firmly against her mouth to inhale its heavenly scent. Why the smell of Parker's cologne calmed her when the man himself infuriated her, she hadn't a clue—but it did. "Go where?"

"Anywhere," he said impatiently. "The porch light just went on." He hooked a thumb toward Mr. Mud Boots's house.

The frilly curtains fluttered. "Mrs. Mud Boots is watching again." Caron fleetingly hoped for another kiss. She even tensed in anticipation.

When it didn't come, she frowned her disappointment. "I'll take you to your car. I saw a fresh twelve-pack of beer on the counter. Decker's good for the night."

"Okay."

She stopped near the black Porsche and waited.

Parker looked over at her. "I'll meet you here at six in the morning."

"Six? That's awfully early." She had been hoping for a little time to work on her own. "Tomorrow's Saturday. People sleep in," she said, trying to dissuade him. "It's after midnight now."

"What did you find?"

She might have trouble reading him, but Parker certainly had her number. His look said he half expected her to lie. But she wouldn't. Even if he was lying about why he was getting involved, he meant her no harm. His having aided her in getting out of Decker's house proved that. She could trust him . . . a little. "The girl's bike, and a phone number. I don't know if the number is important, but the girl's name was engraved on the bike."

"What is it?"

"Misty," Caron said around a lump in her throat. The fear and betrayal she'd sensed so strongly on touching the bike flooded her again now. "Her name is Misty."

Parker's eyes softened. He pulled his wallet out of his jacket and passed Caron a business card. "Call me when you're ready to get started in the morning."

"I thought we were to meet here at six."

"I've reconsidered." His gaze flickered over her face, then lingered on her mouth. "You need some rest. You look like hell."

"You're such a charmer, Parker Simms." If her looks mirrored her feelings, she did look like hell. Her mind had been reeling for days, and there was no relief in sight.

"Charm comes with the tall-dark-and-handsome package. But to tell you the truth, it causes more problems than it's worth."

That remark redeemed him a bit. He accepted his assets and knew that alone they fell short of making a patch on a good man. It was what was inside that really counted.

"Parker." She stared at the speedometer. "Misty doesn't have a lot of time." Caron glanced up to see how Parker took her remark.

His lips pinched together, and he dropped his lids to half-mast, hiding his thoughts. "She's sick," he said, his voice surprisingly soft. "You've told me."

Caron couldn't talk; Parker still didn't believe her. Oh, why did it matter? But it didn't just matter, it hurt. Weary from their battles, she sighed. "See you tomorrow."

He started to reach for her hand, then drew back. He wanted to say something, she could see that he did by the way he twisted his mouth, but he decided against it, nodded briskly and backed away from the car.

So he was shutting her out again. Before she could talk herself out of it, she got out of the car and slammed the door. Breasts to chest, she glared up at him. "I've had it, Parker. Damn it, why won't you believe me?"

"Because I can't. Because—" He clamped his jaw shut.

"Go on, spit it out. Let's get whatever's bothering you out in the open. Then, just maybe we can clear the air."

"We can't." Regret laced his voice. "I don't want to talk about it, Caron."

"Well, I *do* want to talk about it." She clenched her hands into fists and squeezed. "You pour on the charm and wheedle secrets out of everyone, but, by heaven, you won't share your own. That's not fair, Parker." Angry tears stung her eyes. Furious tears, because Parker wasn't any different from the others. "What are you so afraid of?"

"Leave it alone," he said sharply. "You don't know what you're asking from me."

"Then tell me. I'm not stupid, Parker. I know you hate me. What I don't know is why!"

He spun away and strode to his car.

"No." She ran after him and grabbed his sleeve. "No, not this time, Parker Simms. You're not walking away from me without telling me what this is all about."

He stood stock-still. The muscles in his arm were as rigid as steel.

She leaned her forehead against his arm. "Please, Parker. Talk to me."

He blinked, then looked down at her. "You're crying."

He sounded surprised that she could cry. "I'm not crying." A sniffle joined the tears, proving her a liar.

He brushed at her wet cheek with the pad of his thumb. "Okay, you're not."

She raised her face to his hand. "Talk to me."

A frown formed between his brows. "It's best if I don't." A sadness that touched her came into his voice. "It's best to keep this inside me."

Her voice was an explosion of sound in the silent night. "What have I done to you? Can you at least tell me that?"

His hands trembling, he gripped her arms and glared down at her. Anguish warred with rage and flooded his face. "You've made me give a damn about you! That's what you've done, Caron! That's what you've done!"

She expelled a puff of breath, and the fury drained right out of her. Parker was hurting; she could feel it so clearly, so deeply. She softened her voice. "Is giving a damn about me that bad?"

"Yes!" The word seemed to have been ripped from his throat. He let go of her so fast that she nearly stumbled.

When she looked up at him, his face was a bleak mask of desperation. "Go home, Caron. Please . . . just go home."

Frightened by the intensity of his emotions, frightened of not getting help she might need to save Misty, Caron rushed back to her car. Without risking another look at him, she punched down on the accelerator and tore down the street.

By the time Caron crossed the Greater New Orleans Bridge, she'd stopped trembling. But by the time she reached her apartment, she was shaking all over again. Not in fear now, but in anger. She was furious with Parker, but even more so with herself. What good was a partner who didn't believe her? One who wouldn't talk to her? She didn't have time to nurse him along, to probe the depths of his soul to find out what she'd done that had made him so bitter. Her energy had to be focused on Misty.

Inside the apartment building, a bleak yellow light spilled down the dingy stairwell. Caron grabbed the scarred banister and grimaced at all the graffiti on the steps. There were nearly more markings than wood! In a blue funk, she climbed up to her second-floor apartment. Just once, why couldn't a man she cared about have a little faith in her?

It still didn't sit well that Sandy had no report. In every case she'd imaged, he'd always had one. Self-doubt crept in. Maybe Parker was right. Maybe this wasn't real.

Caron fought back. She was *not* losing her mind. Misty *had* been abducted. She *was* sick.

"Nothing like fighting for a life with one hand tied behind your back," Caron muttered, dumping her shoes just outside the door to her apartment. Muddy from Ina's iris bed, they hit the bare boards with a dull thunk and splattered gooey mud. The shoes were ruined. She didn't care to think about what the mud had done to the carpeting in her car.

A creepy feeling seeped through her. She looked both ways down the empty hall. At the far end, near the stairs, a single bulb flickered. It always had, and that flickering always had made her jumpy.

Telling herself to get a grip, she leaned back against the doorframe and dug through her purse for her keys. If it took more than another five seconds to find them, get dry and get to bed, she'd have to paste her eyelids open and tie knots in her knees to stay upright.

As she fished for her keys, her arm banged against the door. It inched open on creaky hinges.

She gave it a blank stare. She'd locked that door; she knew she had. Her heart in her throat, she looked inside from the dim hallway. Dark. Cool. Nothing stirring.

Tense as strung wire, she flipped on the light and took a tentative step inside. Certainty suffused her, and she resisted the urge to shrink back. Someone had been there.

From what she could see, nothing was missing. The stereo, television—even the VCR—were all in place. Nothing had been stolen, but someone *had* been in her apartment.

Her heart hammering in her temples, she walked through the living room, darting her gaze everywhere, then went into the kitchen.

Nothing amiss. Coffeepot still plugged in, its red light glowing. Her cup, still half-full of coffee, sat where she'd left it on the chipped porcelain table. The box of food she'd brought back with her from Midtown was still on the counter, beside the phone. Her palms slick with sweat, she silently eased a butcher knife from the wooden block near the stove, and turned.

The refrigerator's condenser kicked on. Caron jumped. Recognizing the whirring noise, she took a calming breath and warned herself to settle down.

When she'd regained a little composure, she checked the pantry and the hall closet, then moved on to the bathroom. At every corner, every door, she expected someone to spring out at her. But no one did. She found nothing unusual, yet the sense of invasion, of violation, grew stronger and stronger.

A bit more confident, she walked into the bedroom. Her floral bedspread was wrinkled, but she'd probably done that earlier, sitting on the edge to put on her shoes. Her bra and jeans lay where she'd flung them, on the stuffed chair near the window. She dropped to her knees and checked under the bed, then the closet. Systematically she moved on until she'd searched every crevice in the apartment.

She found nothing. But her door had been unlocked, and someone had been here. The question was who? And why?

She put the knife down on the kitchen table and went back through the living room to close and lock the door.

The little hairs on her neck lifted. Her muddy shoes weren't where she'd left them. One was close by, and the other one had been kicked halfway down the hall.

And then she knew, as certainly as if she'd seen it happen. The someone who had been in her apartment had still been there when she'd arrived home. And, just as she had done with Decker, the intruder had slipped past her and fled.

She slammed the door shut and slid the lock, jamming the bolt home. Slumping against the door, she dragged in air, forcing it down to her lungs. Something wet her cheek. It smelled . . . hauntingly familiar.

Queasy with dread, she dragged her fingertips across her cheek, then looked at the bright red streaks on the pads of her fingers. Blood.

Whimpering, she backed away...and stared in horror at the words smeared on her door. YOU NEXT.

Parker crawled into bed and let out a sigh. It had been a long day, but a productive one. After a year of intense effort, he was finally closing in on Caron Chalmers.

He honestly didn't know what to make of the woman. That made deceiving her tough on his conscience. He raked a hand through his hair and stared at the ornate ceiling in his bedroom. If he hadn't known what she'd done, if he hadn't known Harlan's death was her fault, Parker wouldn't have believed her capable. She seemed so damn sincere. But he did know. So why was he suffering these conflicting emotions about the woman?

She was attractive. Slim. Pale. Delicate. But he'd met lots of attractive women, and none of them had tied his stomach into knots. Her courage, maybe? Con artist or no, she had more than her share of guts. Like sex, fear had a distinct scent, and when she'd gone into Decker's, Caron had smelled of fear. But she *had* gone in. Alone. Willing to confront whatever awaited her.

Parker couldn't help but admire her for that, even if the incident had given him a few gray hairs. It'd been a tense few minutes there, trying to get her out before Decker realized she was in the house.

When she'd gotten back into the car, Parker had been even more tense—and suspicious. Could she and Decker be working together? Only a fool wouldn't have considered the possibility. But one look at her and those suspicions had died a natural death. Soaked to the skin, she'd looked so shaken, so damn vulnerable.

It was her eyes. They were intriguing, riveting, lavender, almost translucent when he'd kissed her. But only until she'd regained her senses. Then the shadows had come back. Pain hid in those shadows. Gut-wrenching, soul-shattering pain. What—who—had put it there?

Questions. Always questions about her. But too few answers.

Restless, Parker flipped onto his side, yanked up the comforter and concentrated on the aquarium's droning hum. Usually the sound soothed him. Tonight it agitated.

It was Caron. The idea of busting her had been easier from a distance, when he hadn't yet seen those shadows in her eyes. Maybe that was her attraction. Maybe it wasn't. The shadows confused him. Cold and calculating con artists like Caron Chalmers didn't get hurt. Yet that was what those shadows made him feel. That she'd been hurt and she hadn't recovered. Not that she seemed fragile, so much as brittle and ready to snap.

"You're getting soft in the head, Simms," he muttered, scrunching up his pillow. "Get some sleep." He forced his eyes closed. Tomorrow would be here soon enough, and Chalmers was quick; he had to be quicker.

She'd been ticked about how he'd kept Meriam Meyer busy, and about him not showing a lick of compassion at her near miss with Decker. Parker had had no choice but to play hardball then, though. Caron had looked a beat away from panic, and he had been a beat away from smothering her with relieved kisses. His stomach muscles clenched. After meeting Decker, Parker agreed she'd been right. Kidnapping or no, if Decker had caught her in his house, he would have killed her.

That thought had Parker nearly climbing the walls. He wished he didn't care about her as a woman. Something in her pulled hard at him. Hard, and at gut level. She was attracted to him, too, which was the only thing that made his being attracted to her easier to take. Still, she didn't know him; he hadn't done anything to her. But he did know her, and she'd cost him probably the best friend any man ever had in his life.

That made Parker feel guilty as hell for being attracted to her. Oh, after they'd kissed he'd told her he hadn't been. But he'd lied. He had been attracted. So attracted that if Mr. Mud Boots hadn't nearly knocked the window out of the car rapping on the glass, Parker and Caron would have ended up in the back seat, doing something that would have haunted him as long as he lived.

As aroused now as he'd been when it was happening—and feeling even guiltier—Parker tossed on silk sheets that suddenly felt rough. How could he want her, knowing who she was and what she'd done? What kind of man was he?

It was her, not him. He'd outgrown back-seat tussles years ago. At least he'd thought he had, until tonight.

Parker groaned and again stared at the ceiling. With her sweet curves and sexy moves, Caron Chalmers was hard on his body. But the woman inside was even harder on his soul. She'd cried for him. He rubbed his thumb and forefinger together. Because he'd shut her out and not explained his animosity toward her, she'd cried tears that he'd touched. And he'd been so tempted to open up.

The phone rang.

He considered not answering it, but some sixth sense warned him that he'd better. He reached over to the nightstand and lifted the receiver. "Yeah."

"Parker."

Her voice was high-pitched and cracked, but he recognized it at once. He sat straight up in bed. "What's wrong, Caron?"

"Someone's been in my apartment. They—they left me a message."

He tossed back the covers and jumped out of bed. "Are you sure they're gone?" Hiking his shoulder, he jammed the receiver between the crook and his chin and jerked on his jeans.

"Yes. I—I tried to call Sandy. But he wasn't—"

"Give me your address." He knew it, but right now he just couldn't think.

She reeled it off. He repeated it back to her to make sure he'd gotten it right. "Give me ten minutes."

"I'll wait outside. I—I don't want to be alone here."

"No." She was reacting on emotion, not with logic. "He might still be around."

"It could've been a woman."

Parker grimaced and stuffed his wallet into his pants. "Then *she* might still be around." He pulled on his jacket. "Sit tight. Can you do that?" Where was his shirt? He'd forgotten his damn shirt. "Just sit tight."

"I wouldn't mind if you'd hurry, okay?"

Her voice sounded so tiny, so faint. She was afraid. Hanging up the phone was one of the hardest things he'd ever had to do. Breaking the connection, the link reassuring him that she was safe, was damn near impossible. Why she dredged such strong emotions from him, he didn't know. Nor did he want to know. He just wanted to get to her. If he found a message—and no evidence that she'd planted it herself—then there was a case. Not necessarily a child abduction, but a case. Anyone could be after her. How many cases had she "helped" Sandy solve?

Because he should know the answer to that and he didn't, Parker moved twice as fast. If anyone touched that woman, there'd be hell to pay. She was his, and if anyone was going to bring her down, it was damn well going to be him.

Caron heard the knock. She couldn't make herself touch that door. She wanted to, knew she needed to, but, staring at the dried blood, she couldn't make herself do it. "Come in."

Parker shoved open the door. "Come in? Damn it, Caron, I could be Jack the Ripper and you just invite me in?"

She stood motionless, her arms curled over her chest, staring blankly at the door. In her peripheral vision, she saw Parker. Where was his shirt?

He turned and looked at the message, then stepped close to her. "I thought you meant a note."

Tears burning the backs of her eyes, she blinked hard and looked up at him.

His voice grew soft. "What's that on your face?"

It was blood. From where she'd leaned against the door. Suddenly, she spun and fled to the bathroom. At the sink, she twisted on the tap and snatched up the soap, her hands shaking so hard she could barely keep hold. With harsh, grating swipes, she scrubbed her face till her skin burned, then kept on scrubbing. She wouldn't look up, couldn't look into the mirror until she felt clean again.

"Caron." Parker stepped in and touched her shoulder.

"No!" She jerked away and kept scrubbing. "I have to get it off!"

"Caron!" he shouted. "Look at me!"

She did. Her eyes were wild. Certainty flooded through Parker. This incident wasn't part of any con. The fear and shock in her were real. The air between them crackled with tension. He grabbed a towel hanging beside the sink and moved slowly toward her, speaking softly, in soothing tones. "It's okay. Everything's all right now." Gently he wiped the lathered soap off of her face. "There, it's gone."

"It's not gone," she spat out.

He cupped her chin in his hand. "It's over, Caron."

"It'll never be over." Something flashed in her eyes. "You don't understand!"

He held her face firmly, wet the edge of the towel, then rinsed her face. Her chin quivered, bumping the heel of his hand, tearing at his heartstrings. She was an emotional wreck, but more than just the message had done this to her. Forcing a calm he didn't feel into his voice, he looked down at her. "Explain it to me, then. So I can understand."

"I've been violated. A stranger has been in *my* home. He's touched *my* things." Her face drained of color. "*My* ...personal things."

"What personal things?"

"He'll be back, Parker." She growled deep in her throat. "He'll be back...and next time it'll be my blood on the door."

"No." Pain wrenched in his chest.

"He will, damn it!" She shuddered. "I—I—"

"What?" Parker shook her shoulders. She was bordering on hysteria. "You what, Caron?"

"I...saw him." Her head fell back, and she let out a guttural growl. "Oh, God, Parker, I saw him kill me!"

Her knees gave out. Parker scooped her up and cradled her against his chest. She buried her face at his neck, and he felt her shaking. She was crying, not a sobbing, out-of-control crying, as one would expect, but soft, soul-deep tears that wet his neck, soaked into his skin and squeezed his heart.

Feeling raw and tender, he rubbed little circles on her back. Her skin was clammy. So was his. And he wasn't sure which of them was trembling more. Seeing that message smeared on her door had made mincemeat of his insides. He imagined that was a fraction of what seeing it had done to her. The need to comfort her overwhelmed him, and without thinking of the thousand reasons he shouldn't, he brushed her forehead with his lips. "Shh, it'll be all right. Stop crying."

"He knows about me, Parker. He knows I know about Misty." Caron shuddered and buried her face deeper in the crook of his neck. "We have to stop him before he hurts her." She reared back, away from his shoulder. "I—I don't want her to die." A fat tear tumbled to her cheek.

Parker's emotions nosedived along with it, and he vowed, "She won't, and neither will you. I swear it. Do you hear me? I swear it." And because the need in him was so strong, because he, too, needed comfort and reassurance, he sealed his vow, covering her lips with his.

Her kiss was angry, desperate. He tasted her panic, and wondered if it was his own. She crushed her mouth to his, raked his lower lip with her teeth, and, when he opened his mouth she groaned deep in her throat and swept her tongue deep inside. Her fingers flattened on the bare skin between the lapels of his jacket, then brushed through the hair on his chest. His flesh quivered, and he grunted his pleasure. Their tongues met and tangled in a violent mating that made him weak, enraged his senses and sent his thoughts tumbling.

With a gasp, she eased back. "Parker?" She sniffed, sounding dazed, and brushed a fingertip across his lip.

He swore it brushed across his heart. Her lips were rosy, swollen from the kiss. Her face was flushed, and the irises of her eyes had deepened to the velvety purple of a midnight sky. Feeling too much, he abruptly set her to the floor. "Get some things together."

"Why?" Uncertainty tinged her voice. She straightened her blouse. Water-splashed, the yellow silk clung sheer and outlined the lace on her bra.

He swallowed a knot from his throat and forced his gaze to her face, forced his voice to be less harsh. "I can't leave you here, Caron. Now get some things together, okay?"

"Where am I going?"

Parker expected some flak, but he wasn't giving in on this. They definitely had a case. And she definitely was in danger—from someone. "You're coming home with me."

"You live *here?*"

Parker heard the surprise in Caron's voice, and, looking through the Porsche's windshield, he glanced up at the house. It wasn't much different from the other homes lining Pontchartrain Drive—just three stories of white brick, mortar and verandas surrounded by a lawn no self-respecting weed would dare to grow in and a black wrought-iron gate. Mossy old oaks lined the sweeping drive, and strategically placed lawn lights shone amber on stately evergreens and fragrant magnolias. To him, it was home, just as it had been home to three generations of his mother's family. But to Caron, he was sure, the house reeked of wealth.

He grimaced, sorry that he'd brought her here. She'd be stiff and formal with him now, intimidated, maybe even withdrawn. He'd lost it emotionally for a while back at her place, but he'd calmed down since—at least enough to know that he needed her comfortable, needed her guard down, to catch her cold and prove beyond all reasonable doubt that she was a con artist committing fraud.

Someone *was* after her, and he meant to find out who and why. But that didn't exonerate her for what she'd done to Harlan. Parker had to keep that injustice firmly in mind.

He gripped the steering wheel and compromised, telling her a half-truth. "I stay here." Dishonesty rubbed him the wrong way, but this time the end justified the means.

"Oh."

No disappointment edged her voice, just acknowledgment. That surprised him, too. He drove through the gate and stopped in the center of the circular drive, near the gurgling fountain spurting streams of pink water. At least she was talking again. For most of the ride, she'd sat staring woodenly out of the window, damned near comatose.

Some truth niggled at the fringe of his conscience, as if he ought to be seeing something obvious, but wasn't. Unable to put a finger on the source, he got out of the car, went around, then helped Caron out. Before plunging in, he should have thought this move through. But he hadn't, and what was done was done. At least he wouldn't have to explain this to his mother and Megan. They weren't due back from Europe until after Christmas, so there was no chance they'd drop in on him.

And he wouldn't have to worry about them confiding in Caron, blowing his cover and a year's work.

Caron stepped out. She didn't say anything, but she was scanning, taking it all in, the gardens, the house, the pool.

His fingers stiff on her arm, he grabbed her suitcase from the back seat, then led her in and showed her around.

From her expression, it was clear she recognized that valuable antiques stuffed the rooms, all the way to the attics, that Turkish rugs littered the hardwood floors, and that a Botticelli painting hung on the wall. But she kept her thoughts to herself, not uttering a sound...until they stepped into the garden.

The scent of irises hung heavy on the cool night air. Caron touched the petals of a white iris almost reverently.

"Ina likes irises," she said softly. "I stomped hers."

Parker stepped into a shadow. Caron seemed so fragile. "We'll get her some more."

She looked back at him, still fingering the petal. "Decker stomped them on purpose, but I didn't know they were there. I jumped the fence..." She gave Parker a searching look that tied him into knots. "Do you think Ina will see the difference?"

Doubt, he realized. Shock, too. "Sure she will."

Taking Caron's arm, he led her inside and up the glossy oak stairs. At the bedroom next to his, he stopped and opened the door. "Here you are."

She stepped inside and slowly turned in a circle. Parker's gaze went with her. White oak furniture. A high canopy bed draped in soft pink antique satin. A skirted dressing table and tiny pink floral wallpaper.

"It's pretty."

Her simple remark eased the tense knot from his chest. Seeing the house through her eyes made him feel guilty for having been so fortunate—and acutely aware of how unfortunate Caron had been. She'd been raised by her mother in a shabby four-room house in a neighborhood that spawned drug dealers and prostitutes. Thanks to her aunt Grace's getting Caron in with Dr. Zilinger, Caron had become acquainted with Sanders. And money for the basics soon had become available through him—courtesy of the good taxpayers of the city of New Orleans. Consultant fees for Caron's services.

Harlan had figured Sanders and Caron's mother were having a fling, but Parker wasn't sure about that. The woman was strapped financially and had been ever since Caron's father had taken off for parts unknown. But as far as Parker had been able to tell, Sanders and Caron's mother had never met. On what basis had Harlan pegged them as lovers?

The answer to that question had died with Harlan. But Parker felt sure that lack of money *could* induce a parent to coerce a child into pretending to "see" things she really didn't see. Kids wanted to please their parents. Hadn't Parker played tight end in the championship game with a broken wrist so that he wouldn't disappoint his father?

That could be it. That could be why Caron pretended to be psychic. So that she wouldn't disappoint her mother— her father having already deserted her. Or maybe she pretended for the money. Or maybe for attention? To get back at life for having been so hard on her?

It was possible, Parker decided. But not probable. Caron seemed appreciative of his things, but not overly impressed—except by the flowers in the garden. Frankly, pretense didn't seem her style. But she was a con artist, he reminded himself. Her seeming lack of interest could be intentional.

He dragged a hand through his hair. Hell, what did her reasons matter, anyway? Harlan was dead. She was responsible. That was the bottom line.

"Parker?"

Standing by the window, she looked small and solemn. From the knees down, her white slacks were mud-spattered, and a bit of mustard competed with the water stains on her crumpled yellow blouse. Her hair hung in damp wheaten ropes, and her eyes... Damn those eyes for looking so vulnerable. How could she look so lost and vulnerable?

"I want to thank you for... tonight."

She meant it. He could see that she did. Now he felt guilty *and* like a heel. Wishing she was fighting mad, wishing she wasn't looking at him like she'd lost her last friend, he shrugged. "What are partners for?"

"I'm scared." She gave him a tremulous smile. "I'm not used to being scared."

"I know." The awareness that her words barely pricked the surface of her feelings had the urge to comfort her slamming into him. Parker stiffened against it. But once more she'd touched him. She'd reached deep inside him and wrenched out feelings he didn't want to have for her. And he had to admit that, if only to himself. "Why don't you get into bed? I'll bring you a glass of warm milk to help you get some rest."

Caron nodded, and he left the room.

By the time he heated the milk, called police headquarters to report the break-in and walked back upstairs, Parker was convinced. He was a walking lump of screwed-up contradictions on all matters relating to Caron Chalmers. He wanted her, and knew he shouldn't. He doubted there was a case, yet knew there was a case. He hated her for deceiving others, yet he willingly deceived her. He knew she was a fraud, yet she didn't look or act like a fraud. She looked and acted vulnerable. She *was* vulnerable. And, despite his resolve not to, he felt protective toward her. It was like he'd told her. He gave a damn. He cared. And he had no right.

Deciding he'd definitely lost his mind, he tapped on her door.

No answer. He tapped again. "Caron?"

Still no answer.

Parker eased the door open. She was sitting in the middle of the bed, her legs folded under her, a long flannel nightgown, so faded it belonged in a rag bag, covering every inch of her skin, from chin to toes. Her expression was wooden, so fixed that Parker feared that if she blinked an eyelash would crack off, and her skin was the color of the milk.

"Caron?" He stepped closer, but still she didn't move. He set the milk on the nightstand and sank down onto the edge of the bed. "Caron," he said again, touching her arm. "Don't let this get to you. Not like this."

Something in her seemed to snap. "It's gotten to me, Parker." She glared at him, fury sparking in her eyes. "It's gotten to me way down deep."

"I've reported the break-in. Tomorrow you'll need to do the paperwork." When she didn't say anything, he let his hand slide up the length of her arm. The flannel was soft, and it felt good against his palm. "It's okay to be scared."

"I am scared." The look in her eyes changed. Her irises deepened to a dark purple that bordered on black. "But I'm even more angry. I was violated. So was Misty. That's wrong, Parker. No one should be violated." Her voice grew harder. "Misty can't fight whoever's behind this. But I can, and I will."

Relieved that she was rallying, Parker smiled and gave her arm a reassuring squeeze. "When you get your spunk back, you do it with a vengeance, don't you?"

"It surprised me." He heard her swallow. "We all have a dark side that's dishonest. I should know that in some people dark's about all there is. It's happened so many times." Lines proving she'd received one too many disappointments etched her face, and she let out a self-mocking laugh. "I'm a slow learner." Her gaze, steady and probing, locked with his. "No matter how often it happens, dishonesty always surprises me. Does it you?"

Did she know? A streak of uncertainty shot up his spine, left a bitter taste in his mouth. Had she connected him with Harlan? Instead of answering, he asked a question of his own. "Have you been deceived a lot?"

"Many times." She sighed deeply, avoiding his eyes. "Once people realize you can see things, they're always scheming of ways to use you—usually to get them money." She reached past him for the milk and took a drink. "That's why Aunt Grace took me to Dr. Zilinger's."

So Caron didn't know, and it was her Aunt Grace who'd wanted the money, not her mother. Could Harlan have confused the women? Maybe it was Grace and Sanders who were lovers. Maybe... Caron's hand was steadier now. Parker was glad to see that. "How old were you?"

"Seven." Caron again sipped from the glass. "My father was a heavy gambler. All the family knew about my gift, of course, though my mother drummed it into my head to ignore the images. One night, my father handed me a racing form. I pointed out the winner." A sad smile curved her lips. "That was the last time we saw him."

She rubbed her calf, the same one she'd rubbed in the café and in the car. Parker frowned. "The horse won."

"Oh, yes."

"Why didn't your father come back, then, for more winnings?"

She lifted her chin a fraction. "My mother forbade him to come near me again. He called a couple of times. Once, I even answered." She looked over to the window. "But Mother took the phone and told him not to call again."

Parker's stomach pitched. He was torn. On the one hand, her father had had the right to be a part of his daughter's life. On the other, her mother couldn't be faulted for not letting her father use Caron. This explained a great deal. It was no wonder Caron was reluctant to trust him, or any man. "Your mother blamed you, didn't she?"

"Yes, and no." Caron slumped back against the pillows. "She didn't openly say it was my fault Dad was gone, but I felt guilty." She scraped her lower lip with her teeth. "If I hadn't had the gift, she wouldn't have sent him away."

"And she never let you forget that, did she?"

Caron didn't answer. Nor did she look at him.

She didn't have to; he knew. Anger at her mother burned in his stomach. How many times had Caron paid? How often had barbed remarks, accusations and blame been thrown in her face?

She still felt guilty, he realized. Which was why she continued to send her mother half her salary.

"It wasn't your fault, Caron. You didn't take your father away from your mother."

She cocked a brow at him. "Are you a shrink? You sound just like Dr. Zilinger."

Picturing the tiny Austrian doctor, who had repeatedly refused to answer his questions about Caron, Parker denied it. "No, just an observer of human nature." He plucked a loose thread from the bedspread. "But that doesn't change the facts. It wasn't your fault."

"So I'm told. But my mother would disagree." She tugged the crumpled covers up over her knees, making a tent. "Back then, the images would come so fast I couldn't decipher them. My mother played ostrich—"

"Ostrich?"

"Buried her head in the sand. She nearly buried my sanity with her." Caron squeezed a pillow to her chest. "Do you know how active a child's mind is? What it's like to see flashes of horrible things that make no sense to you?''

"No, I don't." He leaned forward, bracing his elbow on his knee, his chin on his hand. The lady was a class act. The message on her door had rattled her to the core, yet she held it together and trudged along, keeping up her performance. It was damn convincing, too. Or it would have been, had he not known better. "But I would think it would be confusing."

"It was."

"So you went to Dr. Zilinger." The air conditioner kicked on, blowing a steady stream of cold air that ruffled the lacy curtains at the window and the tendrils of hair drying into soft curls and framing Caron's face. His insides warmed. Beautiful.

"Aunt Grace took me. Catch the overhead light, will you?" She reached over and switched on the bedside lamp, filling the room with a warm pink glow. "She told my mother we were going to the movies, of course. But I'd talked to her, and Aunt Grace knew that without help to make sense of all I was seeing I was headed for major trouble."

So Grace *hadn't* connected Caron and Sanders for the money. Back to square one. Frowning, Parker flipped off the light. "Everyone should have an aunt Grace."

"Mmm, yes. She makes awful tea, though. It's so weak you can read a newspaper through it."

The frown faded, and he looked back at her. "That's pretty weak."

"Well, almost that weak."

The smile in Caron's voice skimmed warmth over him. She drank again from the glass; he swallowed with her.

"So tell me about you." She finger-combed her hair back from her face. "Did you have an aunt Grace?"

The lamplight turned her hair gold. "No, I had a mother like her, though. She's as feisty now as she was when I was growing up. 'Never accept anything at face value.' That was her prescription for a happy life."

Parker walked to the window and looked out. A light wind feathered through the trees. Moonlight pooled on the manicured lawn. To get trust, you have to give it. He wanted—no, needed—her trust. "Mom had a bucketful of washboard philosophy. So did Charley."

"Why do you call him by name?"

Parker shrugged. "We were buddies more than father and son." He scratched his temple and smiled. "Charley was a strange kind of guy. He loved his family—don't get me wrong. But it was like . . . I don't know, like he didn't want us to love him back too much."

"Maybe he was afraid he'd have to leave you, and he didn't want you hurt."

"Maybe," Parker said, gaining insight. Maybe that *was* why Charley had given to a certain point, then pulled back emotionally. Parker smiled at Caron. "Are you a shrink?"

"No." She slid him an enchanting grin. "Aunt Grace relies heavily on washboard philosophy, too."

"You're fond of her."

"Sure. She's a terrific lady. A bit eccentric, by most people's standards. But she's always been there for me."

And no one else had. What had it been like growing up with a mother who resented you, and no father?

Parker fingered the wingtip of a fragile glass dove sitting on a chest of drawers. Damn lonely. And, for a kid, frightening.

"Did your mom bake cookies?" Parker asked.

"Are you kidding? My mother thought the kitchen was just a room you walked through to get out to the garage to the car. Aunt Grace did, though. Double chocolate chip with fudge icing."

He pulled a face. "Chocolate."

She wrinkled her nose at him. "Yep."

He sat on the foot of the bed. "In grade school, when I came home, Mom was there with cookies and milk."

"Every day?"

"Yeah." He hadn't thought about that before. She'd given him and Megan time she might have wanted for herself.

"Tell me more."

He saw the hunger in Caron's eyes. Her childhood had been very different. Maybe sharing his with her would keep her mind off what had happened. "I'm too tired."

She patted the bed beside her. "Rest here."

There was nothing sexual in the invitation, but still he hesitated.

"What? Afraid you can't control yourself?"

There was a warm, teasing light in her eyes that he hadn't seen before. "I was worried about your control."

"Don't."

He slid down onto the bed and stuffed a pillow against the headboard, then leaned back. He could smell her perfume, the scent lingering on her skin.

"Did you and your mother talk about what went on at school?" She scooted closer, until she was looking right into his eyes.

He swallowed a boulder that had somehow lodged in his throat. "Yeah, we did." From her smile, he thought that made her happy.

"What did you talk about?" Her voice dropped a notch. A very sexy notch.

"I talked about Johnny Seaberry stealing Lisa Sanger. She was the first woman to break my heart."

Caron laughed softly. "How old were you?"

"Six." He grunted and scooted down on the bed. "I thought I'd never love again. But Mom assured me that I'd be heartbroken at least a dozen times."

"Have you?" Caron snuggled against his side.

"At least a dozen."

"Me, too."

"Really?"

"Uh-huh." Caron tentatively touched his chest with just a fingertip.

He ground his teeth to keep from reaching out. It would be so easy just to lift his hand and wrap his arm around her.

"When I was little, my dad talked about the old days." She yawned and pressed her cheek against his chest, rubbing his hair with her skin. "His father immigrated from Sweden."

The friction aroused him. He looked down and saw that his nipple had peaked. "Um, we're all-American mutts."

"All-American mutts." She stroked his chest. "I like that."

What the hell. Parker gave in to the urge and circled her shoulder. She purred like a satisfied cat. He gave her a smile she couldn't see. "Are you still scared?"

"Yes, but it's better." She gave his ribs a little squeeze. "Tell me more about when you were a boy, Parker."

With her being so close, he thought it'd be a major miracle if he managed to string a coherent sentence together. But she'd stopped shaking, and if hearing his voice would help her through the night, then he'd give it his best shot.

He started talking about his high school days, when Charley was still alive. She seemed to need to hear about his father. He told her about growing up in New Orleans and playing football. And about Peggy Shores, the foxiest cheerleader at St. Nicholas, breaking his foolish heart because he'd failed to score the winning homecoming touchdown. He continued on, revealing the intimate details of his life, his college years at Loyola, and his stint in the Gulf— something he'd never spoken of to anyone.

There was only one facet of his life he avoided: his relationship with Harlan, and the resulting investigation of Caron upon Harlan's death.

By the time he finished, her lids were droopy. "When you want to be," she said, a scant breath away from sleep, "you're a very nice man."

Shadows danced across her face. Beautiful. How nice would she think he was if she knew he was deceiving her? He rubbed tiny circles on her shoulder, feeling guilty as hell.

"Parker?"

Drowsy, he closed his eyes. "Mmm?"

"Tomorrow we need to check out that phone number I found at Decker's. It's important, after all."

An uneasy feeling crept through his chest. He had to force his fingers not to go hard against her tender skin. "How do you know?"

She looked at him through sleepy eyes. Her skin was smudged by dark circles. "It's the reason the man wants to kill me."

Parker's heart skipped, then thudded. "Decker?"

She hesitated. "No."

"Who, then?"

"I'm not sure."

She knew. Feeling oddly betrayed that she wouldn't tell him after the intimacies he'd shared with her, Parker narrowed his eyes and pushed. "But you know he's a man."

"Yes." She licked her lips and burrowed deeper into Parker's chest. "I smell him."

"What?" He sat up slightly.

She frowned, shoved him down onto the pillow and tugged the covers back up over her shoulder and his chest. "Men smell . . . different."

He couldn't disagree. She smelled . . . fresh and warm. A heady mixture of soap and—Passion? He sniffed her subtle scent again to be sure. Yes, Passion. Her choice of perfume surprised him. Hardly the pick for a prim and proper schoolteacher. His voice grew husky. "Give me the number."

She told it to him from memory. Parker stretched over and grabbed the phone. His jeans pinched at the waist, and he wished that, if they couldn't be skin to skin, then at least something softer than denim could be between them.

He could strip down, he supposed. But he'd probably be given his marching orders immediately. Hauling himself off to his room would be the wisest move he could make. Sharing a bed with Caron Chalmers—even if that was all they shared—had to be the dumbest thing he could ever do in his life.

He looked at her sleep-soft face and surrendered. Well, at least it wouldn't be the first dumb thing he'd ever done.

Accepting that he'd made his decision, he dialed the phone and connected with an answering machine. When it had played out and beeped, he dropped the receiver back into the cradle and looked at Caron. "B. J. Hunt's."

She nodded, bumping her chin against his chest. "I'll tell Sandy in the morning and see what he knows about him." With a little yawn, she closed her eyes.

"There's no need." Parker brushed back a strand of hair that was clinging to her cheek. Why did she feel so soft? So warm? So smooth and creamy? "B. J. Hunt's is an investment firm, Caron. They handle only six-figure accounts."

Her eyes snapped open. "What would Decker be doing with their number?"

"I don't know." Parker guided her head back to his chest. "And we won't find out tonight. Rest now, hmm?"

"Will you stay with me . . . just till I fall asleep?"

He felt as if he were being forced to choose. Loyalty to Harlan, or to Caron. But Caron didn't know about Harlan, and she wasn't really asking for loyalty. She was asking for the warmth of another human being to get her through a rough night after a rougher day. "I'll be here," he finally said.

Parker clicked off the lamp, curled Caron's soft body into his arms and stared blindly into the darkness. He didn't like this B. J. Hunt development at all. And he liked even less that his worry for Caron's safety was growing by leaps and bounds. He didn't know why Decker had Hunt's number. But he damn well intended to find out.

Chapter 5

"I don't like it, Parker." Caron adjusted the seat belt in the white limo and nodded to the driver to close the door. "I feel like a kid playing grown-up. Are you sure your mother won't mind?"

"I'm sure. When she and Megan get back from Europe, they'll have half the clothes in Paris with them." Parker smiled. "Stop worrying. You look great."

Stop worrying. Right. It wasn't every day she wore a genuine Chanel suit—and she didn't want to be wearing one today. Especially one that belonged to Parker Simms's mother.

Caron slid him a glare. "Why the show? Why can't we just walk into Hunt's and ask a few questions?"

"Play it straight and aboveboard, you mean?"

"Exactly." She shrugged and quickly checked to make sure she hadn't wrinkled the jacket. If anything happened to this outfit, it'd take her the rest of her life to pay for it. "It doesn't make sense to lie when the truth will do."

"The truth won't do." He tapped on the glass and motioned to his mother's driver, Fred, to go on, then stretched out his legs. "You can't just walk into a place like Hunt's and get answers. Those people are trained to avoid questions—especially ones that might tick off a six-figure client.''

Caron sighed and checked the tilt of her black hat in the window. The brim seemed a shade too wide, but the effect was good. With her hair slicked back smooth, she looked filthy rich. The problem was, she didn't *feel* filthy rich. ''Okay, you've got a point. We play out the charade. But I still don't like it.''

''Stop checking,'' Parker said, giving her a warm once-over that set her to tingling. ''You look great.''

''Thanks.'' There was an easiness between them today that hadn't been there before last night. One she feared a woman could get used to too fast. She narrowed her brows and checked him over just as thoroughly. From the tips of his handmade Italian shoes up to his navy Savile Row suit, he looked perfect. Not to mention gorgeous ... and rich. He'd let her into his life, told her things she instinctively knew he hadn't told anyone else. Warmed by that thought, she straightened his red tie. ''You don't look bad yourself.''

Her fingers brushed his throat. The intimate vibration had her feeling, more than hearing, his chuckle.

''Careful,'' he said. ''You'll give me a swelled head. I might even think you like me.''

''Let's don't get carried away.'' The teasing lilt in her voice took the punch right out of her words.

He lifted a brow and feigned an innocence that set her to worrying. ''Do you always sleep with men you don't like?''

He'd left himself wide-open. She swept a nonexistent speck from her sleeve. ''Only the ones Peggy Shores dumped for blowing the homecoming game.''

''Ouch, that's low.'' His eyes twinkled; he hadn't really taken offense.

''Yeah.'' She smiled and pecked a kiss to the tip of his perfect nose, betting Peggy Shores was eating her heart out regretting that decision now.

The car slid to a halt near the curb on Canal Street. Fred got out, came around and opened the door. He was about sixty-five, Caron figured, tall and lean and very proper.

''Shall I wait, Mr. Simms?''

"I think so, Fred. Mrs. Simms and I won't be too long."

"Yes, sir." The older man touched his fingers to the brim of his uniform hat, shut the door and struck a pose beside the car. A fly buzzed his nose. Like some character out of *The Great Gatsby,* he didn't swat at it.

Amused, Caron linked arms with Parker. "*Mrs. Simms?*"

"That's right." He slid her a sidelong look. "We slept together in my home, Caron. I've got a rep to protect."

"Right." She was excited that he'd given her another insightful glimpse of him. A darling glimpse. Parker Simms—charming and gorgeous and hostile on demand— was terribly old-fashioned.

Wishing he would look her way so that she could read his expression, Caron walked toward the office. "I think your little disclosure shocked Fred." The man hadn't so much as batted an eyelash, but she'd sure sensed his surprise.

"Probably."

Caron glanced back. "If he keeps his knees locked like that for very long in this heat, we'll be peeling him off the sidewalk."

"He won't," Parker assured her. "Once we're out of sight, he'll relax."

She shouldn't push, but of course she would. And, knowing his response *did* matter, she told herself it didn't, then asked the question she really wasn't sure she wanted answered. "Just how many Mrs. Simmses has Fred met?"

The devil danced in Parker's eyes. "One."

"Oh." Her breath shriveled to a puffy wisp.

Smiling, Parker paused. "Surprised, I see. You really do have me pegged as a womanizer, don't you, Caron?"

That was exactly what she'd thought. But his saying it openly had heat rushing to her face.

"I'm not, you know."

She was beginning to doubt it herself. And, though she wondered, *how* he intended to explain her absence to Fred later was low on her list of priorities. A flip answer was definitely required. She hiked her chin. "Time will tell."

"Yes, it will. For both of us." The smile became a leer. Just on the other side of a brass nameplate bolted to a tall

column—and just out of hearing distance of the doorman—Parker again paused. "Remember, Mrs. Simms,
you're a little eccentric, a little dazed— No, don't object.
They'll be less cautious if they think you're an airhead."

She squinted against the strong sunlight. "I think there's
a backhanded compliment in there somewhere."

The look in Parker's eyes heated, became lazy and dangerous. "I'll help you find it later. For now, you're an eccentric airhead who's crazy about me."

If he kept looking at her the way he was, the crazy-about-
him part might be too easy to play. Caron groaned. "This
pretending really rubs me the wrong way. Can't I just be
me?"

Something odd flashed in his eyes, a hard glint that told
her he couldn't believe what she'd said. He rolled his gaze
heavenward, then dipped his chin and gave her a quelling
look. Still, when he spoke, his voice was softened. "We've
been through this, and we agreed this way is best."

They had. At dawn, and again at seven this morning.
Both times, Parker had made a strong case. "All right, all
right." Caron plastered a smile on her face. "But, for the
record, I don't like lying. So let's get this over with."

The doorman swung the tinted glass door wide. A blast
of cool air raised gooseflesh on Caron's skin.

The interior of the building was as sleek and angular as
the smoky-mirrored exterior. Cool white tile floors gleamed
glossy and smelled of wax. Black leather sofas and chairs
were arranged in three groups and separated by small gardens of lush green foliage. And at a desk near the far wall
sat a woman who could have modeled for the swimsuit issue of *Sports Illustrated.* By no stretch of the imagination
did her being seated mask her assets: tall, perfect bones,
and elegantly dressed in a quiet blue suit that perfectly
matched her eyes.

Caron straightened. Parker had known. If she'd come in
here in her mackintosh and jeans, she would have been
disregarded. Her time with her students had dulled her
memory. Rich responds to rich. Upscale firms take only
upscale people seriously. And for the first time since she'd
put on the cream Chanel suit, Caron was glad that she had.

Parker spoke to the receptionist, his voice cordial but authoritative. "We have an eleven-o'clock appointment with all of your counselors."

Caron clamped her jaw to keep from gaping. What lies had Parker told to finagle an appointment with *all* of the counselors? If she could keep her libido intact when she looked at the man, she'd *know* what he had done—and what he was thinking. Unfortunately, she hadn't mastered that control—at least not so far.

She slid him a sidelong look. He wasn't smiling. Taking her cue from him, she lifted her chin, doing her best to look snobbish, and certain she only looked ridiculous.

"Mr. and Mrs. Simms, yes." The receptionist flickered her gaze over Caron, then it landed on Parker and warmed.

Caron resisted an urge to groan. Did he affect *every* woman he met that way? As she followed the receptionist into an inner office, Caron decided he did. He had so far.

The office looked like a living room. No sleek angles here. Warm greens and browns, conservative and luxurious, in the manner of an old-time gentleman's club. The carpet was thick and plush. Sinking into it, she tottered on her heels and grabbed Parker's arm for support.

They sat down across from the fireplace on a leather sofa. Though the air-conditioning whirred softly, a fire snapped in the grate. Atmosphere, Caron figured, and a shameful waste of good trees.

A grandfather clock's pendulum marked the passing seconds. Parker looked totally relaxed, but with every click she grew more nervous. She was in over her head. Rich was a way of life, a thousand unspoken mannerisms. Mannerisms and attitudes that, though they were natural to Parker, she didn't have, and had never particularly wanted. But Caron needed those assets now, to find a connection between someone here and Decker, to find Misty.

Three men entered the room. Parker put a proprietary hand on her knee. She didn't object, and she chided herself for taking comfort in his touch—and for wanting more touches.

While the receptionist handled the introductions, Caron studied the men. One was about sixty, very distinguished, very reserved. Sensing that he was benign, Caron dismissed him, betting herself that every suit in his closet was three-piece and some shade of gray.

The other two men, both somewhere in their thirties, appeared polished and refined—though they were totally different-looking men.

One was a blond boy-next-door type, clad in a perfectly pressed black suit and a creased white shirt. Keith Forrester, the receptionist had said.

"Thank you, Jillian." Forrester dismissed the receptionist with a nod and a cool smile that didn't reach his eyes. "I'll take care of things from here."

Plastic, Caron thought, watching Parker shake Forrester's hand. When he turned to her, Caron accepted his hand. His fingers were limp. She'd never trusted a man who shook hands with limp fingers, or one she sensed was insincere.

"My pleasure." She drawled the lie, then withdrew her hand and looped it around Parker's arm. His biceps was thick and tense, but he still looked relaxed. And if he found her suddenly pronounced accent odd, he didn't show it.

"May I introduce my associates, Brian Cheramie—" Forrester motioned toward the other young man, then motioned to the older one Caron had sensed was benign. "And Charles Nivens."

Caron nodded, sure they could see she was a phony. Parker's smoothing her hand with his thumb didn't stop her from trembling—or from studying Brian Cheramie.

Small and dark-skinned, he looked typically French. He rubbed at his graying temple, and a ring on his finger played in the firelight, glinting colorful prisms. Interesting, that. From the five-plus-carat stone winking at her from his pinky, it was clear that Brian Cheramie was rich in his own right. But upon clasping hands, again she sensed insincerity. Was the trait common to all brokers?

Keeping her expression passive, she accepted Charles Nivens's outstretched hand—and sensed guilt—and the reason for it. The stoic Mr. Nivens was having an affair.

Surprised, Caron met his gaze. He hadn't seemed the type. He stepped out on his wife, but he was faithful to his work; she knew that the moment she saw his eyes.

The men sat down in traditional wingback chairs across from the sofa. The fire in the grate snapped, and a log crunched, shooting a spray of sparks up the chimney.

Parker nodded. "I don't believe in wasting time—yours or ours—so I'll get right to the point, gentlemen."

"Yes, sir."

Forrester alone had answered. Caron didn't like him. She didn't like Cheramie, either. She wasn't sure why...yet. Did it have anything to do with Misty?

Parker sent Caron a look so warm it conjured up a stellar flush inside her. "My wife and I are seeking a broker to handle some of our stock transactions. We're considering all three of you. What we want are your personal dossiers and a status report on all the accounts you've handled in the last, oh—what do you think, darling? Five years?"

He didn't believe in being timid. Or in asking for just the sun, not when the moon and stars, too, were hanging there, ripe for the plucking. Forrester's brazen attitude had irked her, but Parker's seemed second nature, unassuming. Admiring him for that, she nodded. "Five years sounds reasonable, darling."

Parker smiled at her, then looked at the men and sobered. "Five years."

Mr. Nivens lifted a haughty brow. "Releasing personal information is a violation of the Privacy Act, Mr. Simms."

"Only if a third party releases it, Mr. Nivens. The typical prospectus is too dry— Boring is deadly, don't you agree?" Without waiting for an answer, Parker went on. "We don't require your client's names or copies of their portfolios, only proof of how you've managed those portfolios." Parker leaned back. "The information is a requisite. We dabble with roughly ten million. But we won't spend a dime with people we don't know and trust."

Eager, Forrester leaned forward on his chair. "If you have a few minutes, I'll get the information together."

Brian Cheramie jumped on the train. "So will I."

Mr. Nivens stood. "My client list is full at present, but thank you for thinking of me."

Parker nodded, avoiding Caron's gaze.

She understood why Mr. Nivens felt compelled to withdraw. His wife's family was Mafia-connected. Mafia-entrenched, more accurately, straight from Sicily. Nivens was an outsider with an ill wife. That prohibited him the right afforded married "family" men to dally in affairs. If they learned of his infidelity, the family would take it as a personal slight. And Charles Nivens feared the costs of offending the family.

Under the circumstances, Caron deemed that wise.

The gleam in Forrester's eyes, and in Cheramie's, Caron catalogued with one word: *greed*. Rubbing Parker's arm, she focused, hoping to sense a connection between Decker and one of the men. Both wanted the account, and would do anything to get it. That sensation came through loud and clear. But nothing came that connected either of them to Misty.

It was *their* focus that was limiting her. They had blocked all thoughts not pertaining to acquiring the Simms account.

Reaching down, she rubbed the tender spot in her leg. Misty? Again Caron saw the little girl crouched down in the corner of the tool shed. And again Caron's heart ached. She had to try harder, she told herself. She couldn't let Misty end up like Sarah.

A knock on the office door had the men falling quiet.

Jillian ducked her head in. "Pardon me." She looked at Forrester. "I'm sorry, sir, but you have an urgent call."

"Thank you." Forrester stood. "If you'll excuse me?"

Caron watched him leave. Something in his swagger, in the tilt of his head, alerted her senses. And, though she had no proof, instinctively she knew he was their connection.

She forced herself to be patient for a few moments, then interrupted the talk between Parker and Brian Cheramie. "Darling," she said, "I'll be right back."

The men stood when she did, and Caron left the office. The look in Parker's eye said he wasn't surprised.

She walked down a short hallway and heard Forrester speaking to someone.

"Vanessa," he said, "will you stop panicking?"

The phone, Caron realized. He was on the phone. She checked to make sure no one had entered the hallway behind her, then stepped closer to Forrester's office door, pretending to be interested in the artwork lining the wall.

"Come on, sugar," he said in a cajoling tone that grated on Caron's nerves. "Now isn't the time for cold feet. We're almost home free."

A shiver streaked up Caron's spine. An image was coming. She could feel herself tottering on the brink.

"Mrs. Simms?"

Jillian!

Caron jerked, then lifted her foot to check her pump. Forcing it to wobble, she looked up into the receptionist's cold gray eyes. "Yes?"

"Broken heel?"

"No, it's just loose." She didn't wear pumps often, and her arches ached like the dickens.

"The conference room is this way." She pointed toward the office Caron had left.

"Yes, it is." Caron slid her a saccharine smile. "But the ladies' room is that way." She pointed in the opposite direction.

"Shall I show you?" Jillian's eyes hadn't warmed.

She knew Caron had been listening in on Forrester. Faking bravado, Caron smiled. "I can manage."

Jillian stood waiting. Caron waddled like a duck to the ladies' room, waited a minute, then exited.

When she returned, Parker, Forrester and Cheramie were standing outside the conference room door.

"Are we leaving already, darling?" Caron asked.

"Yes." He held up two folders. "I spoke with Mr. Nivens, but he's elected not to participate."

"Well, I'm sure we've found our broker." She deliberately focused on Forrester and took Parker's arm.

"I'm sure we have." Parker looked at Cheramie.

Nothing like a little competition to bring out the fangs, Caron decided. Parker was clever. Now, if he'd dangled a one-million-dollar account before the men, rather than a mind-boggling ten-million-dollar one that usurped their every thought, then she would have thought him brilliant.

He started toward the door, and Caron glanced back at the two men. Certain they would hear, she sweetened her voice and said, "I rather like that Mr. Forrester, darling."

"Cheramie's our man, my love."

Parker had given her a license to flirt. Using it, Caron nuzzled closer and fingered the hanky in his pocket. "I suppose I'll have to change your mind, then. I really do want Forrester. He has an excellent crease in his slacks."

"Maybe I'll change your mind." Parker looked down at her, his eyes twinkling that beautiful dove gray. "Forrester has creases, but Cheramie's an aggressive broker." Parker dropped his voice to a husky growl. "We both know how much you appreciate aggressiveness."

She stopped and stroked his lapel with her fingertip. "Now, honey, I'm sure Mr. Forrester's aggressive, too."

Parker dropped his voice so that only she could hear. "Kiss me, Caron—to make it look good."

The kiss wasn't for Forrester and Cheramie, and Parker and Caron both knew it. But, since it was the handy excuse she'd been looking for since the Mr. and Mrs. Mud Boots incident, Caron covered his mouth with hers. His hand at her waist tightened, and he let out a little grunt of approval.

"How's that?" she asked, giving him a genuine smile.

He smiled back. "Better."

Caron focused. The image came easily. Behind them, Forrester and Cheramie stood watching... and smiling. Parker had been right about this ruse, too. He held the personal dossiers on both Forrester and Cheramie, didn't he?

Before the door leading outside closed behind them, an upright Fred had the rear door to the limo open. Caron slid in, kicked off her pumps and wiggled her toes. She could get used to this curbside service. And more so, she feared, to Parker's kisses.

When he settled beside her, she let out a relieved breath, glad the charade was over and eager to measure its success.

"I'll take Forrester." She reached for the file. "You take Cheramie."

"First things first." He took her hand. "You make a lousy airhead, Caron."

"Excuse me?"

"You were supposed to act dippy."

She frowned, trying to keep her temper tamped. "I told you I didn't want to playact. It goes against my grain."

He gave her a doubtful look that quickly changed to a smirk. "I guess we'll have to practice that, too."

That tilt was curling his lip again. Torn between biting it and kissing it, she frowned. But before she could decide, Parker tapped on the glass between them and Fred.

It glided open. "Police headquarters," Parker said.

Caron's stomach lurched. Watching the glass slide back into place, she felt something inside her closing, too. For a while, she'd been able to push aside the fact that someone meant to kill her. But she couldn't deny it anymore.

Parker lifted the car phone and passed it over, his soft voice insistent. "Let Sanders know we're on our way."

Acknowledging the incident by signing a statement somehow would make it more real, more menacing. She licked her lips, her hand hesitant.

"You have to face it, Caron." The receiver in one hand, Parker opened Cheramie's file and thumbed through the pages with his free one. "Then you can start to heal."

He understood her feelings, the sense of violation that was eating away at her. "I know. It's just—" She paused, searching for the right word to describe how inadequate she felt facing a second unknown enemy.

"Disconcerting?" Parker suggested.

"Yes!"

His voice lowered a decibel. "You could drop your investigation."

Caron cringed and rubbed her arch with her other foot. "I can't just forget that Misty's in trouble, Parker. What kind of woman would that make me?"

"Then take the phone."

Staring at the receiver, she forced her fingers to wrap around the cold, hard plastic. Her hand shook. Cursing the tremor, she dialed Sandy's number.

Parker wasn't watching her. She appreciated that thoughtfulness. He was studying Brian Cheramie's file, but she didn't fool herself; he'd listen intently to every syllable she uttered. And if their positions were reversed, so would she.

Parker flipped the page and, without a word, lifted her foot onto his thigh and began massaging her arch. She nearly purred. Did he even realize what he was doing? No, she decided. His brows knitted, he scanned the page, his focus and his attention completely on Cheramie.

She stretched and replaced the phone. "No answer."

"Here's our man," Parker said, then passed the file to her. "Cheramie."

His fingers still working their soothing magic on her foot, Caron read through the file, then reread it. "I'm not sure. Just because he's been in trouble before doesn't mean he's doing anything wrong now." She dropped the file in her lap and rubbed her leg. "My money's on Forrester."

"Why?"

"Just a feeling." Parker was looking at her calf. Caron moved her hand back to the file. "Forrester's too eager, for one thing. For another, his dossier makes no mention of a wife, and the man's definitely married. He was wearing a wedding band."

"A ten-million-dollar account can make a man eager."

"Not Nivens." Inhaling the smell of the leather, she inched down in the seat. "And even for a ten-million-dollar account, Forrester's *too* eager." She tilted her head. "I was sensing something about him. I almost had it . . ."

"Had what?"

"The image. I don't know what it was. He was on the phone with someone named Vanessa. The gist of the conversation made me think they were into something crooked and Vanessa was getting cold feet. In fact, Forrester himself said as much."

Parker's eyes narrowed. "Something crooked?"

"I don't know for sure. Jillian interrupted before it came to me. The important thing is that I was sensing something. I didn't with Cheramie—at least, nothing more specific than that he wasn't being sincere."

"Sensing something doesn't make Forrester a conspirator in a kidnapping. He could have been talking to an anxious stockholder who wanted to dump a block of stock too soon. It could have been normal business."

Caron weighed her options. Considering that every time she talked about imaging, Parker pulled away from her— mentally and physically—she wasn't enthusiastic about discussing the matter with him. But he was her partner. She had been attracted to him from the start, and last night she'd come a long way toward respecting and admiring him. Their relationship had to be planted on solid ground, on mutual understanding. Just as she must accept him—assets and flaws—he must also accept her. The images were a part of her, a part of what had shaped her into the woman she'd become. And, yes, she admitted to herself, she wanted him to understand that—and to approve of her.

The seat was butter-soft. Smoothing it with her hand, she opted for the truth. "If I can connect Decker and Forrester, me sensing something does make him a conspirator."

"If *we* connect."

Even his arrogance had become less irritating to her. "If we connect them," Caron repeated. She had to explain. Yet, if Parker still didn't believe her about Misty afterward, Caron wasn't sure she would be able to hide her reaction. It would anger and hurt her.

Lowering her foot to the carpet, she looked out the window at the blur of trees they were whizzing past. "You don't understand about my images. I rarely sense ordinary people." Her throat locked shut. She swallowed and forced herself to finish. "I sense victims."

Parker's hand stiffened on Cheramie's file; the folder crunched. "Forrester's a victim?"

Solemn, she looked over. "Forrester *causes* victims."

"I see." Loosening his tie, Parker sighed, then freed the top two buttons on his shirt.

"You don't see," she said, contradicting him. "Not yet, but you will."

"We've checked with all your neighbors," Sanders said to Caron, "but no one saw or heard anything."

Parker stepped into Sanders's office and touched Caron's shoulder. "About done?"

Strain etching her face, she nodded. Parker hated seeing it, and gave her shoulder a reassuring rub. Suspicion glimmered in Sanders's eyes, but Parker couldn't resent the look. Caron and Sanders were friends; Sanders knew Parker had been after Caron for a long time. And after getting to know her, Parker better understood Sanders's anxiety. Caron was a strong and courageous woman, but there was still something very fragile and feminine about her that made a man feel protective.

"On the abduction." Sanders rocked back and slid his cigar into the ashtray, burying its tip in cold ash. "Have you imaged anything else, Caron?"

"Nothing important." She didn't meet his gaze.

Though her denial surprised Parker slightly, he held his tongue. Caron *had* imaged other things. And she'd *seen* Misty's bike. But outside Decker's last night she'd said that without a missing-persons report Sanders wouldn't believe her, or even attempt to get a warrant to search Decker's house. Decker could be Misty's uncle, maybe. Caron had thought they were related when she'd first mentioned him, and without a report, who was to say he wasn't? Caron could just be imagining Decker meant Misty harm. But, Sanders's doubt had hurt her; pain had shadowed her eyes. Was that hurt the reason she was withholding information from Sanders now?

Instinctively Parker stepped closer, until the back of her chair brushed against his thighs.

Sanders noticed, and pursed his lips. "I'm still keeping tabs on the reports. So far, nothing's come in that could be your girl."

Parker looked over the top of Caron's head to Sanders's desk calendar. Several names had been scribbled in, and tons of doodling. John Dryer. A ship. Linda. A star. Marcus Theriot. A question mark. Linda, again. Another star.

"Have you checked with surrounding towns—Metirie, Kenner, Bridge City?" Caron shifted in her seat and absently patted Parker's hand.

On seeing that, Sanders grimaced. That he didn't approve was obvious. But what were his specific objections? Parker wondered. Did he fear he would hurt her? Take revenge on her because of Harlan? Sanders should know Parker better. But, Parker admitted, he had put the fear of God into Sanders, warning him against blowing Parker's cover by telling Caron about his connection to Harlan. And it wasn't a bluff. If Sanders did tell her, he *would* think this sweltering shoe box of an office was paradise.

"Caron, look," Sanders said. "Maybe you should let this one ride. I talked to Dr. Z., and she wants you to call."

"Not yet. I'll call when I've got a fix on Misty."

Parker watched them interact. Sanders almost kowtowing. Caron defiant. Was his objection something else? Something darker? Could he be in love with Caron himself?

Parker considered it. Sanders didn't look at Caron like a father, or even like a fond uncle. He didn't look lovesick, either. Parker narrowed his eyes. In fact, Sanders didn't *look* at Caron at all. Not into her eyes. Now that was an interesting observation.

"And I can't let this ride. How could I let a child's life ride?" Seeming more than a little annoyed, Caron jerked a pen from her purse and poised it over a notepad. "What have you learned on Cheramie and Forrester?"

Sandy retrieved his cigar and bit it between his teeth. "Word on the street is that Cheramie's been doing a little inside-trading. Nothing solid on that. Strictly rumor." Sandy thumbed through a sheaf of yellow legal sheets. "Forrester's squeaky-clean."

"Nothing?"

Parker heard Caron's surprise. She seemed so sure Forrester was the connection to Decker. Parker's money had been on Cheramie...until now. Something subliminal in Sanders's behavior niggled at Parker's investigator's instincts. What, Parker couldn't have said. But this didn't happen often. And when it did, he sat up and took notice.

Caron stood. "Thanks, Sandy." Her eyes were shadowed, the skin beneath them dark-circled. She hadn't slept much last night. "If you hear anything..."

"I'll call." Sanders stood and nodded.

Parker had no doubt that Sanders would call. But he had grave doubts about the good detective's motives for doing so.

The phone at his ear, Parker cracked two eggs into a heated skillet and waited for Fred to answer the phone at Caron's apartment.

"Chalmers residence."

Parker smiled. Fred would be formal in a tent. "It's me. How are things going over there?"

"Ah, good morning, Mr. Simms. The police finished an hour ago, the new locks have been installed, and Helga has just informed me that she requires an additional quarter hour to finish cleaning."

"Great." Picturing his petite maid, with her steamroller personality and her gray waffle hair, Parker switched phone ears and arranged the sizzling bacon on a bed of paper towels to drain. "Tell Helga I owe her."

"Indeed you do, sir. She's requested a coat."

"A coat." Parker salted the eggs. Nothing was simple with Helga. The woman demanded, she didn't request. "A mink, right?"

"A sable, sir," Fred said. "Full-length."

Remembering the blood smeared on Caron's door, Parker agreed. "Tell her she's got it." He'd learned years ago not to barter with Helga. She'd wind up with the fur *and* diamonds.

He hung up the phone, gave the eggs a final turn, then left the kitchen.

Slinging a dishcloth over his shoulder, he stopped at the foot of the stairs, leaned against the banister and looked up. "Caron."

No answer. Why didn't she answer him? "Caron?"

Still no answer.

Maybe she *couldn't* answer. That grim thought had him taking the steps two at a time. The dishcloth went flying.

He knocked on her door. "Hey, Caron."

Muffled sounds came from inside.

Fear fueling his moves, he kicked hard. The wooden door cracked and splintered, then banged open and slammed back against the wall.

Bent double and twisting, she screamed.

"It's me!" he shouted. "It's me!"

"God, Parker!" She whirled around, giving him a view of more than her jean-clad backside. "What are you trying to do, scare me to death?"

Feeling like a fool, he muttered. "You didn't answer." She couldn't see. The ribbed neck of her red sweater was twisted around her ears, clinging like a band around her forehead and completely covering all but the crown of her head. The bottom of the sweater was hiked, baring her middle and resting just beneath her breasts. His palms itched to touch her naked skin.

"Has it ever occurred to you to turn the doorknob? Kicking down doors! Geez, Parker!"

Muttering, she gyrated and bumped into the bed, banging her shin. She grunted, and her stomach muscles tightened, then flattened, with the sound. More creamy skin. Very nice.

Hot and cold at once, he folded his arms over his chest, leaned against the doorjamb and narrowed his eyes. She looked like a ticked-off turtle wedged inside its shell. "At the risk of sounding stupid, what's wrong?"

"My sweater's stuck."

"Ahh." Did she think he hadn't noticed? He'd have had to be made of stone. And just looking at her vividly reminded him he was one hundred percent flesh-and-blood man.

"On my earring."

He smiled. "I see."

"I wish I could," she growled, twisting herself into the bed again. "Would you mind?"

Chuckling to himself, he walked over to her. She'd just showered; he smelled soap and some soft and sweet-smelling powder that dusted her skin. He edged his fingers into the neck of the sweater. Her skin was as warm as it was silky smooth. He dragged his fingertips down.

"Ouch!" She grabbed at her neckline.

The fabric cut into his hand. "Sorry."

"Me, too. I could've choked to death."

He hiked his brows. "I'd revive you."

"I'll bet you would."

Something shiny near the sleeve of the sweater caught his eye. Her backside brushed his thigh, and his knees went weak. "Wait. Be still a second. I see the culprit."

Her buttocks rested firmly against his thigh. Sweat beaded his brow, and his hand trembled. How could getting a snagged earring out of a woman's sweater do this to him? He'd had sex without feeling so aroused.

"Okay. Just get it, will you?"

Her voice was none too steady, either. That pleased him. "Patience, Caron."

"Not one of my best virtues."

So he'd noticed. He anchored his hand on her bare waist. His fingers automatically kneaded, and warm heat flowed up his arm and down his middle to his loins. "My hands are too big." His voice sounded gruff and grainy.

"You're a large man." Her flesh quivered under his hand. "But you do have your gentle moments."

Her skin was soft, as smooth as good Scotch, and even more warming. Desire curled low in his body, and his hands began to shake. Slowly he twisted the shiny silver star through the knit. "Got it."

"Thank God. I thought I'd be wearing this as a turban for the rest of my days." She let out a relieved sigh and jerked the sweater down, trapping his hand underneath.

Their thighs brushed, their gazes met, and they stilled.

"You're caught."

Afraid she was right, he nodded and lifted the earring in his free hand. She didn't notice, so fixed was her focus on his eyes. She really was a beautiful woman. Especially fresh from the shower. Worse, she smelled as good as she looked, and her scent had his stomach in knots. Her hair was still damp and wisps curled around her face. He liked that. A lot. Too damn much, in fact. "Did you mean it, Caron?" He let his fingers drift over her abdomen and up to her ribs.

She sucked in a breath that concaved her tummy. "What?"

"About me being gentle?" There was nothing quite like the feel of her naked skin. Satiny-smooth. Soft. Supple.

She licked her lips. "You have your moments." Her gaze never left his mouth.

"Thank you." The urge to kiss her, all sweet and soft and sexy, body-slammed him. What would she do if he did?

"You're welcome." She took the earring. "Thank you."

He stepped closer and cupped her chin in his hand, then rubbed her lobe between his forefinger and thumb. "Your ear's red."

"I, uh . . . I guess I tugged a little too hard."

Her voice husky, she settled her hand at the waist of his jeans and looked up at him, her eyes that translucent lavender that turned his mind to mush—and his conscience into a prickling itch easily ignored.

Figuring that his odds were fifty-fifty, and that fifty-fifty odds weren't bad, he took the plunge. Not because he wanted to, but because he had no choice. "Caron—" he leaned closer, and their noses touched "—I want to kiss you."

She dipped her chin and rubbed her cheek against his jaw. Her breath warmed his chest. "We tried that." She lowered her lids, but, even as she rejected him, her mouth parted for his. "It didn't work."

She was saying no, but her fingers, gently squeezing his waist, were shouting *yes*. "I want to try again," he whispered, lifting his hand and tracing the soft hollow of her throat. He let his fingertip trail and brush across her cheek. It flushed a rosy pink. Delicate. Nice. "It wasn't that bad at Hunt's," he reminded her.

"So we're improving. But kissing now . . . here . . . It wouldn't be wise."

She didn't want him. She wasn't feeling all of the things her eyes promised him she was feeling. And she was right. Considering their situation, a deeper intimacy wasn't wise; it was crazy. He wanted this kiss more than he'd wanted anything in a long time, but he'd never push her, or any woman. He let his hand fall to his side.

Caron cocked her head, and worried her lip with her teeth. Her eyes were stormy. "Parker?"

He couldn't answer. He'd say too much. What had she done to him? How had she gotten inside him like this?

"I'm not Peggy Shores, Parker." Her shell-pink lips curled. "I won't run out on you."

She was trembling. It hadn't been easy for her to lay open her soul for him. But beautifully and bravely she'd done it; she'd stepped toward trust.

Desire poured through his body, hot and thick. He damned himself for it, and for wanting her more than he wanted to avenge Harlan's death. She was beginning to trust him, and he was deceiving her. Bitterness churned in his stomach, and guilt quilted his chest. He had been lying to her since the moment they'd met.

She stepped closer, wrapped her arms around his waist and let them slide over his back to his shoulder blades. "I'm not always wise," she whispered, rising up on her toes and grazing his mouth with her soft lips.

He balled his hands into fists at his sides. His knees nearly folded. This was a first. They'd kissed before, but only when intensely emotional, or for someone else's benefit. This time, their kissing was her idea . . . and just for them.

Unable to resist, he leaned forward and met her mouth with a gentle pressing of lips. She softly sighed. Shudders of pleasure ran rampant through him; she tasted sweet, and as warm and delicious as he'd remembered. Even better; this time she wasn't holding anything back.

He was lost.

Drifting through the hair at his nape, her fingers gently scraped his scalp. She rested the heel of her hand flat against his shoulder, then squeezed, telling him she wanted more.

He tightened the circle of his arms and drew her closer until they met chest to breasts. She whispered something he didn't hear, but understood perfectly.

Her parted mouth welcomed, beckoned, lured. Their tongues met in a fury of motion, a warm and wet and joyful union, like flame and log, each feeding on the other. He wanted her. Really wanted her. The need pounded through his veins, swept through his pores. God help him, he wanted her more than he'd ever wanted a woman in his life.

She let out a sexy little moan that had him rock-hard and reeling, and then, just as suddenly, ice-cold. What was he doing? He couldn't make love with Caron, not without telling her the truth. To her, he'd be no better than her father!

Furious with himself, Parker pulled back, angry and bitter that circumstance, not feeling, forced him to stop.

Sensing his withdrawal, Caron stilled. After a long moment, she straightened her sweater and managed to look up as far as his chest. "What happened?"

He heard her confusion, and it left him sick of himself. He shouldn't have let things get out of hand.

"Hmm?" Grunts were infinitely easier right now than words. He wanted to kiss her again. Just once more; then she'd be out of his system and he could think straight.

Because he was lying to himself now, as well as to her, he scowled.

"Parker?"

The distrust was back in her eyes; she thought he didn't want her. Her expression, the tense set of her shoulders, the disillusionment in her voice, spoke as clearly as if she'd said the words. It was for the best, he told himself. Still, something heavy and hard blanketed his heart. He hated it; the warmth had felt so good and right. But it hadn't been. This was right; this leaden emptiness was all he could afford to feel for Caron.

She twitched her nose. Cocking her head, she blinked, then sniffed again. "Do you smell something burning?"

Burning? No, not any— Then what she'd said hit him. "Burning! Damn, that's your breakfast!" He bolted from her room, then down the hall.

Caron followed him downstairs. Seeing a dishcloth on the landing, she picked it up and draped it over her shoulder. To think that kissing her, a mere seminormal woman, could have such an effect on a hunk like Parker Simms boggled her mind. It invigorated and dazzled, too—until she remembered that he'd stopped.

Her spirits sank. For a while, she'd thought he wanted her; no man in her life had ever kissed her the way Parker had. But he didn't. She'd known it an instant before he'd stopped kissing her. Something beautiful had nearly happened between them, but at the last moment, Parker had retreated.

Once more she'd opened herself up to a man, and once more she'd been rejected. But this time it was different. Before she'd been disappointed; now she hurt.

Yet she wasn't despondent. Probably because when Parker had turned cold, she'd sensed his bitterness *and* his confusion. He was having as hard a time with their chemistry as she was. Maybe Charley keeping Parker at arm's length, not letting him show his love openly, had been the reason for Parker's sudden withdrawal. Maybe she'd gotten too close. When they'd kissed, the dazzle had been unlike anything she'd ever before experienced. Being dazzled once in a while, she decided, could do a woman good. A man, too...if he'd let it.

Turning the corner at the foot of the stairs, Caron frowned. Unless she was deluding herself. Maybe Parker hadn't been dazzled. Maybe he'd pulled back because he just plain didn't want her. It hurt to admit it, but from the start he hadn't liked her. Oh, they'd warmed to each other since then. But that didn't mean that Parker felt anything more for her than lust. And maybe for him lust was short-lived, a fleeting thing.

She pondered on the matter all the way down the hall and paused at the kitchen door. By then the truth had settled. She'd let him into her heart, but Parker hadn't let her into his. He didn't want her. The truth was as simple and as awful as that.

In the kitchen, the smoke was thick. Caron waded through it, her eyes tearing and her throat burning, and opened the back door. A warm wind whipped into the house, filling it with fresh air.

Parker was at the sink, drowning what was left of what had been ... What had it been? "Parker?"

"What?"

From his tone, he wasn't ready just yet to be civil. He was angry with himself for burning breakfast . . . and for wanting to kiss her. She could hear him mumbling, but she knew that the rambling, disjointed comments she was hearing weren't being spoken; she was hearing his thoughts.

Excited by this rare glimpse inside him, she stood very still. But when he looked down at her, what she sensed was pain. Desire was there, yes, so was confusion and . . . and something else. But, first and foremost, she sensed pain.

Busying herself, she located the cups on the second try, poured herself a cup of what smelled like—and she prayed was—coffee, then rummaged through the fridge and scarfed up a fried chicken leg.

Munching, she sat down at the oak table. The chair rocked on the tile. Parker was scrubbing the skillet, his back to her. Caron chewed slowly, enjoying the view. He had great shoulders. Really great shoulders. She swallowed and took another bite. How would they feel, bare against her hands?

That she'd never know had her sinking into the depths of despair. She shifted on her seat and lifted her mug. Inhaling the steam, she tuned in on Parker.

The pain had lessened, but he was still calling himself forty kinds of fool for not taking her. What he wanted was to make love with her; lust burned strong in him. That truth had her face hot and her body fluid. It had her mind drifting, entertaining fantasies again. But lust was all she sensed, so she was glad they hadn't made love. Lust wasn't enough.

Making love with Parker Simms. Now that was the stuff of a woman's dreams. She set the chicken down and sipped from her mug. It wouldn't happen, of course. The very idea of them making love was absurd. They were both against it. He didn't even like their kisses. Depressing, that, but true. At least, she inwardly sighed, she confused him as much as he confused her. There was a certain comfort in that. Still, she couldn't help wishing that just once a man could want more than her body or her gift, that he could want *her*.

Parker slapped at the faucet, cutting off the water. As abruptly as the flow stopped, he knew what he had to do. His body was geared for a primal mating with Caron, and it refused to be ignored. He'd fought the feelings, and failed. So he'd do what he'd always done. Face the inevitable head-on, and suffer the consequences later.

He turned away from the sink. Her legs folded under her bottom, Caron was nibbling at a chicken leg. He wished it were his skin. His body sprang to life, every nerve ending raised to full alert. Without a word, he grasped her hand and lifted her to her feet.

She dropped the chicken onto her plate and looked up at him, dazed. He gripped her shoulders and primed his mouth to warn her, but the words wouldn't come. All he could think about was how it would feel to sink himself into her and to forget the reasons he should hate himself for wanting her.

He kissed her hard and fast, deep, then deeper. She gravitated to him, her soft breasts flattening against his chest. Leaning back against the table, he spread his legs and tugged her between them, nestling her body to his. She fit perfectly, and she kissed him back with a hunger that drove desire through his core. Lust, he told himself, immensely relieved. It was lust.

She broke their kiss and nuzzled his chest. "You've changed your mind. You do want me."

He slid his hands over the swell of her buttocks, pulled her closer, and rocked his hips, letting her feel his heat. With a little gasp, she looked up at him.

His body went rigid, statue-still, and his heart hung suspended in his chest. He saw too much. Oh, God, too much. For the first time ever, there was no distrust in her eyes.

Caron pulled away, sat down at the table and picked up her chicken leg. Without a word—and as though nothing had happened between them—she began nibbling again.

Parker turned his back. What had he done to her? To him? He'd crossed the line, broken down the barrier between them. He had to tell her about Harlan, about the investigation. The time had come for a fresh start.

Caron's stomach was quivering. It was happening again. The sensation of being on the brink started deep in the pit of her stomach and rippled outward. *Not now,* she begged. *Please, not now. Parker wants me now!*

It wouldn't go away; it grew stronger. She cast Parker's back a resigned look, wanting to call out, but knowing he could do nothing to stop the image from coming.

Setting her cup down firmly, she stared into its depths. The swirling brown liquid coiled around and around, forming a vortex and winding deeper and deeper into itself. And then, in it, she imaged a park. Misty swinging. The homely man in his expensive clothes, pushing her.

A woman was there, too. Caron couldn't see her face. It was as if she were inside the woman, seeing the scene through her eyes. Caron's heart began to hammer, her breathing grew shallow, rapid, and the strongest sense of hatred she ever had felt permeated every cell in her body. Evil. Dark. Ugly. But was it focused on Misty? Or on the man pushing her swing?

"Caron," Parker said. "I think we should talk. There are things I should tell you. Things that need saying. Caron? Caron? Caron, what's wrong with you?"

She ignored Parker, willed him away until his voice faded, then focused harder on the image. She couldn't tell who the woman hated. But the hatred was real. And so strong.

"I've got to get back to work now." The man in the image stopped the swing, walked with Misty to a long black car, and lifted the lavender bike into the trunk.

Misty nuzzled him. "I love you, Daddy," she said, then went to the woman and took her hand. Caron felt the warmth of Misty's fingers, the vibration as she waved goodbye.

Her father waved back, and smiled. His smile, so tender and loving, had warmed Caron's heart earlier, but now, when she saw it through the woman's eyes, it enraged her. The woman's hatred was for Misty's father.

Caron's hands began to quiver, then to shake. Through the woman's eyes, Caron looked down...and saw a greasy rope in her hands.

"What are you going to do with that?" Misty looked up, her head cocked, her trusting eyes curious, her golden-brown hair blowing in the gentle wind.

Checking and not seeing the man, the woman grabbed Misty's arm and yanked, then began wrapping the rope around Misty's wrists, cinching it tighter and tighter.

Caron fought the feelings. It was as if she were winding the rope. And yet she knew this had already happened, that nothing she did now could change anything.

"What are you doing?" Misty began screaming, crying, trying to twist herself free. "What are you doing to me?"

And then Caron was Misty. The ropes were binding her wrists. Caron jumped out of the chair, screaming.

Elbow-deep in soapy water at the sink, Parker swung around. She ran into his arms, buried her face at his chest. "It's a woman. A woman!"

"Shh, calm down." He stroked her head, her shoulders. His hands were wet and dripping soapy water. "I can't understand you."

"I thought Decker took her from the shopping center. He *did* take her from the shopping center." Caron licked her lips. Her heart was nearly pounding through her chest. "But a woman tied Misty up, Parker. A woman tied Misty up and *brought* her to Decker at the shopping center. The woman caused all of this. She intentionally had Misty abducted. And she's someone Misty *and* Misty's father know!"

A deep frown creasing his face, Parker searched Caron's eyes intently. Her arms were propped at his waist, but her hands hung limp, palms up and away from his body. "Caron, what's wrong with your hands?"

She looked at him, despair flooding her eyes, fear rattling her voice. "The ropes are too tight...."

Parker sat quietly beside Caron in the Chevy near Decker's. Caron had insisted that they use her car, that it would be less conspicuous. Parker supposed she was right; no one had given them a second glance all afternoon. Decker was still inside. Probably laid back in his recliner, his feet hiked up, a can of beer balanced on his belly, with the TV tuned to the Saints game.

Caron was still dozing, her hands resting limp in her lap—right where they'd been since this morning.

He grimaced. Several times during the day he'd tried to trip her up, but she hadn't fallen. The look in her eyes when she'd told him about the ropes should have convinced him she was telling the truth. He'd never seen such gut-wrenching fear in a woman. It had nearly ripped his heart right out of his chest. And it did again, every time he recalled it.

That should have convinced him, but it hadn't. Harlan had been so damn sure she was a fake. He'd sworn that if Sanders hadn't been following Caron's phony psychic...

Ah, what the hell good could come from rehashing it again? Parker scratched at the steering wheel with his thumbnail. The bitter taste in his mouth seeped down and lay like a rock in his stomach.

In the twelve years they'd been partners, Harlan had never once pegged a person wrong. If he said they were guilty, they were guilty. If he said they weren't, they weren't. His hunches always panned out. Hadn't he collared the thug who'd killed Charley? Hadn't he saved Parker's neck on the Grimes divorce case? Grimes had wanted back some incriminating photos that his wife had hired Parker to take—wanted them badly enough to kill for them. Hadn't Harlan taken a bullet in the arm meant for Parker's heart?

Hell, the list went on and on, all the way back to John Thayer's party, back in college. Harlan had jerked Parker out of Harry Sampson's car that night. Parker had been madder than hell, and he'd fought him, but back then Harlan had been stronger. If the incident had happened a few years later, after Parker had beefed up his muscles and learned to fight, he would have won the fight with Harlan—and he would have died. Harlan had said Harry Sampson was too drunk to drive; he'd been right.

The day Charley died, Harlan had become Parker's rock, the glue that held him together. Though only older by six years, Harlan had been more of a father to Parker than

Charley had ever been. Harlan had held nothing back. He'd stood unobtrusively on the sidelines, letting Parker feel his way. But when he was needed or called upon, Harlan had never hesitated to step forward.

Swamped by a bitter sense of loss, Parker glanced into the rearview mirror, then back out into the night. Why did everything have to be so foggy? Wasn't anything black-and-white anymore? Harlan had had sharp instincts about people. Unfailing instincts. And he'd pegged Caron as a fraud.

The trouble was that Parker had instincts, too. And he wasn't so sure about her anymore.

Caron whimpered in her sleep. Unable to stop himself, he reached out and gently stroked her neck. Harlan never before had pegged as a con artist a woman who looked like an angel.

Parker let his thumb wander to the soft spot behind her ear. He was a man with a problem, he admitted. A serious one. He should hate her. By all that was right and decent in a man, the very sight of her should make him sick—for Harlan. It was wrong, indecent, disloyal, not to hate her. And Parker had tried—God knows, he'd tried—but he just couldn't do it. He just couldn't hate this woman.

He didn't love her; he could never love her with lies and half-truths and Harlan between them. So what *did* he feel? No attraction had ever wound him up inside like this.

Maybe it was lust, and it just felt different because he was emotionally involved in this case. On the surface, that seemed logical. He looked over at her. She was a beautiful woman. Long, lean legs, nice curves, a pretty face. He'd always had a thing for leggy blondes. Especially intelligent leggy blondes who couldn't even pretend to be airheads. The thought took root. Yeah, he assured himself. It had to be lust. Different, more emotional because of Harlan, but definitely nothing more than lust.

The car was moving. Caron forced her eyes open. Her hands throbbed and hung limp at the ends of her arms. She groaned and used her elbows to sit up straight on the seat.

"Hi." Parker tapped the turn signal.

It was dark. The lights from the dash cast an eerie green light on his face, and still he looked handsome. It wasn't fair. The steady click of the blinker pounded inside her head. "Where are we?"

"On the way back to my place."

He hit a pothole. Her stomach lurched, then rolled. She broke out in a cold sweat. "Stop the car."

"I can't. We're on the bridge."

"Stop the car. Please!" She leaned against the window. Clammy. Dizzy. Queasy.

He swerved into the emergency lane and braked to a stop. "What's wrong?"

"Sick." She gasped. "Open the door."

Parker reached over her, snapped the handle and shoved. The metal hinge made a grinding sound, and the door pivoted open. Cool air blew across her face. "Oh, God. Oh, God."

She gagged, her muscles spasming, then locking. Her head swam, she swayed against the open door and heaved onto the street, heaved until she just couldn't heave anymore.

Parker kneaded her muscles, massaging tiny circles on her back. "Done now?"

She still hadn't caught her breath, and her head wasn't clear. "I think so."

"Here, swallow." He pressed a thermos cup to her lips. Her nose protested before the cool liquid touched her lips. Herbal tea. Afraid she'd vomit again, she tried to turn her head.

Parker held it firm. "It'll help. Come on, sweetheart, just a little."

Sweetheart. Such tenderness in his voice, such concern. To hear that again, she'd walk through hot coals barefoot. She opened her mouth and felt the cool tea slide into her mouth. She swished it around, spit it out, then took more. It soothed, gliding over her tongue and back toward her throat. She had to force herself to swallow.

"Good girl," Parker praised her, stroking her hair.

Something red flashed behind them, reflected in the rearview mirror. She couldn't look back, but she didn't have to; a police officer was walking up to Parker's window.

"Car trouble?"

"No," Parker told the officer. "My wife is ill."

"She's not having a baby?"

Her eyes were closed, but his tone told Caron that if she was having a baby, she'd likely have to pick the officer up off the street.

"No," Parker said. "Just a stomach virus. Caron, are you okay to go on now?"

Just the thought of moving had her queasy again. "Yes."

"Good," the officer said, sounding relieved. "Good."

Parker reached over her and shut the door. She brushed his shoulder with her forearm and cranked open her eyes. It took a monumental effort. "You're a very nice man, Parker."

Something dark flickered in his eyes. He looked away, slapped the shift into drive and merged back into traffic.

Had that look really been guilt? No, she must have misread it. What did Parker have to feel guilty about? Oh, he'd lied to her about his reasons for getting involved; his reasons went deeper than just wanting to help Misty. Caron had told him she sensed that someone he loved had been abducted. He hadn't admitted it, but he hadn't denied it outright, either. That look couldn't have been guilt. Yet she had seen something there, and now he seemed about as warm as an icy arctic blast.

"Any idea what made you sick?"

His voice sounded strange. She didn't want to answer, but considering he'd helped her—again—she should trust him enough to tell him the truth. "I'm not sick."

"You can't use your hands, and you just heaved all over the bridge, but you're not—" He propped his elbow on the armrest and rubbed his temple. "The girl, right?"

"Right." Caron snuggled down and closed her eyes. Maybe, if she just didn't think about riding, if she practiced the exercises Dr. Z. had taught her, her stomach would stop rolling and pitching like a ship in a storm.

Parker chanced a covert look at Caron. Her arms lay folded over her stomach. Even when she'd been heaving out of the car door, she hadn't used her hands.

He frowned and sped up to get through a caution light. If these empathy pains of hers were faked, she was carrying them a bit far. He'd seen the sweat sheening her skin, seen her ribs heave, her muscles contort. She hadn't been faking it.

The candy bars. That was the only explanation. Her physical symptoms were real. That didn't mean she was psychic, but her pains *were* real. Yeah, too damn much candy. Of course.

"You said we were going home."

He glanced over. "We are."

"I need to go to the apartment, Parker. To *my* home."

"But you're sick."

"I need to, Parker." She rubbed his thigh with her forearm. "Aren't you the man who said I had to face this?"

"That was before you threw up all over the street."

"My apartment, Parker," she insisted, closing her eyes and mumbling something about smooth roads. "I'm through running."

Parker clenched his jaw, whipped the car around and drove to her apartment. The slot next to his Porsche was empty. He pulled in and turned off the ignition. Caron was sleeping, half on his shoulder, half against the seat. He hated admitting how good she felt beside him. And how guilty he felt because she felt good beside him.

He looked down at her, at the fringe of lashes dusting her cheeks. Half the health problem could be the candy bars; she hadn't eaten right all day. But he had the feeling she didn't eat right many days. That could explain her illness in part. But not completely. And it couldn't explain his concern.

He got out of the car and walked around to her side. Yeah, that was probably all there was to it. If he'd stuffed three candy bars into his stomach in one day, he'd be sick, too. He opened the door, wishing he believed it.

"Caron." He touched her shoulder. "You're home."

She grunted but didn't awaken fully. Parker reached in and scooped her into his arms, then carried her into the building. He gave the steps a wary look. Before, he'd been so frantic to get upstairs to her that he hadn't noticed the condition of her building. Looking at it now, he had half a mind to buy the damn thing just to get it up to code and make it safe. But, just as quickly, he decided against it. Caron would resent his interference.

He looked down at her face. She was exhausted. That, too, could be making her ill. What had been faint smudges under her eyes this morning were dark circles now. She'd slept some last night—he'd watched her—but she hadn't rested. She'd tossed and turned, fitful. Whether it was real or imagined, this abduction business with Misty was eating at Caron.

He dug through her purse for the keys, then opened the door. A damn amateur could pick the new lock with a toothpick; the dead bolt barely penetrated the wood. Yet anyone who really wanted in would just cut a hole in the wall. Locks kept honest folks honest. Criminals were more persistent.

Irked, Parker kicked the door closed, then immediately flinched. But Caron didn't seem to hear it slam. She was still sleeping, her hair hanging over his arm like a golden waterfall. Very pretty. Very touchable. Why couldn't he get a firm grip on his feelings for her and keep them tamped?

He walked straight through to her room. Standing beside her bed, he considered undressing her. But his body's reaction to just the thought of that had him shoving back the flowered coverlet and putting her down on the bed.

He eased off her shoes, then stepped back and looked at her. His heart swelled. She looked so . . . peaceful.

That thought had him frowning, narrowing his eyes. He hadn't noticed it before, but when Caron was awake, she never looked peaceful. Why was that?

When she'd been teaching at Midtown, she'd seemed happy. Personally, he'd thought her life a little lonely. She didn't have any close friends, just her students, her mother and her aunt Grace. But her relatives were in Mississippi, too far away to visit more than once a month.

Her lashes fluttered, but Caron didn't open her eyes. Was she dreaming? She was a likable person. A bit testy when people were slow to catch on to what she was telling them, but likable. She was dynamite-looking, yet she emitted a strong signal that discouraged men from getting close.

He let his gaze wander around her room. A bulletin board with drawings the kids had done nearly covered the far wall between a dresser and a desk. She had welcomed her students with open arms and an open heart; even from a distance, Parker had seen that clearly. He looked at the pictures. One drawing faintly resembled a frog, and it conjured up the memory of her playing leapfrog with the kids. She'd been in her glory. Her hair in a swinging ponytail, her oversize pink sweater flopping around her thighs, her laughter . . . He could still hear her laughter.

It was getting harder and harder to reconcile the woman Harlan had believed her to be with the Caron Chalmers Parker was coming to know.

Thoughtful, he glanced back. Curled on her side, she was sleeping comfortably. Tempted to crawl in beside her, he turned and headed for the door.

Halfway there, he paused for a long second, then turned and walked back. Before he could think of all the reasons he shouldn't, he bent over and placed a tender kiss on her forehead, then left the room and softly closed the door.

Caron heard the click and smiled. What he'd been thinking she couldn't tell; her hormones were humming, and the shield hiding his thoughts was firmly in place. But that tender kiss told her his thoughts hadn't been bad ones, and for now that was enough.

Parker was coming around. He might not believe her just yet, but he was coming around. And Misty was sleeping soundly. Caron could rest easy for a time. She scrunched her pillow and let herself drift off.

For the first time since Sarah James's death, Caron forgot to remind herself not to dream.

Chapter 6

Parker stood in the dark at Caron's living room window. Staring down at his Porsche, he hoped it would still be parked there in the morning—unstripped.

Rubbing his neck, he walked back to Caron's bedroom door. In the morning, she'd be mad as a hornet at him for staying. But he couldn't leave. What if she got sick again?

His hand on the knob, he bent to the door and listened. No noise. Nothing stirring. He peeked in and saw her curled on her side, in the same position she'd been in hours ago.

Winding back to the sofa, he bumped his shin on the corner of the coffee table and plopped down, then shifted and squirmed, trying to find a comfortable position. But he'd already proven that six feet of man couldn't get comfortable on five feet of sofa.

He propped his head on the armrest, scrunched up his legs and, giving up on finding a place to put his arm, crooked it over his chest. Christ, he'd be stiff for a week.

A lump tortured his spine. The sofa had more lumps than his mother's gravy. Helga, now, could make good gravy. His stomach growled, reminding him that he'd missed dinner.

He closed his eyes and recalled the Thanksgiving Helga had been down with the flu and his mother had cooked. Classic rubber turkey; dry as dust. Megan had wrinkled her freckled nose and demanded their mother promise never to cook again—except for baking cookies. He chuckled softly and wondered what Caron's Thanksgivings had been like. Her days after school had been very different from his. She'd soaked up every detail of his tales like a love-starved sponge.

Knowing that she had been starved gnawed at his stomach. He gave it a rub, but the ache didn't go away. "You've got it bad, Simms," he told himself. "Really bad."

The red light pulsed, setting the raindrops beading on the sign to flame. "Rue de Bourbon," Caron read, knowing that she was dreaming, that this had all happened before... the night Sarah James died.

But this time it would be different. This time the spellings on signs wouldn't confuse her. This time Sarah wouldn't die.

It was dark, after midnight. Cold and rainy. Blustery winds whipped at electrical lines strung down the street, at tree limbs, making a shimmering, eerie sound.

Driving slowly down the street, Caron saw the man in dirty jeans leaning against the lamppost, his booted foot propped. He tugged the bill of his cap low over his eyes and took a drag from the cigarette cupped in his hand. Its tip glowed orange.

She saw the bar, the sign above its door. Two men ambled out, a woman between them. Her hair was long and black, dusting the hem of her short skirt. They were drinking from paper cups, laughing, celebrating Christmas.

Caron was not. She was frantic, fighting for breath, her arms aching as if her blood circulation had been clamped off too long. Her head swam, her breasts and thighs burned as if branded by white hot pokers, and her jaw throbbed. Sarah had been struck. Again.

Caron veered right, pulled up to the curb and parked.

"No," she told herself, feeling herself tossing on the sheets. On some level, she knew she was in her apartment, in her own bed, asleep. She could feel the cotton sheets, stiff from the clothesline, pricking at her back. She knew, and yet this was too real, too different, to be a dream.

She felt the car's cold metal door handle against her hand. Heard it snap open. Saw the rain splattering onto the street. She screamed at herself. "Don't get out. Don't go in. *Sarah is not here!*"

But she did get out.

And she did go into the bar.

Hot tears blurred her eyes, pooled, then tumbled down her face. "I made a mistake," she cried. "It was the street sign, not the bar. It was the street—" Deep sobs grew to hopeless wails. "Sarah! Oh, God, please! Please, I made a mistake!"

He heard something.

Groggy, Parker opened his eyes. His shoulder was numb. He grunted and half rolled, half fell off the sofa.

"I made a mistake!"

Caron? He jumped up and ran into her room.

He heard her sobs. Deep, pitiful cries of despair, anguish and regret. "Caron, what's wrong?" He moved to the bed and reached for the lamp to turn on the light.

"No, don't," Caron said. "Don't."

He sat on the edge of the mattress. She rolled toward him and put her hand on his knee, shaking hard. He covered it with his. "What's the matter? Are you sick again?"

She didn't answer.

Parker rubbed her arm, her shoulder. At some time while he'd slept, she'd put on one of her flannel gowns. He was coming to like them. "Talk to me."

"It won't help. It . . . happened."

Her voice, weak and thready, tugged hard at him. He wanted to hold her, but did she want to be held? She needed it, he decided. He needed it, too. Seeing her like this tore him apart and made him ashamed. Shifting around to lean against the headboard, he pulled her into his arms. "Come here, Caron."

When she snuggled close and buried her head against his chest, he knew he'd done the right thing. God, but he hated feeling her tremble. He rested his chin on her head and whispered against her hair. "Shh....it was just a dream.... Don't cry, talk to me. At least trust me with your dreams."

"It wasn't just a dream." Her voice was a mere wisp of sound. "It was—"

A loud crash of thunder rolled overhead, shaking the walls, and it began raining again. Parker waited for her to go on, stroking her delicate shoulders and her spine. Shadows played on the ceiling. Watching them, he wondered. Why did holding only Caron Chalmers, of all the women in the world, feel so right?

"It was another case," she finally said. She cleared her throat, but tears still choked her. "A year ago, I imaged a woman. A very beautiful woman. She had blond hair and green eyes and a beautiful smile."

Sarah. His heart nearly stopped. Caron was telling him about Sarah! He forced his voice to be calm. "What happened?"

"I was trying to find her. She was so pretty, and so...scared." Caron's tears seeped through his shirt and wet his chest. "She'd been at the mall, Christmas shopping. She'd bought a wood carving—a mallard drake. I imaged it."

He'd seen it. It had been returned with Sarah's personal effects—her Christmas gift to Harlan. Parker's heart ached.

"A man hit her from behind in the parking lot, dragged her into a van and took off. He took her to this seedy place. It was dirty and smelled sour. He lived there.

"She was tied up—her hands, like Misty's," Caron went on. "Once, she sawed through the rope by dragging it across the metal frame, again and again. But he found out. He chained her. Sometimes, when I imaged her, I could see the room she was in, see her chained to...to that bed."

Caron's voice cracked. "I'd been looking for her for three days. There wasn't a break—no rest. And I was so tired. At night, he would be there. And he'd do...horrible things to her.

"The first two days, she fought him. She tried so hard to be brave. But on the third day, she got so...quiet."

Parker squeezed his eyes shut. The coroner's report confirmed that Sarah had been tortured for three days. A sick feeling burned like acid in Parker's stomach. He wanted to tell Caron to stop, wanted to shove the ugliness, the gruesome truth, away. But he couldn't. He had to hear it from her. His eyes burning hot, his face wet, he tightened his hold on Caron. Whether he meant to soothe her or himself, he wasn't sure, but he began sweeping her scalp with long, gentle strokes.

Caron sniffed and rubbed her nose. "Then I saw the sign—Rue de Bourbon. The street name doesn't have the 'de,' and I didn't catch that it had been painted in. I told Sandy. There was a bar with that name off of Desire Street. We went there." She shuddered. "Oh God, Parker," she cried. "We went there!"

He wanted to tell her the truth, tell her that she didn't have to explain. He *knew* what had happened. And he knew it haunted Caron; he could see that clearly now.

Her sobs grew deep, racking her slim body. "The red light confused me. The bar had a flashing red light. We went inside. It was smoky and dark and the smell of beer and sweat made me dizzy. I saw an image and felt a stabbing pain in my throat. My neck burned. I—I started gasping. I tried to tell Sandy it was a traffic light. That we were in the wrong place. It was the street, not the bar."

She gulped in ragged breaths, then went on. "But my throat—" She swallowed hard. "I couldn't talk. I couldn't tell him, Parker. And . . . and she died."

Again Parker felt the pain, the hollow emptiness that had carved out his insides, the anger that Caron's interference might have slowed down the police investigating hard evidence that might have saved Sarah. And again Parker felt the bitterness that had filled him at the morgue when Harlan identified Sarah's body. He'd never forget seeing her like that. Bruises muddying her arms and legs, her face. Cigarette burns peppering her breasts and thighs. And never, not if he lived a thousand years, would he ever forget the jagged wound splitting her neck. Her throat had been slashed.

Caron's sobs eased, and Parker brushed at his face with the back of his hand. He was shaking as hard as Caron. Would remembering ever get easier?

"I found her too late."

Parker's hand stilled on Caron's shoulder. Cold dread seized his chest. "You saw her?"

She nodded against his chest. "I scribbled down that it was the street. Sandy took me there, and I pointed out the house. He told me to stay in the car, but I couldn't."

"You followed him in." The dull ache behind Parker's eyes began to throb, and he dropped his lids. "Ah, Jesus, Caron..." The need to shield her had him tightening his hold, pulling her closer until she nearly draped his chest.

"I don't know what happened after that. The last thing I remember was walking into that awful room and seeing her on the bed." Caron shuddered. "I woke up at Dr. Zilinger's institute. They told me two days had passed."

Her voice had calmed now, so much so that the dull tone had knots forming in Parker's stomach. "Did you remember?"

She hesitated a long time before answering. "Yes, I remembered," she said, dragging in a ragged breath that heaved her shoulders. "I still remember."

Caron had had this dream before, he realized. Many times. Whether she suffered from a guilty conscience because she pretended to be psychic when she wasn't, or because she was psychic and she'd made a mistake that might—or might not—have cost Sarah her life, Parker wasn't sure. But guilt was guilt. And that he understood.

Caron had seen Sarah in the hellhole where she'd been tortured and murdered, not in a sterile morgue. He wished he could have spared her that. He wished he could have spared Harlan, too. The word *devastating* didn't begin to describe what they had suffered. God, poor Harlan. Sarah had been his wife! To see his wife that way. How that must have twisted him inside.

Parker's throat clogged with tears. It had twisted Harlan. Hadn't he called Parker that Christmas morning and said that without Sarah life wasn't worth living? Hadn't he said that she'd been everything good in him, that he had died with her? He had been reaching out, crying for help.

But Parker hadn't heard. He'd been confused by the signs . . . just like Caron.

He stared blankly at the ceiling. His voice thick, he gave Caron what he could give her. "It wasn't your fault."

"It was."

"Why?"

"I made a mistake, and she died."

A long silence filled the room. Rain pattered against the bedroom window, tatting against the pane. The drops beaded, glistening in the light from the streetlamp.

Caron felt guilty because Sarah had died. He felt guilty because Harlan had died. And Parker's guilt deepened. Lying there in Caron's bed, holding her in his arms, he realized what it was that had been niggling at the fringes of his mind since that first night at Decker's: Caron had never lied to him.

But *he* had lied to her. He was still lying to her. She hadn't given him Sarah's name, but Caron had given him everything else.

The urge to tell her the truth, to tell her about Sarah and Harlan and the yearlong investigation, burned on Parker's tongue, begging to be spoken. But he swallowed the words, forced them back down his throat. They were tearing holes in his belly, but he couldn't tell her. Not now. It was too late.

Though the evidence pointed in that direction, he wasn't convinced she was psychic. She could have found and suppressed evidence pointing to Sarah's whereabouts to protect her image. Sanders could have given her enough to send her in the the right direction. She was tenacious. All she would have needed was a thread. But she was carrying around a ton of guilt. She needed someone. And, though he had no right, God help him, he wanted to be the someone she needed.

Caron sniffed, rolled over, then cranked an eyelid open. Bars of light shining in from between the blinds slanted across the room and her bed. Her head ached, her stomach felt queasy, and memories of last night were rushing back to her. Parker. She'd told him about Sarah.

Groaning, she turned onto her side and reached for the covers. If he hadn't been sure she was a certifiable flake before then, he surely was now. Her hands throbbed.

Misty. Caron kicked off the covers and dragged herself out of bed. Some awful smell that wasn't coffee was coming from the kitchen.

Parker was still here. She should give him a hard time for staying, but the truth was, she was glad he had. After the dream, he'd held her. Safe, secure and content, she'd gone back to sleep. She usually paced the floors until dawn.

After a detour into the bathroom she stumbled into the kitchen. Parker was at the stove, stirring something in a pot. Without a thought to her reasons, she walked up behind him, curled her arms around his waist and pressed her cheek against his back. "Morning."

"Morning." He turned and brushed a kiss to her forehead, then cast her an appraising glance. "You should've slept longer."

She moved to the cabinet, pried it open with her wrist, then reached for a cup. Pain bolted up her arm, and she whimpered.

"Here." Parker grabbed a cup and filled it from the pot.

"Is it coffee?" She couldn't keep the skepticism from her voice.

He smiled. "Yeah, it's coffee." He turned her toward the table. "Sit. Breakfast is ready."

She sat down in her usual chair. When he put the cup in front of her, she looked up at him. He was every bit as gorgeous first thing in the morning as he was at midday, and in the dark of night. Feeling like a frump, she pouted. It wasn't fair. She felt like a zombie, like something the cat had dragged in, and was certain she looked worse. Yet he looked gorgeous.

She shrugged her sleep-tossed hair back from her face. "Thank you, Parker."

Stirring the pot, he arched a brow. "For what?"

"Specifically?" With luck, maybe he'd let her off the hook. Considering she hadn't yet had coffee, that would be the decent thing to do.

He nodded.

No such luck. Resigned, she winced against the light and looked up at him. "For being here for me last night. For giving a damn." The muscles in her throat clamped, and her eyes burned. He'd been so tender and gentle, and she knew he'd cried with her. "For not skating out on me like Mike and Greg and my father did."

So other men had hurt her, too, reinforcing what her father had done. Parker nodded, turned back to the stove and let loose a silent stream of curses. When he felt he could talk without betraying his resentment, he asked the question that had been on his mind all morning. "You have many nights like that?"

"Some." Caron stared at his back. He was reacting to her at gut level. Somehow she knew that—not by any image, but by emotion. And his emotions were as raw as hers. He rinsed his hands at the sink, stretching his shirt taut across his shoulders. A little fire sparked to life in her stomach.

He looked back at her, his eyes probing. "Many?"

"Many." Her cheeks warm, she braced the cup between her forearms and lifted it to her mouth.

A frown threatening his lips, he spooned the oatmeal into bowls. "Honey and cinnamon, butter, or milk and sugar?"

"None of the above." Her stomach rolled. "Just coffee, thanks."

"Caron, you can't exist on coffee and Butterfingers." He wiped his hands on his makeshift apron—a dishcloth tucked into the waist of his jeans. "You'll be hypoglycemic."

"Hypo-whatever, I can't eat that stuff." She pointed a disgusted finger at the bowls.

He tugged the dishcloth free from his pants. "What can you eat, then?"

"There's pizza in the fridge. I'll have a slice."

Frowning his displeasure at that disclosure, Parker got the pizza out and lit the oven.

"I like it cold."

"God, Caron." He gave her a look of sheer horror. "Cold?"

"Cold." She drank again from her cup. "Would you hand me the phone and dial Sandy?"

Parker got the phone, dialed the number, then sat down across from her and started doctoring his oatmeal with honey.

While listening to Sandy, Caron ran her fingertip around the honey jar, then licked her finger. When she hung up, she relayed the conversation to Parker. "There's still been no missing-persons filed, and he doesn't have anything new on Forrester or Cheramie." Caron *knew* they were connected somehow; she felt it.

"It really irks you that he won't believe you without the report, doesn't it?"

"Yes. We've worked together since I was seven years old. If the man doesn't know me by now, he never will."

Parker agreed with a grunt, then added another dollop of honey to his oatmeal. "So why is he holding back?"

"Because I screwed up last year."

"We all make mistakes, Caron." And as the hours passed with them being together, he wondered if he hadn't made the biggest, most unforgivable mistake of all.

"I know."

She was sinking again; her shoulders were slumped. "Then accept it and get on with your life." She hadn't touched the pizza. Hoping to sidetrack her, he lifted the slice and pressed it against her lips. "But first, eat."

"You're always shoving food in my face." Caron glared at him, sighed and sank her teeth through the cheese and into the crust.

When she licked at a drop of tomato sauce on her lower lip, he figured she'd realized she was hungry. And if he could keep her mind off Sarah, Caron might actually eat a decent—more or less decent—meal. "Do you feel up to checking out Cheramie this morning?"

Still chewing, she grunted her opposition. "Forrester's our man, Parker. I feel it."

"No, it's Cheramie." Parker slathered butter onto his toast. The light scraping sound filled the kitchen. "Did you see the rock on his finger?"

"It's a zircon."

"How do you know that?"

"He was flaunting it." Seeing Parker's perplexed look, she explained. "A man who owns a rock doesn't flash it. Wearing the ring is second nature. He forgets he has it on." She dipped her chin. "Another bite, please."

Parker put down his knife and lifted the pizza. "Okay, you have a point about the ring. But I still think—"

Parker suddenly noticed that the top button on her nightgown had come undone, exposing the soft hollow at her throat.

"So what were you thinking?"

"Cheramie," Parker said, staring at that soft hollow and grasping for cohesive thoughts. "We should start with him."

Caron drank from her cup before answering. "We'll compromise."

Anything would be fine with him. Her eyes looked dull. Beautiful, but dull without their normal sparkle. Did she have any vitamins around here?

"Parker, quit staring. You're making me self-conscious."

He grabbed for his spoon, then noticed she was smiling. The tips of his ears burned.

"You're blushing."

"What?" he asked. "Real men can't blush?" She pulled a face, and he slid her his best dastardly look.

She laughed in his face.

"Knock it off, Snow White. You've had your fun."

"Okay." Threads of laughter lingered in her voice. "How about we check out Cheramie this morning, then switch to Forrester this afternoon?"

"Sounds reasonable." Gracious, she'd let it drop. And, for the umpteenth time, he wondered how her Mike and Greg could have willingly hurt her.

The phone rang.

Chewing a bite of toast, Parker lifted the receiver and tucked it against Caron's ear. "Hello."

She lifted her chin. "It's for you."

Parker took the phone. "Simms."

"Fred here, Mr. Simms. Millie just called from your office. She says she has the owners' names on those two trucks at the Decker residence you asked about."

"Yes?"

"Butch Decker owns the '79 Ford. The other one belongs to a Keith Forrester."

"Thanks." Parker dropped the receiver onto its cradle.

"Did that phone call have anything to do with the case?"

He nodded and folded his arms across his chest.

"What? Misty?"

"No. About the trucks."

She stepped to his side. "Who owns them?"

He looked up at her looking down at him. Her hair swung forward, caressing her cheeks. "Eat another slice of pizza and I'll tell you."

"That's blackmail."

He grinned. "It sure is."

"I've been blackmailed before, Parker Simms. I didn't care for the feeling."

"Who's the culprit? I could use a good fight."

"My father, for one."

"Fathers are exempt," he replied to suit his own purposes, telling himself that it didn't matter. "We're talking loves or lovers here."

"I didn't get good at spotting a Judas until college." She rubbed her wrist over Parker's shoulder. "That's when I clashed with Greg Cain."

"Uh-huh." He watched closely for signs of distrust, but saw none.

She cocked her head. "I should've known about him. Cain and Abel—remember?"

"I remember." The similarity between himself and Cain stung. "So what did the traitors do?"

The shadows came back to her eyes. "Pretty much the same thing my father did. They made me care about them. And when I did, they used it against me to get what they wanted."

Her forearm stilled against his shoulder. He gave it a gentle pat. "We all make mistakes, Caron. I've been hustled into bed a time or two—"

"Not my body, Parker." She gave him a frown that could have felled a tree. "My gift. They used me to get to it."

There was a question in her eyes; she was asking if he was using her, too. He was, but not the way they had. He didn't want material gain. He wanted peace.

Because he couldn't be totally honest, he said nothing.

Caron realized he wasn't going to answer, and she sighed. "I guess I'm still a slow learner, after all. I've got to risk it." She stepped closer, bent at the waist and pecked a chaste kiss on his cheek.

The man in him was elated that she thought he was worth the risk. When she would have pulled back, he looped an arm around her hips and tugged her closer. She fell across his chest. "Now, do it right, sweetheart," he growled out in a sorry imitation of Bogey, "and I'll spill the works."

Smiling, Caron kissed him. She was getting too used to this, to sharing meals and spending time with Parker. He was getting too close, learning more about her than she'd ever exposed to any man. He was a good man. A slick charmer with a convenient code of ethics, but a good man. And if she wasn't careful, she warned herself, she could find herself falling in love with him.

He broke their kiss and nuzzled her neck. How she'd ended up in his lap, she hadn't a clue. But the hardness at his hips, pressing against her bottom, told her that he was equally glad she had.

Parker breathed against the hollow of her throat. "One of the trucks belongs to—"

"Forrester." She smiled and tweaked Parker's nose. "I told you so." Then she motioned for another slice of pizza.

"Twenty-four hours of intense research, and we still don't know *how* they're connected." Parker ran his hands through his hair, pushed back from Caron's kitchen table, stood and stretched.

"It's got to be easier than we're making it. We've missed something simple, something basic." She rubbed her temples. Her eyes felt as if someone wearing sandpaper-soled shoes had spent the night hiking across them. "Toss me Forrester's dossier again."

"You've checked it a dozen times."

"Thirteen's a baker's dozen." When Parker reached over several stacks and started looking through the wrong one, she added, "No, the one on the end."

He opened the file and spread it out before Caron. "You're hung up on Forrester's not listing a wife on his dossier. But that doesn't make him guilty of abduction."

"No, it doesn't. And, yes, I am hung up on that. A man shouldn't deny he has a wife."

"Maybe when he completed the dossier he hadn't married. Maybe he's still not married."

"And maybe dead pigs fly. How many singles do you know who wear wedding bands?" Caron tossed back at him. "Would you?"

"What?"

"Deny having a wife on a dossier."

"I might." Parker drank from his cup. "If I thought admitting it would hurt her."

Caron cocked her head. "Have you ever come close to getting married?"

"Once." That tilt curled his lip. "Peggy Shores."

"She dumped you!" How could he almost marry a woman who'd dumped him?

"Yeah, she did. But I later inherited a trust fund from my maternal grandparents. Peggy tried coming back."

"Really?" That explained two things. One, how Parker's family lived on an estate on a cop's pay—it *was* Parker's house; he'd said that he only lived there, but it was his—and why Parker was skittish when it came to trusting. Between Charley pushing Parker away to keep him from becoming too dependent and Peggy Shores coming back for the money, Parker had almost as much reason not to trust others as Caron did! "Did you let Peggy come back?" He'd said he'd almost married her.

"Almost. But right before the invitations went out I came to my senses. I figured if she'd run out on me once, at the first sign of trouble she'd run again."

"Do you ever wish you had married her?" Why had she asked that? Did she really want to hear a man she was dopey about say he wished he'd married another woman?

"No." He blinked, then blinked again. "Maybe once in a while, when the nights get long, I wish I'd married someone."

"Me, too." Caron rested her arms on the table. The refrigerator's condenser kicked on. The wall clock near the stove hummed. "Trust is a fragile thing, isn't it?"

"Yes." He stood up. "I've got to check in at my office." Parker took his cup to the sink, drained it, then tossed a used tea bag into the trash. "Come with me."

The intimacy was gone, but his nonchalance wasn't fooling her. Nor was his asking her to his office. He was afraid to leave her here alone. Feeling tender, she shook her head. "I've told you before, Parker, I don't need a keeper." She smiled to soften her refusal. "I'll be fine."

"Are you forgetting—"

"I'm not forgetting," she said quickly, interrupting him, hoping he wouldn't mention the message left on her door. Somehow thinking about it wasn't as bad as hearing about it. When they spoke about it out loud, the incident became too real, too frightening.

"I don't want you alone. Until we tag whoever—"

His worry brushed over her heart. "Tell you what. You can drop me at the café by Forrester's office."

"What for?" Parker leaned against the counter, folded his arms across his chest and set his expression in stone.

He meant to be answered. "Ina said Lily Mae's friend works there. Maybe she knows Forrester. Since it's close, he might lunch there."

"Who's Lily Mae?"

"She lives on the other side of Decker."

"Why didn't I know about her?"

"Ina told us at her house the other night." Amused, Caron pointed a finger to his chest. "But you were too busy stuffing your mouth with rolls to pay attention."

He lifted a hand. "Guilty."

"Yes, you are. Now, dial the phone, Parker."

He didn't move a muscle. "Who are you calling?"

"Ina."

"What's Decker's neighbor got to do—"

"Humor me," she told him. "I've got a . . . a hunch."

"Okay."

"Okay?" She'd expected, at the least, one of his grunts.

"I have hunches, too." He shrugged, then grabbed the phone and passed it to her.

When Ina answered, Caron greeted her.

"I was wondering what happened to you, child. You ain't got pneumonia, have you?"

"No, I'm fine." Caron nudged the receiver Parker held at her ear. "Ina, what's Decker's sister's name?"

"Linda. I told you that when you and Parker—"

"Linda what? Do you know?"

"Oh, my. I've heard it, child, but this old mind ain't what it used to be. I could ask Lily Mae. She'll recall. Her mind's like a steel trap, takes everything in and spits it out whenever she wants it."

Caron tensed. "Is it Linda Forrester?"

"Yes, yes. It surely is."

"Good." Caron smiled and nodded to Parker.

"Did Linda ever have a little girl with her when she came to visit Decker?"

"No. She's not one for kids. I thought I'd told you that."

"You did, Ina. I was just double-checking." Caron frowned. "I need to talk to someone about her. And I remembered you mentioning a friend of Lily Mae's down at the diner." Ina called the café a diner.

"Mary Beth."

"Mary Beth," Caron repeated, her heart thumping faster. "Yes, that's it. Would you do me a huge favor?"

"Depends on what it is. I don't hold with giving my pledge till I know exactly what I'm pledging."

"Just a phone call. Would you call Mary Beth and ask her if she'll talk to me?"

"I ought to be asking why, but I'm thinking if your Parker is at all like his daddy, I'm better off not knowing."

Caron grazed her lip with her teeth. "That's probably true, Ina."

"I'll call. You go on down there. Mary Beth works the lunch shift, so she'll be there. Get you a slab of her apple pie. It's mighty fine."

"I will. And thanks, Ina. You're a doll."

"Have you found the girl yet?"

"Not yet." Caron's smile faded. They had a few more days. Misty *had* to be home by Christmas. Otherwise, it would be a day of mourning, not of joy. "Soon, we hope."

Parker whispered. "What's her favorite color?"

"Well, you just call if I can help."

"Thanks." Caron said. "Ina, Parker wants to know your favorite color."

"Parker's there? I've been meaning to talk to him about smooching you in the car. Mrs. Klein's got a powerful crick in her neck from watching, and Mr. Klein's miffed with her 'cause he's having to do all the cooking. You tell Parker Simms that smooching in the car with a lady ain't proper now, you hear?" Without missing a beat, she rushed on. "And tell him pink's my pick of the litter. Not them blue pinks, now. Can't abide them blue pinks. I like the clear pinks."

"Okay. Clear pink." Caron's face burned. "I'll tell Parker about the, er, smooching, too. Bye, Ina."

Parker tapped the hook button, grinning. "Smooching?"

"It ain't proper." Caron mimicked Ina. "Mr. Mud boots, alias Mr. Klein, is miffed with Mrs. Mudboots, alias Mrs. Klein, because she's got a powerful crick in her neck and he's having to do all the cooking."

Parker laughed. "Did you tell her it didn't count?"

"What didn't count?"

"Our kisses."

"What?" Sometimes the man was as dense as a board.

He shrugged. "We didn't like them."

"Shut up, Parker."

Chuckling, he punched in a number. When Fred answered, Parker winked. "I need a favor, Fred. I want you to see to it that Ina Erickson has as many clear pink irises planted as her heart desires and her lawn will hold."

He tilted the receiver. "I need Ina's address."

Caron reeled it off, unable to resist smiling at him.

Parker repeated it, thanked Fred, then hung up.

Caron stood up. "For a lousy kisser, you're a soft touch, Simms."

"Who, me?"

The warm look in his eyes had her breathless. "You."

He began tidying up the kitchen. "Come with me to the office, then we'll go to the café together."

"I can't." She wished she could. Oh, how she wished she could.

The bowls rinsed, he turned off the water. "Why not?"

Her smile faded. "We're running out of time."

The café was old-fashioned, in a charming sort of way. Wooden tables with little mason jars filled with white daisies, potted palms scattered here and there to give the diners an illusion of privacy, and a jukebox that had to be one of the first ever installed in the city of New Orleans.

Caron slid down onto the green plastic seat and waited for the waitress to come to her table. If her hunch was anywhere near the target, when she left here, she'd know a lot more about Keith Forrester than she'd learned reading his trumped-up dossier, which, in addition to not mentioning he had a wife, she felt sure glamorized his brokering accomplishments during the past five years. That she'd have to adopt Parker's methods to learn the needed information still grated on her, but it was urgent. Misty was sleeping more and more—just as Sarah had the day before she'd died.

There wasn't much time.

The waitress's sensible shoes squeaked on the tile floor. "Yes, ma'am," she said to Caron, though her weathered face suggested she was Caron's senior by thirty years.

"Mary Beth?" The woman nodded.

"I'm Caron. Ina's friend."

"Oh, yes, she called just a few minutes ago." Mary Beth looked around. "What can I get you? They're sticky about visiting while on the job around here."

"Coffee and apple pie?" Caron asked.

"Peg baked today. Hers ain't bad." The woman smoothed her pink uniform skirt. "If you like tart apples."

Caron concentrated, focused on the woman. Her air conditioner at home was out of commission. She was looking forward to finishing her shift in ten minutes; her feet hurt. But she wasn't looking forward to sweltering in her sultry apartment. She needed money.

"Mary Beth," Caron said, "do you know Keith Forrester?"

"Ina says you're okay, but—" She dropped her lids to half-mast. "Why are you asking? Friend or foe?"

"Neither. Objective third party." Caron fished a fifty out of her purse. Using her hands had sharp pains bolting up her arms and through her shoulders. The money was supposed to go toward next month's rent, but desperate situations called for desperate measures. Misty was desperate. Mary Beth, who was susceptible to heat exhaustion, was desperate. And Caron, who had made a fatal mistake last Christmas, was desperate not to repeat that mistake this Christmas.

"I need to know about him." Caron laid the fifty on the table. "When you get off, can we talk?"

"Sure." Mary Beth watched the money. "Sure, we can talk. But I don't want your money."

Passing down the cramped aisle between the tables, a man brushed against Mary Beth's shoulder. She bumped the edge of the table. "Coffee and apple pie," she said, steadying herself. "Be right back."

Caron waited, watching the comings and goings-on in the café. A young boy clearing tables carried a brown plastic bucket from one table to the next, methodically dumping soiled dishes and linens. He should be in school. Someone dropped a glass. It shattered on the tile.

"Here you are." Mary Beth set Caron's cup and pie in front of her, then sat down on the other seat. "What do you want to know?"

"First, how well do you know Keith Forrester?"

Mary Beth smiled. "Everybody in the place knows more than they want to about him *and* his wife."

A funny feeling inched up Caron's spine. "Why?"

Mary Beth leaned forward across the table and dropped her voice. "Let's see, today's Tuesday, so it must have been Sunday that this happened. Keith was here for lunch. He comes in a couple of times a week."

"Alone?"

"Most of the time. But once in a while his rich redhead comes in, too. They don't come together, though."

"Do you know her name?"

"No, I never heard him call her anything but 'Sugar.'"

In his office, Forrester had called Vanessa 'Sugar.' Was it a generic term with him?

"Did she ever have a little girl with her?"

"No, she didn't."

"Okay, what happened on Sunday?"

"Well, we thought it was odd, Keith coming in on a weekend and all. He looked upset when he got here. Kind of mopey and scared at the same time. Then his wife, Linda, comes in." Mary Beth's eyes widened. "She was madder than a virgin bride hitched to a drunk groom. She sure didn't talk like a virgin, though. Before we knew what was happening, she was screaming and throwing dishes at Keith. Ranting on like a lunatic. Crazy things about him getting her brother mixed up in some scheme."

Caron's whole body tensed. "Could you make out what it was all about?"

"No, it didn't make a nickel's worth of sense to any of us. But Linda told him that if he didn't stop it, she would. That he could rot in jail for his five million." Mary Beth guffawed. "Can you imagine? Keith Forrester ain't got no five million."

"How do you know?"

"Because he ain't paid Chuck in over two months."

"Chuck?"

"The owner here."

"I see." Caron tapped the fifty. "Have you seen Forrester or Linda since Sunday?"

"No. And he ain't been in at the office, either."

"Oh?" How would Mary Beth know that?

"Chuck told me—Charles Nivens, my boss."

Genuine surprise had Caron cocking her head. "Charles Nivens owns this restaurant?"

Mary Beth nodded. "Do you know him?"

"No, but I've heard he's a very nice man."

"He is." Mary Beth's cheeks turned pink. "His wife is in De Paul's, you know."

The mental institution. Caron didn't miss Mary Beth's familiarity, or her pet name for Charles Nivens. Here, she thought, was the other half of Chuck's affair. "Has she been there very long?"

"Twelve years." Mary Beth propped her chin on her folded hand. "She'll be there forever, but Chuck won't divorce her. He's Catholic, you know."

Mafia-connected, she knew. Catholic, she didn't. "I'm sorry." Caron pushed the fifty toward Mary Beth. Why didn't Chuck buy her an air conditioner? "Thanks for your help."

"I wouldn't take this, but my air conditioner's on the blink." She scrunched up the money and shoved it into her pocket. "I'd just as soon nobody knew we'd talked...."

Ah, pride. Mary Beth wouldn't let Charles Nivens help her financially. "I understand."

Caron watched Mary Beth leave through the front door, then sat watching the window, her pie and coffee untouched. Her hands hurt too much for her to try lifting the fork or the cup. Remembering how Parker had fed her, she eyed the pie longingly. He'd be here in a few minutes. That thought made her feel much better than it should have. Accept it, she told herself. There's something very special about Parker Simms.

And something very weird going on with Keith Forrester.

He had a scheme. He'd gotten Decker involved. And learning about it had made Linda Forrester, Decker's sister, a very unhappy camper. Vanessa, whoever she was, hadn't been happy, either. She'd had cold feet.

Caron rubbed her wrists, then stilled. If she had one, she'd bet another fifty that Vanessa was Forrester's redhead. That she was involved, and the scheme was Misty's abduction.

Unfortunately, Caron would also bet that she wouldn't get far talking to Linda. The woman wasn't apt to point a finger that would land her husband and brother in prison. What could Caron do? She could, via Mary Beth, ask Nivens about Vanessa. But he was a stickler about confidential matters, and getting the mob interested in what was going on was a very bad idea, especially when five million dollars was the sum being thrown around. No, that was too dangerous; Misty would surely be killed. To confirm her suspicions, Caron had to get Linda to talk. The question was—*how?*

Parker swaggered in through the front door. Spotting her, he smiled and started over to her.

Female heads turned to watch his progress. Caron's spirits lifted, and she smiled. Of course. Parker.

Parker got into Caron's car. "Okay, Snow White. Forrester just called me back on my mobile. I told him we wanted to meet his and Cheramie's wives before deciding which man we'll hire to broker our investments."

"Didn't he wonder how you knew he had a wife? It wasn't in his dossier, Parker."

"Sure he did."

"Well, how did you explain knowing?"

"I didn't *explain* anything. I reamed him a new rear end for not *telling* us about her." Parker slid her a wicked grin. "When in doubt, attack."

"Your mother's washboard philosophy."

"Right." He checked his watch. "Cheramie isn't married. But I'm meeting Linda at the café in fifteen minutes. I want you to go stay with Fred until I get back."

"I'm going to stay here." She looked through the Chevy's window, past Parker's shoulder to Decker's door. Killer was running along the fence, deepening the ruts.

"Caron, don't be stubborn, okay? You can't even use your hands without hurting, and you know Decker isn't going anywhere. He never goes anywhere except to the corner store for more beer and chips."

"I'm staying, Parker." She propped her wrist on the steering wheel.

"Damn it, I need to know you're safe."

She looked up into his eyes, smiled and rubbed his jaw. Parker was worried about her, and he wasn't used to being worried. Well, she understood that. She was worried, too. She hadn't forgotten that someone wanted her dead. But if Decker moved, Caron wanted to know it. He was their direct link to Misty. "You're going to be late."

Parker squeezed his eyes shut for a scant second. "All right. But by tomorrow morning, you're going to have a damn phone in that car, and if you say one word against it, I'm going to tape your mouth shut."

He was still upset because she'd been less than enthusiastic about the new dead bolt he'd had installed at her apartment. He cared. He didn't want her, but he did care. She forced herself to act indifferent. "If you want to waste your money buying me a phone, it's fine with me."

"Be careful."

"All right, Parker."

She watched him walk back to his Porsche, muttering something god-awful about a woman testing a man's sanity.

Smiling, Caron leaned her head back against the seat, and watched Killer hike his leg against Decker's truck tire.

A man down the street was mowing his lawn. The gentle breeze carried the smell of freshly cut grass back to her.

At twenty past one, the growls in her stomach grew to roars. She worked with her forearms to get a Butterfinger out of her purse.

Her hands started tingling, then burning like fire. She gasped and dropped the candy into her lap, started rubbing her hands together. For a moment, she panicked, and then it hit her. Tingling. Burning.

Blood circulation.

The ropes were off. Misty's hands were free—and she was swallowing some pills!

Horrible visions of Sarah flooded Caron's mind. She cranked the engine and rushed toward police headquarters. She needed to talk to Sandy.

* * *

At midnight, down from Decker's house, Caron pulled up behind Parker's car and cut the engine. Her head swam. Her leg throbbed. She was queasy and in a cold sweat.

Parker stormed up to her window, his expression as grim as death. "Where the hell have you been? I've been half out of my mind—Caron, what's wrong?"

Caron tried to talk, but managed only a whisper. "She's sick. So...sick."

He opened the driver's door, slid into the car and scooted Caron over on the seat. "You're burning up."

"Misty." Through glazed eyes, she looked at him. "Misty has a fever."

Parker cranked the engine. "It might be Misty, but *you're* going to the hospital."

It took a monumental effort, but Caron managed to squeeze his arm. "Institute. Dr. Zilinger."

"Okay. Okay, I'll buy that." He slammed the gearshift into Drive and peeled out, leaving fifty dollars' worth of her tires on the street.

Parker walked into the institute carrying Caron in his arms. "Dr. Zilinger," he said to the nurses at the desk.

The heavier of the two stood. "Bring her this way."

Parker carried Caron through the brown swinging doors and into a room filled with machines and instruments built into the wall. "Where's Zilinger?"

"We'll take care of the patient, sir. As soon as we fill out the paperwork."

Parker gently put Caron onto a gurney. Then he turned on the squat nurse. "You have three minutes to get Zilinger in here, or I'll buy this damn hospital and fire you."

She squared her shoulders and glared. "Who are you?"

"Parker Simms." He pointed to Caron. "The patient is Caron Chalmers. Now move your behind."

Dr. Zilinger barreled into the room. "Ah, Mr. Simms. I thought I recognized your bellow." She looked up at him through smudged glasses. "What's wrong with Caron?"

"She's sick. She says it's Misty—the girl supposedly abducted. But Caron's the one with the fever."

The doctor put the earpieces of her stethoscope in her ears and listened to Caron's heart. She checked her pulse, then her eyes and ears and her throat.

Parker cringed with every grunt.

Finally the tiny Austrian turned and craned back her neck to look up at him. "Caron's fine."

"What? She's unconscious, for God's sake. How can you say she's fine?"

"It's not Caron who's ill, Mr. Simms. It's Misty. To cure Caron, Misty must receive the medication. We can medicate Caron and numb the pain, but we can't eliminate it."

Caron groaned. Parker stepped closer, took her hand. "It's okay. We're at Dr. Zilinger's." He hoped Caron took more comfort in that disclosure than he did. Personally, he thought the doctor was a quack. Caron was fine? Right.

"Dr. Z.," Caron whispered faintly. "Explain. He doesn't understand."

"All right, Caron. I've ordered something for the pain. Just try to rest now. I'll talk to your young man."

The doctor looked up from the chart where she'd been busying herself scratching notes that, to Parker's way of thinking, only a chicken could read.

"Well, Mr. Simms. It appears that you'll finally be getting your answers."

Half an hour later, Parker frowned. "So what you're telling me is that she's worked a lot of these cases, and successfully solved them?"

"That's exactly what I'm telling you." The doctor refilled her coffee cup.

Parker felt hollow. Harlan had been so sure. Parker himself had been so sure Caron was a con artist. He dragged his hand through his hair. No, he hadn't been. From the start, he'd had a hard time reconciling the woman Harlan had thought Caron was with the woman he'd been getting to know.

She was *not* a fraud.

God help him, he had to tell her the truth.

And the truth was that *he* was a fraud.

"Parker—" Dr. Zilinger joined him at the window "—Caron's resting comfortably. The medication blocks the pain. It'll make her woozy, so I'm keeping her overnight."

"Okay." His heart felt wrung out, and he admitted what his heart had known for some time. Somewhere between coffee at Shoney's, oatmeal at her apartment, and here, he'd come to care about her. He didn't love her; he'd never allow himself to love her. "She'll be all right, won't she?"

The tiny Austrian met his gaze. "I'm not sure. She can't take much more, Parker. Neither, I'm afraid, can Misty. You know that we almost lost Caron when Sarah died?"

He snapped around. "Almost *lost* her?"

"When Sandy brought her in, Caron was in respiratory distress." The doctor laced her hands behind her back. "It was close. Too close. Caron's empathy with the victim is so strong that she suffers their trauma." The doctor let out a heartfelt sigh. "I was hoping . . ."

"What?" Parker stuffed his hand in his jacket pocket. God, but he felt helpless. He was out of his depth here. He understood too little. And he had no one to blame but himself. Caron had tried to explain. But he'd refused to listen.

"I was hoping Caron's gift wouldn't return."

Return.

The word echoed in his mind like a death knell, and the hollow pit in his stomach filled with a leaden knot. Parker swallowed hard. "What do you mean—return?"

Dr. Z. tugged on her stethoscope. "From the night she saw Sarah, until this started with Misty, Caron suffered from traumatic psychic burnout."

"In English?" Parker prompted her, motioning with his lifted hand.

"Seeing Sarah mutilated shocked Caron. So much so that she subconsciously blocked her ability to receive any psychic images."

"Oh, God." Every ounce of strength ebbed right out of his body.

The doctor frowned up at him. "What's wrong, Mr. Simms? You've gone pale."

"You're telling me that for a year Caron hasn't imaged." Ah, Christ. She hadn't been pretending, she hadn't been imaging!

"That's correct." Dr. Zilinger's frown turned curious. "Where are you going?"

His stomach hanging somewhere around his ankles, Parker cleared his throat. "To see Caron."

"I'm right here, Parker."

He turned around. In a white hospital gown, she stood not ten feet from him. He rushed forward, took her by the arm. "Are you all right?"

She gave him a weak smile and rubbed her hand over his jaw. "I've had better days."

He loved the way she touched him. He covered her hand with his and pressed his lips to her palm. "You shouldn't be up. You look like hell."

Her smile reached her eyes. "He's quite a charmer, isn't he, Dr. Z?"

"Indeed." The doctor stepped closer, studying Caron intently. "And he's also right. You should be resting."

"I can't. I have to go."

"Go?" Parker frowned. "Go where?"

"To Decker's." She looked up at him. "I have to touch Misty's bike."

Dr. Z explained. "The images are strongest when she's touching something that belongs to the victim."

Parker clenched his jaw. "You're not going back in there."

"I have to, Parker."

"Then let's call Sanders and get a warrant. We can do this right, without endangering you."

"He won't do it. You know that as well as I do. Without a missing-persons report, Sandy would be putting his career on the line—and he won't do that. And you shouldn't blame him for it."

"Be reasonable, sweetheart. You can't expect me to let you go back into that house, knowing what I know about Decker. He could be the man who left the message on your door."

"I'm not asking for your permission. Don't you see? I have no choice. I have to risk it." She stroked his face. "Look at me. No, damn it, really look at me."

He did. Her eyes were dull, listless. The dark circles beneath them were deeper now, and strain etched her face. She looked weary and worn out.

"Misty is worse, Parker," she said. "If I don't find her soon, she's going to die." Caron swallowed hard. "And, this time, so will I."

Chapter 7

Caron rested her head against Parker's shoulder and watched the city lights twinkling below. There wasn't a prettier view of New Orleans than from the bridge. With a little shiver, she prayed this wouldn't be the last time she saw it.

"Cold?" One hand on the steering wheel, Parker reached with the other and rubbed her thigh.

"No," she said, wondering why it was so easy to confess her deepest feelings to him. "Scared."

"Me, too." He tapped the signal, then switched lanes.

She had a hard time imagining Parker Simms afraid of anything. It was comforting, having him admit to a weakness.

"I can't stand the thought of you going back into that man's house, Caron."

Scooting closer, she linked their hands. He laced their fingers and pressed their palms together. A knot shifted into her throat. Too tender!

She changed the subject. "You didn't tell me." The medication had kicked in. But was that why she was feeling better? Or was it Misty? "How'd the meeting go with Linda Forrester?"

"All in all, I suppose it was productive. She's hiding something, Caron, and she's scared witless."

As soon as Misty crossed her mind, the pain redoubled. Was focus the key to controlling the pain? "For her brother, maybe?"

"I don't think so." Parker braked, slowing the car. "It— Hell, I don't know. You're the one who senses things."

So finally he'd accepted it. She gave his fingers a little squeeze. "Maybe she's worried about Forrester."

"That was easy enough to pick up on," Parker agreed. "I don't know about that fling we suspected with Vanessa, though, sweetheart. Forrester's wife's a knockout, and she's crazy about him. From her clothes, they're loaded, too." Parker grunted. "What else could the man want from a woman?"

"I don't know." Caron felt oddly content. Considering their situation, she should be frantic, but she wasn't. Parker's endearment soothed, mostly because it had rolled so naturally off his tongue. "Do you have something of hers? Something she touched?"

"No." Parker passed a truck, then eased back over into the right-hand lane. "Wait. Yes, I do." He pulled something from his jacket pocket. "This."

Caron took the book of matches, closed her eyes, and concentrated. Fear flooded her. Anger followed it. Then the images were coming so fast, she couldn't decipher them, just soaked them up like a sponge.

She dropped the matches and opened her eyes. Parker was about to exit onto Belle Chase Highway. "Don't turn," Caron said, her voice pitched high.

"Why?" He glanced her way. "Caron, what is it?"

"The woman you met wasn't Linda, Parker. I don't know who she was, but she wasn't Linda."

"Okay, but—"

"She's the woman who took Misty to Decker."

"Oh, God."

"She knows where Misty is." Caron's heart nearly thudded out of her chest. "Turn around."

"Where are we going?"

"First to my apartment."

Parker whipped off the road, waited until it was clear in both directions, then turned and headed back toward the bridge. "I don't get it."

Caron kissed his shoulder. "When in doubt, attack."

"That I get." He lifted his brows. "But attack *who?*"

Parker looked out Caron's window. The sun had come up, streaking the sky with soothing golds and pinks. The shower had stopped a few minutes ago; Caron had gone into her bedroom and closed the door. She hadn't said any more about what was going on, and, though he hated to admit it—and he'd thought of nothing else—he still didn't have a fix on exactly who she meant to attack.

Trust her. The thought came and held. Parker stared at the sign at the store across the street. He was more than relieved that she hadn't gone back into Decker's to touch Misty's bike—especially after Dr, Z. had told him that they'd nearly lost Caron when Sarah died.

His stomach curled and rumbled at the thought, and his chest felt compressed. If he lived forever, he'd never forget Caron telling him that if Misty died, this time she'd die, too. He'd nearly crumbled, nearly fallen to his knees the way Harlan had in the morgue.

Frowning, Parker watched two kids ride by on bicycles. A man wearing red suspenders hung up the phone on the outside wall of the store, then shuffled to the bench near the door. How could Parker trust her? She'd been willing to risk her life. She'd known the danger in touching that bike, but she'd been willing to do it—for Misty.

The objective man in him should have admired her courage. But where Caron was concerned, there wasn't any objective man in him. And the unobjective man was terrified of losing her, and forbidden to tell her or show her how he felt, because he hadn't been honest with her. It was a hell of a dilemma.

The man on the bench rose, looked at the sign and scratched his head, then sat down again.

"I'm ready to get started," Caron said from behind him.

Parker turned and caught his breath.

Caron was standing beside the sofa, wearing a white sundress with thin straps and a scoop neck. Her skin was flushed from the shower, and she'd brushed her hair until it gleamed. She looked beautiful. If he hadn't seen her just hours ago at the institute, he wouldn't have believed how sick she'd been.

Perplexed by it all, he frowned. "What happened?"

"Excuse me?" Now it was her turn to look confused.

"Caron, a few hours ago you were unconscious. I feared for your life. Now..." His voice trailed off.

"Now, what?" Her skirt swished against her thighs.

"Now you look... healthy."

"I think I figured out something in the car. It's a matter of focus. If I concentrate on Misty's condition, the empathy pains control me. But if I think about you or the case, I can minimize the effect—at least sometimes."

If she spent half as much time thinking about him as he did thinking about her, she might just make it through this case unscathed. "I'm glad." And then he gave her something he'd never given anyone else: power over him. "You scared me, Caron."

"I'm sorry." The look she gave him was genuine.

She knew, and she wouldn't use it as a weapon against him. "What now?"

"Let's put on a pot of coffee and make some plans. First on the list is Sandy. It's time we filled him in."

In the kitchen, Parker noticed the answering machine. "Maybe you should answer your calls first." He pointed. "Light's blinking."

Caron rinsed the coffeepot, then filled it with water. "I will in a minute. Can you grab a filter for me? Second cabinet on the left."

Parker opened the cabinet door and pulled out a box of filters. They clung together. He raised a small stack and blew on them until one broke free of the rest, then passed it over. When she took it from him, Caron smiled. He smiled back. There was something good about being in her kitchen together, about them smiling at each other.

They were on their fourth pot of coffee after an all-night vigil of studying documents when the doorbell rang.

"I'll get it." Parker shoved back from the paper-strewn table, then went out to the living room. He glanced at his watch. No wonder they were wired. It was nearly noon.

"If it's a solicitor, give him an earful." Caron's voice followed him. "I put up a sign."

"Okay," he called back, then cracked open the door and stepped aside. Sanders. And from the look on the detective's face, this wasn't a social call. Parker decided to dispense with the amenities. "Come in."

"Where's Caron?"

Caron recognized Sandy's voice. The little hairs on her neck lifted. Logically, she knew that Misty was safe for the moment; she'd imaged her sleeping comfortably not more than three minutes ago. But emotionally, Caron knew neither of them was safe—not yet. Not until everyone involved in Misty's abduction was behind bars.

Caron walked into the living room. Sandy was chewing on a stubby cigar. He never took his cigars out of the office...unless he was deeply disturbed.

Misty! Fighting a sense of panic, she focused every ounce of concentration she could muster, every fiber of energy, on Sandy. "Is Misty—" She couldn't say it.

"I don't have any word on Misty, Caron."

Parker shut the door. It took a full minute for Caron to calm down. Seeing her that way grated Parker's insides raw. One second she was fine, the next she was devastated. Her eyes held as much fear as he'd ever seen in any human being, and she was shaking like a blender on the high setting. Dr. Z. had warned him of what to expect; during a case, Caron always stressed out. But his instincts were telling him that her reaction was more than anticipated stress.

To cut the tension, Parker offered Sanders a chair.

He took one, a chair beside the sofa. "Parker tells me you had a close call yesterday."

"Yes, I did. But I'm fine now." Her voice was strained.

She wasn't fine, Parker thought; she was falling apart before his eyes. Parker led her to the sofa, sat down beside her, then lied with a clear conscience. "We were just about to leave, Sanders. Did you need something, or is this a social visit?"

"I was hoping you'd fill me in on what's been going on. I've left several messages, but—"

"We've been out," Parker said. Caron was as white as a sheet, and if she held her back any stiffer it might just snap.

Caron put her hand on Parker's thigh. Her grip was strong, but when she spoke, she sounded at ease. "We know about Decker and Linda and Keith Forrester, Sandy."

"I figured you did." He looked toward the window.

The sense that Sandy had done something seriously wrong grew thick, palpable. Parker looked at Caron, but she stared straight ahead at Sandy.

"She's why I'm here." Sandy didn't meet Caron's gaze. "I thought you'd want to know..." His voice faded away, and he looked at Parker. "Linda Forrester was murdered yesterday afternoon, about two o'clock."

"What?" Caron gasped.

"Her husband's been out of town on business since Sunday. He found her at his house about six last night."

Caron's chest heaved with forced breaths. Parker clasped her hand. He'd talked to Forrester yesterday morning. The man hadn't been in the office—according to Nivens, via Mary Beth—but he had returned Parker's call within minutes of Parker's leaving the message. "Any suspects?"

"Not yet." Sandy took his cigar out of his mouth. "She wasn't killed at home. There were no signs of any struggle, or any valuables missing. I talked with the coroner this morning, and from the amount of skin he found under her fingernails we believe there would have been a struggle."

Caron stiffened. "How was she killed?"

Sandy grimaced. "She was strangled with a dog leash."

Caron frowned. Strangled. No blood. Sandy's hand was trembling. This didn't make sense. "Was there blood?"

"A lot of it—all hers. She took a rough beating."

Parker grunted. "But there was no blood at the house."

He was confused, too. She tightened her grip on his hand.

"No," Sandy said. "No oddball fingerprints, either."

Parker narrowed his eyes. "And the coroner fixes the time of death at two o'clock Tuesday?"

Sandy nodded and clamped his teeth around his cigar.

Parker looked at Caron. She'd caught it, he realized. When she'd imaged the woman who'd taken Misty to Decker, she'd thought the case was winding down. But it wasn't. They'd barely scratched the surface.

"I've got to get back," Sandy said. "I just thought you'd want to know."

Parker walked Sanders to the door. "Keep us posted."

"Sure will." He headed down the stairs.

Parker looked back at Caron.

"It was half past one when my hands quit hurting," she said. "Someone freed Misty's hands from the ropes then."

"And it was 2:45 when I left Charles Nivens's café and the woman I thought was Linda Forrester." Forty-five minutes *after* the time of her death.

"That woman wasn't Linda Forrester."

"You knew that from the matches."

"Yes." Caron wanted to stand, but she knew her legs wouldn't hold her. "But now we have proof."

Parker frowned. "Sanders didn't bat an eye when you connected Decker and the Forresters."

"No, he didn't." It was hard to admit, but Caron couldn't deny it anymore. "He knew they connected."

"Yes."

The regret in Parker's voice encouraged her to continue. Caron rubbed her palm over the scratchy sofa arm. The fabric was rough, abrasive, suiting her mood. "He was deeply disturbed by her death. Deeply disturbed." Those sensations had been too strong not to be accurate.

"Yes, he was."

Sharing the knowledge that Sandy was involved in this was somehow, oddly, a relief for Caron. She tucked her foot under her bottom. "You talked to Forrester yesterday morning. He set up the meeting with you and Linda. He wasn't out of town."

"I left a message, and he returned the call. He could have been anywhere."

"He wasn't."

Parker slumped his shoulders. "More images?"

"No, just a supposition." Caron let her head fall back against the sofa cushions. "What about Vanessa?" Caron was speculating on the mystery woman's identity.

"Maybe." Parker sat down beside her and propped his hand on her thigh. "The morning we were at Hunt's he was talking to her about getting cold feet."

Caron tossed his own words back at Parker. "That could have been about selling stock too early. Normal business."

"Yeah." She saw in his eyes that he remembered the conversation. He sat back down beside her. "Or it could've been about Misty's abduction."

She rested her head on his shoulder. "What next?"

"We take five to think." He lifted her chin with a fingertip until she looked up at him. "For a long time, I doubted you, Caron. I regret that. I believe you now. And I want you to forgive me."

She blinked hard and nodded. "If you haven't experienced it, being psychic is a hard thing to grasp."

It was. But now that he had, he was as afraid for Misty as Caron had been from the start. There was too much going down at once, and if they weren't careful, they could miss a vital clue. They'd pay the price. But so would Misty.

He hated to ask—focusing would bring her pain—but he had to know. "Is Misty doing okay?"

Caron gave him a watery smile. "She's sick, but she's okay. Her fever is down, and her leg isn't hurting so much right now."

"Good." He let out a breath he hadn't realized he was holding. "I don't like the way this is shaping up."

"Me, either. Forrester needs five million for some unknown reason. He has some woman—let's say for the moment Vanessa *is* Forrester's redhead—who knows Misty's father and Misty bring Misty to Decker, Forrester's brother-in-law, so that if something goes wrong, Vanessa and Decker will go to jail for kidnapping."

Parker took over. "Then Forrester's wife, Linda, somehow finds out. She opposes the kidnapping and ends up dead. Forrester 'finds' her body, and maybe lies about being out of town at the time of the murder."

Caron scooted closer to Parker and propped her chin on his shoulder. "Logic tells me Forrester killed Linda. So why doesn't it feel right?"

Parker kneaded Caron's nape with his free hand. "Sandy's gut-deep in this, Caron. You do realize that."

"Yes, I do. All the way up to his cigar stub. But Sandy *isn't* capable of murder." She paused for a second, then went on. "It could have been Decker."

Parker explored the possibility. "He does have it in him to kill, but he doesn't seem the type to kidnap a child for anything other than his own gain."

"Linda died on Tuesday." Caron plucked a speck of lint off Parker's lapel. "Ina said Linda visits Decker every Tuesday. And he has Killer, so he likely has a dog leash."

"If Forrester was offering Decker part of the ransom, then, yeah, maybe." Parker grimaced. "We still have too many *ifs* and *maybes*."

"We'll eliminate them." Caron patted his shoulder, then stood up. "Let's get some coffee."

Parker followed her to the kitchen. "The more we find out, the muddier the waters seem to get."

"Isn't every case like that?" At the cabinet, Caron pulled down two fresh mugs, then reached for the coffeepot.

"I guess so." He pulled out a chair and sat down. "We haven't discussed the Vanessa angle much. What if she *is* the redhead Mary Beth said comes into the café with Forrester?"

Caron sat down across from him and slid one of the mugs over to him. "The word you're looking for is *mistress*."

"Okay, then." Parker sipped from the steaming mug. "What if Vanessa is Forrester's mistress? And what if she wants to elevate her position to that of his wife?"

Caron tipped her head and kicked off a sandal. "Women have been known to kill for a man." She wiggled her toes, then slid them between Parker's legs and rubbed her arch with his calf. "I guess it's possible."

"What we need is a better fix on her." Under the table, he lifted Caron's foot to his thigh and began rubbing her instep. "Mary Beth didn't know anything?"

The firm sweep of his fingers over her foot was a slice of heaven. Caron shook her head. "Not even her name. Our only clue is that she has red hair."

Parker's hand slid to her ankle, and the strangest expression lit his face. "No, that's not our only clue. Forrester identified the body, Caron. The woman I met with, who I believed was Linda Forrester, was a redhead."

Her mug in midair, Caron pursed her lips. "What color is Linda Forrester's hair?"

"I don't know." Without rising, Parker stretched and grabbed the phone, then passed it to Caron. "But Ina does."

Her heart sped up a notch. Caron called, spoke with Ina, then hung up and looked at Parker. "Ina says thanks for the irises. They're beautiful."

"Linda Forrester's not a redhead."

"Blonde." Caron squinted. "What about a wig?"

"No way."

"They make very good wigs, Parker. Are you sure?"

"I grew up with two women, Caron. Trust me, I know about these things."

She wanted to laugh, but Parker chose just that moment to let his fingers dance across the back of her knee. "Okay," she said, working to keep her voice steady. "I know a woman is behind the entire abduction. She bound Misty's hands at the park and took her to the shopping center, to Decker. And I'm positive that she's someone Misty and her father know and trust. But, really, that's all I know."

"*We* know. Not I, Caron. *We.*"

"The way I see it, we've got a choice to make." He rubbed his lip with his thumb. "You're sure Misty's all right for now?"

Caron focused. Finally, Misty's image formed. She was lying on the floor in the wooden shed, sleeping peacefully. There was a red plastic glass near her left hand, and the remnants of a hot dog on a plate beside it. Caron concentrated harder, pulling herself deeper into the image, but couldn't see anything else. Misty's breathing was steady, at least, settled. And the pain in her leg was better.

Caron opened her eyes and looked at Parker. "She's okay. Actually, she's better. But don't make too much of that. I've seen this happen before, and then suddenly things take a downturn."

"She's okay right now. We have to go with that."

Caron could have kissed him. "What's our choice?"

"We'll need to do two things. It's just a question of the order we do them in. We can pay Hunt's a visit and try to get a fix on the Vanessa who called—maybe she's a client—and then go to the morgue and see if the victim is a redhead or a blonde, or flip around and visit the morgue first."

"Jillian isn't going to be overjoyed to see me, or to answer any questions. She caught me listening in on Forrester's conversation. But the morgue doesn't appeal, either." Caron drank the last of her coffee. "You choose."

"The morgue," he said. "I want to know who died."

Startled, Caron snapped her gaze to Parker. "Sandy said it was Linda Forrester."

Parker slid Caron a level look that rocked her to the core. "And who identified her?"

"Forrester."

"So does he tag his wife, or his lover, as the murder victim?"

A cold chill crept up Caron's spine. "It could be either one."

Parker couldn't forget.

The last time he'd walked through these corridors he'd been with Harlan. They had taken these same steps down these same stairs to the basement. They'd gone through these same heavy swinging doors and walked into the same cold room.

"You okay?"

He looked at Caron. "What?"

"You're shaking. Does being here bother you?"

He considered lying to her; it would be so easy. But he couldn't do it. His days of lying to Caron were over. "Yeah, it does."

She rubbed the back of his hand with her thumb. "It bothers everyone with an ounce of compassion and half an ounce of sense."

"We should've waited until morning."

"We couldn't wait, Parker. We've discussed this. They're not about to let two people off the street come in and view a corpse. You've got to pretend to be Sandy."

"What if the attendant knows Sanders? The guy's been around since God was a baby."

"I'll sense it," she said calmly. "You're going to have to trust me on this."

Parker wasn't a man given to trusting easily. But he intended to try. Caron wrung feelings out of him that he didn't know he had. After all he'd done *against* her, the least he could do *for* her was to try to trust her. "Okay."

"Really?" She gave him a smile that wrenched his heart. He'd given other women diamonds and not seen as much pleasure in their eyes.

"Really." He squeezed her hand.

The guy on duty was named John Davis. He was about forty, and stoop-shouldered, and he was chewing the hell out of a toothpick. He was pleasant, and hard-nosed, too, Parker imagined, considering his line of work.

After a brief conversation, Caron gave Parker a go-ahead nod. John Davis didn't know Sanders. Relieved, Parker cut the chitchat and got down to business. "Detective Sanders," Parker said. "Can we have a look at Forrester?"

"Sure thing. She's right over here."

They walked into a room that was even chillier than the office. White walls, white floor, square silver refrigerated tombs with long shiny handles.

John stopped at the third one, middle row. "Forrester," he said, checking the name marked on the orange paper inserted in a slot just above the door. "Move a little to the left, please."

Caron urged him, and Parker moved. Sarah had been just two silver doors down.

John rolled the toothpick to the opposite side of his mouth, then opened the door and pulled out a sliding tray. On it was a woman's sheet-draped body. Parker read the tag attached to her toe, which was sticking out from under the edge of the white shroud. "Forrester."

"Ready?" the attendant asked, looking at Caron.

Parker heard her swallow, watched her nod. How many times before had she done this alone? He reached over and took her hands.

The man lifted back the corner of the sheet.

Parker stiffened, half-afraid that when he looked down it would be Sarah he'd see. He wouldn't let that happen. He couldn't. He forced himself to lower his gaze, then frowned.

A thin line of choke marks dappled her neck. Her face wasn't damaged. She was blond and beautiful. But she was *not* the woman he'd met at the café.

Caron squeezed his hand. "Is it her?"

"She was a redhead." Strained, his voice grated.

"A wig?" Caron suggested again.

"No. I'm sure. Her face was shaped differently, more square than oval. And her lips were thicker. It's not her."

Parker was in a cold sweat. He nodded, and John Davis pushed the tray back into the wall and closed the door.

"I thought she'd lost a lot of blood," Caron said.

"She did," Davis said with a nod. "The back of her head was pounded with a heavy object."

Caron thanked him. Parker couldn't seem to find his voice. His mind was too full of memories of Harlan, and how he'd reacted on seeing Sarah here. The man had crumpled right before Parker's eyes. And the moment Harlan had fallen to his knees was the moment Parker had decided to burn down the building where Sarah had died.

He couldn't bring her back. And he couldn't collar the guy who'd murdered her; he'd already been arrested. But there was something Parker could do to comfort her husband and his friend. Parker could see to it that no other woman ever suffered as Sarah had suffered in that hell-hole. He could see to it that when Harlan drove by that building—as any husband would countless times—he wouldn't ever have to look at that building again. Parker could do those things for his friend. And he had.

Caron frowned. What was Parker thinking? His expression had closed, and his eyes had grown hard; whatever it was, it was wicked, and he'd had to bury his emotions deep. Before they'd arrived, she'd suspected that coming here would be hard for him. Only now did she realize how hard. Parker's father came to mind. Had Parker had to identify Charley in this room? She hoped he would talk to her about it, but she wouldn't push. When he was ready, when he trusted her, then he'd talk. And that would be soon enough.

She led him outside, through the parking lot, and to the car. "Give me your keys, Parker. I'll drive."

He passed them to her without a word.

Caron got in and shut the door. Parker was sitting there, looking as wooden as a cigar-store Indian. She considered waiting, then decided against it, and reversed her earlier decision not to push him. The more time that passed between now and whenever he talked to her about this, the deeper he would bury his emotions. And she knew firsthand how important it was to give emotions free rein. Burying them spelled disaster.

She covered his hand with hers. "Was it Charley?"

He seemed surprised that she'd noticed, and he tried to pull his hand free. But Caron held on tight. "Don't run from me, please. We've been through too much together for you to run from me."

He didn't answer for a long time. When she figured he wasn't going to, he did. "She was...more than a friend."

"You identified her in that room." He nodded. Caron's heart ached, and she wrapped him in her arms and held him close.

She sensed more than felt or saw his tears. Though his eyes were dry, the tears were real, welling up from his heart. "God, I'm so sorry."

He needed rest. They both did. They were running on sheer adrenaline, and that, as she'd learned from Sarah's case, was a breeding ground for mistakes.

Caron started the engine and headed toward home. Misty was safe for now. They could afford a few hours' sleep.

During the ride, Parker didn't say a word. Not when, unfamiliar with standard transmissions, Caron ground the

Porsche's gears. Not when, testing the handling of the car, she nearly had them airborne. And not when, sidetracked by a kid shooting across the street on his bike, she bumped the curb parking at her apartment. But it wasn't until he climbed the stairs without griping about the graffiti and the rickety banister as he usually did that she started worrying.

Inside, she tossed her purse onto a chair in the living room and walked straight into the kitchen. From the fridge, she called out, "Hungry?"

Parker paused at a mirror in the hallway. On the way back to Caron's, he'd seen nothing but the flames of the burning building. But he was okay now. Tired-looking around the eyes, and bone-weary, but back on solid ground emotionally. "Yeah, I am," he said.

Grabbing a slice of pizza from the fridge, Caron bit off the tip. Parker put water into the kettle and rolled his eyes back in his head. "God, she's *trying* to make me sick."

"I am not. If you don't want pizza, help yourself to whatever you do want." Caron looked at the phone. The red light on the answering machine was blinking.

"How old is it?"

A wrinkle furrowed her brow and she shrugged. "Not sure." She grabbed a can of cola from the fridge and tapped the button on the answering machine.

A recording of a woman's voice filled the kitchen. "Caron, ain't you ever gonna get home, child?"

"Ina," Caron told Parker.

"Call me right away, you hear? No matter what time it is. Right away!"

"What's that all about?"

"Beats me." Caron set the pizza on the counter and punched in Ina's number.

Ina answered the phone right away.

"Caron?"

"Yes, Ina, it's me." Caron straightened and reached for her cola. "Are you all right? You sounded—"

"I have something to tell you," she said, breathless. "Whew! I was in the tub."

"Take your time."

"I'm fine now." Ina breathed deeply. The phone crackled. "I called Tuesday. Where've you been?"

"Everywhere." Caron glossed over the whirlwind she and Parker had been living in. "What's up?"

"I said I'd call if anything unusual happened at Decker's. Well, something did. Just after one—Tuesday, I'm talking about—Linda came over to see Decker, like usual. But she was madder than a horny bull penned up away from the cows. Stomping and spewing curses on Decker's head—some I never even heard of before.

"Then this man drives up in a shiny Lincoln. He was dressed to the hilt. Quite a looker. But I didn't think much of him for long. He gets out of the car yelling. Then they all start arguing. Have themselves a free-for-all right there in the driveway outside the garage.

"Mr. Klein was outside giving Fluffy a bath with the water hose, and he heard the whole thing. They didn't see him, of course. Mr. Klein wouldn't embarrass nobody, letting on he's hearing family business."

"What were they arguing about?" Caron had missed them by minutes. Mere minutes!

"I couldn't hear, and Mr. Klein won't say. 'A body's dirty laundry ought be kept behind closed doors,' Mr. Klein told Mrs. Klein. She says he's a stubborn cuss. He'll take it with him to his grave. But Lily Mae was out watering her begonias—not that they need watering, what with all the rain we been having. But she heard the man—that Forrester fellow, she says—tell the others that if they didn't all keep their mouths shut, he'd kill them."

"The others?"

"Linda and Decker. Ain't you listening, child?"

"Her own husband?" Shock streaked up Caron's back.

"That's right," Ina said with an indignant snort. "Lily Mae knew it was Forrester, because he drove up in that shiny Lincoln. Mary Beth had told her all about it."

The first time she'd been to Decker's, before she'd met Parker, there had been a black Lincoln in the drive. "Have you seen Decker since then?"

"He's been home. Killer treed Fluffy on the shed roof, and she got muddier than a slopped pig—that's why Mr.

Klein was giving her a bath on Tuesday. Well, the fool cat still ain't learned her lesson, 'cause last night she was right back up there, treed again on Decker's shed.''

Caron rubbed her temple. "But have you seen *Decker?*"

"Sure did, just last night. You really ought to pay closer attention, child. The fool emptied a double-barrelled shotgun, trying to shoot Fluffy off the roof.''

"Good God! Did he hit her?"

"Naw, he missed her by a mile. Put a hole the size of a penny through the side of Lily Mae's garage, though." Ina sighed. "Decker never could shoot worth a switch. Mainly 'cause he's usually drunk."

"Mmm, too much beer, I suppose."

"Exactly." Ina harrumphed. "I called the police. Decker knows it, too. I been keeping watch, but he ain't stomped my irises again, least not yet."

Caron smiled. "Have the new ones taken root?"

"You know they have. Fred put 'em in, didn't he? They sure are pretty. You tell your Parker I said that, you hear? Fred's a nice man. Likes my lemonade. Most say it's too tart, but Fred had two glasses. Fine man, yes, indeed."

"Good." Caron took a drink of her cola and polished off the last bite of pizza.

"Have you found the young'n?"

Caron imaged Ina crossing herself. "Not yet. But we think we're getting close."

"Fred tells me Parker won't have family around for Christmas. His mama and sister are still in Europe. I'm figuring you won't, either."

"No, I won't." Caron fought the memories of last year. She'd been unconscious all through Christmas, and her mother hadn't even called.

"Well," Ina said, "I'll expect you both here by noon Christmas Day. Tell your Parker now, you hear?"

"Thank you. I'll tell him."

"I'll call if I hear anything more before then. I told that scum I'd called the police. I'm half expecting he'll stomp my irises again, so I'm keeping a close watch."

"Ina, you be careful. Decker could be dangerous. Stay away from him, okay?"

"I didn't roll out of the swamp yesterday, child. I know not to kick a mad dog when he's foaming at the mouth."

"All right." Caron smiled. "See you Christmas." Caron hung up and turned to Parker. "Ina expects us at noon for Christmas dinner."

"Okay with me, if it's okay with you. I'm due a square meal." Parker crunched down on a cracker.

There was no justice. Even pouting, he was gorgeous. "Tacky, honey."

"Truth, sweetheart." He smoothed peanut butter onto another cracker. "What else did Ina have to say?"

"Around noon Tuesday, Decker and Keith and Linda Forrester had a whopper of an argument in Decker's driveway. Forrester threatened to kill Linda and Decker."

Parker stopped chewing. "And two hours later she turns up dead."

Caron brushed a crumb from his lip. "Right." She grabbed her purse, took out the pills Dr. Z. had given her, then dry-swallowed two. "I know Forrester looks guilty, but . . . it just doesn't feel right."

Parker shoved back his chair. "I think it's time we had a chat with Decker."

Caron downed a swig of Coke. "So do I. But he won't talk to us. Why should he?"

"Because we're going to put the fear of God into him. Attack, remember?"

"The sooner the better, Parker. Misty's awake."

"Is she—?"

"She's scared and in pain, but she's holding on."

So was Caron.

Parker pounded on Decker's door. Inside the house, Killer started barking. "Come on, Decker," Parker shouted. "I know you're in there."

Decker swung the door open. Killer bounced against the screen, popping it with his front paws. "Get outa here." He kicked at the dog, then growled at Parker. "What the hell do you want?"

The beer in his hand foamed from his hand gestures. Caron squeezed Parker's hand, then let go.

"Straight talk, buddy." Parker's expression darkened. "You helped Keith Forrester and a redhead kidnap a kid named Misty. Her bike's in your garage. Your sister, Linda, found out. She didn't like it. Now she's dead. In a few minutes, cops are going to be crawling all over your ass. And we're the only thing standing between you and the electric chair. Now talk."

"I didn't kill her."

"Well, it's your hide Forrester nailed to the wall."

Decker narrowed his eyes. "Who the hell are you?"

Avoiding Parker's gaze, Caron barged in. Sometimes, the truth just wouldn't do. "We're private investigators."

"I don't have to talk to you."

"No, you don't," Parker agreed. "But you're in this up to your earlobes, and every cop in town knows it. We're the only chance you've got, and probably the only people in the world who figure you *didn't* kill Linda."

Decker's eyes misted. "I didn't."

Caron challenged him. "But you know who did."

Decker looked torn between talking to them and telling them to go to hell. Caron pressed. "Someone is going to go to jail for kidnapping Misty and murdering your sister, Mr. Decker. If you don't help us, that someone is going to be you."

He dragged a hand through his hair and stepped back from the door. Parker opened it and went inside. Caron followed.

Decker plopped down in his recliner. Caron watched Killer. He sat alert at his master's feet, his ears pricked, but he wasn't growling. She didn't trust either of them.

"Linda was all I had." Decker's red-rimmed eyes proved he'd been doing some heavy-duty drinking, or mourning, or both. He shielded his eyes with his hand and rubbed.

Caron started to say something, but Parker's glance had her keeping quiet.

Decker's chest heaved. "That friggin' cop offed her." He pounded the arm of his chair with his fist. "I'm gonna kill him. Just as soon as I find that slimy bastard, I'm gonna rip his heart right outa his chest and feed it to my dog."

Caron swallowed back the knot of revulsion clogging her throat. Her knees went weak. He was talking about Sandy. She knew it as well as she'd known Sandy was involved.

"Sanders?" Parker asked, not sounding at all surprised. He walked to the television and lifted a gold-framed photo.

"Yeah, Sanders." Decker took a long draw from the beer.

Parker raised the photo. "Is this Linda?"

Caron saw the long blond hair, the same beautiful face they'd seen lifeless in the morgue. It was her.

Decker pursed his lips and nodded.

"Why do you say Sanders killed her?" Caron couldn't believe in her heart that Sandy could kill anyone; there had to be another explanation.

"He was sleeping with her." Decker shook his head. "It's kind of complicated."

Needing the support, Caron leaned back against the door. "We have time."

"Keith got into a little trouble at work. Played hotshot with somebody else's money. Sanders found out, and was gonna have Keith arrested."

Parker looked at Decker. "Sounds reasonable, so far."

"They knew each other from way back. Sanders and Forrester and Linda."

"It can't be that far back," Caron insisted. "Sandy's a good twenty years older than Forrester."

"No, he ain't." Decker made a scissors motion with his fingers. "Keith's touchy about age. He's had everything lifted that can be lifted. So's Linda."

Parker shrugged. "That doesn't explain why Sanders would kill her."

"He's in love with her. Always has been. And when he went head-on with Keith about the money, Keith used that. He told Linda he'd 'learned his lesson,' that he'd never do anything crooked again. And he sent her to Sanders to patch things up and take off the heat."

"*Sent* her?" Caron cocked her head. "What do you mean?"

Decker sighed. "Keith told Linda that she was the only one who could keep him out of jail. She had to pretend she'd fallen in love with Sanders to get him to give Keith a little time to fix things."

"And she did it?" Caron couldn't hide her shock.

"Yeah." Decker sniffled, then cleared his throat. "She was crazy about Keith. She did anything he asked her to do. Always."

Parker stuffed his hand into his pocket. "So Linda became Sandy's lover and persuaded him to keep his mouth shut about Keith and the money."

"Yeah." Decker took a long swallow of beer, then crunched the can between his palms. "Then Sanders found out Linda was stringing him along. He dropped by her house. Keith was supposed to be out of town."

"But he wasn't," Parker said.

"No. He was popping it to Linda on the sofa. Sanders saw them through the window."

Decker twisted his lips. "So Sanders waited till morning, then came here looking for her. Everybody knows Linda comes over here every Tuesday." Sending Caron a leering smile, he added, "Considers it her family duty to straighten me out."

Caron grimaced. Could it have been Sandy, not Forrester, Ina's neighbors had seen arguing with Linda and Decker?

"So what happened?" Parker put the photo back.

"She wasn't here. She'd gone to the beauty shop first. I told Sanders. He was messing around with Killer's leash. Said it was just what Linda needed to keep her in line."

Caron blinked, then blinked again. "Where is it now?"

Decker shrugged. "I don't know. That's the last time I saw it."

"So Sandy left, right?" Parker prodded.

"Yeah. But first he called Linda and told her to meet him at their place." Decker got out of the recliner. "I'm gonna grab another beer."

He'd be in plain sight, but Caron still tensed. Parker nodded.

"Their place." Decker guffawed. "Sandy acted like it was a big secret. Hell, everybody knew they went to the camp. Even Keith knew it."

Caron condemned Decker; in her heart, she blamed him for not protecting his sister. "You let her meet him?"

Decker guffawed again. "Honey, it's clear you don't know Linda. Since she was sixteen and Keith popped her cherry in the back seat of his daddy's Caddy, ain't nobody been able to tell her nothing. I couldn't stop her. Nobody could. But I did follow her."

"So you saw Sandy kill her?" Parker picked up a seashell from a shelf covered with trinkets and put it to his ear. He sounded calm, but his hand wasn't steady.

"No. I got caught behind a wreck and lost her. By the time I got up to the camp, Linda was dead. Piled on the grass, deader than dirt." He snapped the top off the beer and took a long swig.

"What time was that?"

Decker lowered the can from his mouth and swallowed. "About three-thirty." He shrugged. "Maybe four."

It didn't fit. Something was very wrong here. But what? Caron licked her lips. "You've explained everything except why you got involved in the kidnapping."

"Because of Linda. Keith told me he'd fixed the papers to make it look like *she'd* stolen the money. He's got one of those fancy computers. He said that either I went along, or Linda went to jail. So I went along."

"Where's Forrester now?" Parker returned the shell.

"I don't know. Probably shacked up with the redheaded whore who started all this."

"Vanessa?" Caron asked, playing a hunch.

"Who knows? He don't tell me his sluts' names. But the money was her old man's."

"Do you know his name?" Caron tensed, tempted to shake the truth out of Decker.

"No. Never heard it."

Parker stepped to Caron's side, as if sensing she'd need him close. "Decker," he said. "Who is Misty—and where is she?"

Caron's heart skipped a full beat, then pounded against her ribs. She was scared to breathe, to so much as blink.

"I don't know who she is or where they have her." He shook his head. "I swear, if I did, I'd cut her loose like Linda wanted."

"Misty was here," Parker said, in a flat tone.

"Yeah, until Linda saw her. Couple hours later, Keith picked the kid up. I don't know where he took her."

Caron squeezed Parker's arm. She believed Decker. He didn't know where Misty was now. But he was wrong about Sandy; he hadn't killed Linda.

"Where's this camp?"

"Uh-uh. No way you're getting that out of me. Forrester will kill me. Or Sanders will."

Caron smelled Decker's fear and knew he wouldn't change his mind.

"We aren't going to tell the police what your involvement in this is, Decker—at least not yet. But don't take off."

"My sister's funeral's tomorrow. I'll be there."

"Parker." Caron nodded toward the door.

He gave her a perplexed look, but followed her outside.

She didn't say a word. They got into the car and closed the doors.

Then Parker looked Caron straight in the eye. "Vanessa is Misty's mother."

"What?"

"It fits."

"Parker, you're making a hell of a mental leap here."

He covered her hand on her thigh. "Just listen, okay? Then, if I'm out in left field, you can be the first to tell me you told me so."

"Okay."

"Vanessa and Misty's father are loaded, like Decker said. Forrester's their broker. He starts trading with money he doesn't have—five million, like Mary Beth said at the café. He needs money, so he gets involved with Vanessa and puts the pinch on her. Vanessa decides she wants Linda out of the picture and Forrester to herself. If she pulls his fanny out of the fire, she'll own him. This she doesn't tell Forrester, of course. So she and her lover arrange for her daughter to be abducted. Then she and Forrester can extort the five million he needs to cover his buns from Misty's dad. But Forrester doesn't want dirty hands, just in case something goes wrong. So he enlists a pair he can control—Decker's.''

Caron picked up where Parker left off. ''But Forrester didn't bank on Linda finding out, or objecting. And when she did, and confronted him in the café, he knew he had to move Misty someplace Linda couldn't find her, or the whole scam would blow up in his face.''

Caron slapped the armrest with her hand. ''Exactly.''

''It fits.'' Parker gave her a nod. ''Caron, where's Misty?''

''I don't know, Parker.'' Her elation faded. ''I just don't know.''

He gave her thigh a little squeeze, then laced their fingers together. ''Sanders isn't looking good in this, Caron.''

''No, but Decker lied. Sandy didn't kill Linda.''

Parker cocked his head and cranked the engine. ''I know you've been friends with Sanders for a long time, but him killing her fits. From the nonexistent kidnapping report all the way to the affair with Linda, it fits.'' Parker snapped on the headlights. ''Sanders wouldn't be the first man to bury a report, or to kill a woman for duping him.''

''I'm not sure about the report. But Sandy didn't kill Linda,'' Caron insisted. ''Decker's lying about that, I just know it.''

''Okay. Let's talk this through. Decker said he hadn't seen Killer's leash since Sandy had it at his house, right?''

''Right.'' The gearshift clicked into drive.

''He said it before we mentioned it, Caron. He knew she'd been strangled with a leash.''

Caron frowned. ''The police wouldn't release that information, not yet. Sanders was breaching protocol in telling us about it.''

''Right. But he did tell us. And if the police know it was a dog leash, then they must have it.''

''Decker made it a point to mention that he hadn't seen the leash since Sandy was at his house—*before* Linda had been killed. The police don't know where she died, Parker. Decker said he saw Linda 'deader than dirt' in the grass, but by the time he got to the camp—remember? That puts him at the murder scene, Parker. And the leash had to have been wrapped around her neck. I mean, she wasn't likely to have removed it after she'd been murdered, then replace it after she'd been moved to the house.''

''Maybe it was a slip of the tongue. Maybe Sanders told Decker, too.''

''Sandy didn't tell Decker. It was a slip of the tongue. But it was also the truth. Sandy didn't kill Linda. He probably buried the report. But if he had killed her, he would have buried the leash, too. He'd never have told us about it. Decker saw that leash around Linda's neck, Parker. And it wasn't at any three-thirty or four. It was at two, exactly as the coroner said.''

Parker slid her a sidelong look. ''You know who killed her.''

''No, but I'm close. Something's niggling at me.'' She dug into her purse for a candy bar. ''I'll figure it out.''

''No, ma'am.'' Parker stayed her hand. ''No candy. We're going to eat a decent meal and get some rest.''

''But we're getting so close to Misty.''

''We're running on nerves. We need fuel. Not mistakes.''

''Look.'' Caron pointed through the windshield.

A group of carolers were singing 'Silent Night' on a brightly illuminated porch. Caron hoped it was a good omen. Three days till Christmas and, more than anything, Caron wanted Misty safe and sound.

Parker turned the corner, then looked over at Caron. ''Okay, don't pout.'' He checked his watch. ''It's nearly midnight. We'll eat, rest for a couple of hours, then get back to business.''

''Okay,'' Caron said reluctantly. He was right. They did need food and rest. If they were tired and hungry, they were more apt to make mistakes. They'd come too far and gotten too close to mess this up now. ''But first thing in the morning.'' Caron shifted her gaze and looked out the window. "It'll be Christmas soon, Parker. I want this wrapped up. I need peace this Christmas."

Parker captured her hand, lifted it and pressed his lips against her fingers. "Peace sounds good to me, too."

She didn't say it; neither did Parker. But it was there between them. The investigation of Linda's murder had bought them some time. With Forrester finding the body, he'd be afraid he was being watched by the police—which he probably was—and that would keep him from harming Misty. But they were closing in, and if Forrester realized his house of cards was collapsing around his upper-crust ears *before* she and Parker found Misty, there was no doubt about what Forrester would do.

Silence the victim.

Chapter 8

"Psst, Parker, wake up." Caron bent over the sofa and touched his scrunched shoulder.

He opened his eyes. "What's wrong?"

"We've got to go." His hair was mussed, and the curls clung to his scalp. She ran her fingers through them.

He glanced at his black diver's watch and squinted at its illuminated dial. "It's 2:00 a.m.," he groaned. "We just got to sleep."

The fog lifted, and he sat up straight. "Is it Misty?"

She stepped back. Two hundred and twenty pounds of muscled man in motion was too much, especially considering what she was about to say. That he wouldn't like it was a blatant understatement. "I've got to touch the leash."

His expression flashed from worried to grim. "Caron, I'm asking you not to do that."

Asking had been hard for him. She sank her teeth into her lower lip and touched his shoulder. The muscle was hard-packed, tense. "If I didn't have to, I wouldn't, Parker." God, but this was hard for her to admit, too. "Because you asked me. But I was thinking. Someone untied Misty's ropes and gave her medicine to reduce the fever. If it was Linda, by touching the leash, I might—''

He grabbed Caron's wrist. "You might go through her death. Have you forgotten what happened? Misty was just sick. But Linda died, Caron. She died.''

Caron wrapped her arms around his head and held him to her stomach. He was shaking. Or was it her? She couldn't tell, but it didn't matter. They both understood.

After a long moment, he looked up at her. "Caron.''

One word. But the emotion behind it was so forceful, so strong, that she nearly cried. She bent down and pressed her lips to his. He dragged her to him, kissing her hard and deep. She tasted the turmoil inside him, the anger, the rage, the fear. He plundered her mouth, his hands on her hips hard and demanding, and she let him.

When he gentled, regaining control, she pressed her forehead to his. "I care about you, Parker. So much. But I'll never be able to look myself in the mirror again if I turn my back on Misty. Can't you see? If I start running again, I might never stop.''

"It's Misty.'' His eyes were accusing. "Isn't it?''

"Yes.'' Caron hadn't wanted to tell him, hadn't wanted him to feel the gripping fear she felt. But she wouldn't lie, not to him. "She's worse. She's hallucinating.''

"The evidence room is locked up tighter than a sealed drum, folks, and it will be until 7:00 a.m.''

Caron leaned against Parker and glared at the portly desk sergeant. She was so tired her knees were wobbly. "We can't wait. Please, call Detective Sanders.'' She'd asked before and been refused. Maybe this time he'd soften.

"I told you, Jeff's wife just had a baby about thirty minutes ago. He's the only one on watch with a key, and I'm not calling Sanders down here at two-thirty in the morning when I don't have a key to let him in.'' The sergeant shrugged. "What's the point?''

Jeff was the guy responsible for evidence. And Parker knew the sergeant wasn't going to budge. That Caron sensed Misty was sicker had Parker worried. That Forrester, the redhead—Vanessa?—and Decker were still floating around out there, ready, willing and able to harm Misty had Parker downright scared for the kid. And for Caron. He hadn't forgotten the message left on her door. Or the empathy pains. Or the way he'd felt when she told him that this time she'd die, too.

Sanders *had* to be gut-deep in this or he'd already have arrested Forrester and Decker. Even if the sergeant called, Sanders wouldn't let them into the Evidence Room. He didn't want Caron to sense anything on this case—or did he? Maybe that's why he'd told them . . . Yes!

Parker grabbed Caron's arm. "Thanks anyway, Sergeant. We'll come back at seven."

Looking immensely relieved, the sergeant nodded, dismissing them.

Caron looked at Parker as if he'd lost his mind. Before she could protest, he tugged her out of earshot of the sergeant.

"Parker, what are you doing?"

"Sanders isn't going to help us, Caron. At least, not outright. Neither is the sergeant."

"Somebody damn well is. I have to get into that evidence room, Parker. If I can touch the leash, I might sense where Misty is!"

"I know that. And we're going to get in, okay? But I have to tell you something. You were right, Caron. Sanders didn't kill Linda. He told us about the leash because he wanted you to touch it. He *wants* you to find Misty."

"That's it!" she shouted in a whisper. "That's what's been niggling at me. In all the years we've worked together, Sandy's never revealed classified information." She frowned. "But why didn't he just tell us to come down?"

"That, I don't know." But Parker had his suspicions. If they were right, he knew why Sanders hadn't arrested Decker or Forrester. "Lower your voice, and follow me."

Suspecting what he had in mind, she clasped his arm. "Parker, we can't!"

Two uniformed cops walked by and gave Parker and Caron curious looks. On cue, they smiled, and the cops walked on.

When they were out of sight, Caron fired at Parker again. "Have you lost your mind?"

"Probably."

"We can't break into the evidence room!"

"Okay. What's your plan?"

He knew darn well that she didn't have one. He'd pulled the same stunt at Meriam's about the street index. "I don't know."

"There's no other way to get in there."

"Right." She bit down on her lip and grasped a convenient, if feeble, excuse. "I don't know where it is."

Parker hiked his brows. "Downstairs, in the basement."

When she twisted her mouth, Parker pecked a kiss on it. "I know. Just for the record, you don't like this any more than you like lying." He curled her to his side, then turned toward the elevator. "Just for the record, I don't, either."

She'd never know just how much he meant those words. Not telling her what he'd done, not telling her about Harlan and Sarah, was eating holes in his stomach. But if he confessed, he'd lose her. He knew that now as well as he knew that Misty was in serious trouble. And losing Caron, he realized, was not something he wanted to do. The knowing stunned him. He stared at her.

"What? Have I sprouted two heads?" Caron reached up and patted her hair. It was a tangled mess, and she half expected Parker to tell her she looked like hell. But he didn't. In fact, he didn't say anything. And darned if he didn't look as if he *couldn't* say anything.

A bell sounded, and the elevator doors slid open. Caron stepped inside. Parker didn't move. She tugged his sleeve.

When the doors slid closed, she pressed the button. It lit up, and she looked back at Parker. He was still staring at her as if she were an alien. "What's the matter with you?"

He stepped closer, until his chest was against her breasts, and cupped her chin. "I need to do this, Caron. I know my timing's rotten, but . . . I need to . . ."

His lips brushed ever so lightly over hers, grazed her chin, then returned to her mouth. He planted his hands at her shoulders and let them slide around to her back, then pulled

her into the cradle of his arms. He'd kissed her before, but
not like this. There was a new tenderness in his touch, and
there was awe in the gruff groans vibrating in his throat, in
the tips of his fingers as they worked the flesh at her side.

He reared back enough to mumble her name, then bore
down on her mouth and crushed her lips beneath his. The
attack on her senses had her legs going weak and her heart
careening, and every pore in her body seemed to be
stretching toward him, sensually gravitating, wanting to
absorb the feel of him.

The elevator hit bottom with a little jerk, and the door
opened. Parker set her away from him, looking, for all the
world, totally calm.

Caron slumped against the wall. How could he do this to
her and look so calm? If the man didn't want her and still
managed to turn her to putty, she shuddered to think of
what he'd do to her if he *did* want her!

He caught her hand in his. "You okay?"

"Uh-huh." Mumbles she could manage. Words were an
entirely different matter. Good grief, his kisses were po-
tent. Her head was fogged.

"Ready?"

"Uh-huh." Better, but not quite coherent. Her lips still
tingled, and her insides were still hot and fluid. There was
no way she could walk.

Parker smiled and tweaked her nose. "Come on, honey.
Snap to."

Snap? She couldn't slither. "Right."

"The evidence room." He hooked his thumb left.

Evidence room. Misty.

The fog faded, but the glow remained. "Right," she said,
more firmly, then followed him down the hall.

Parker turned down a short hallway, then stopped. Caron saw a sign on the wall above the door: Evidence Room.
The recessed wire door had a wooden frame and a formi-
dable-looking hasp lock. Her heart sank. Without a saw or
a keg of dynamite, they'd never break that lock.

"You keep watch on the hall," Parker whispered.

How was he going to get in there? Deciding she was better off not knowing, Caron went to the corner where the

two halls connected. The corridors were empty. The gray tile floor looked glossy and slick—freshly waxed.

Hearing a rustling sound behind her, she looked back. The bottom half of the wire in the door hung loose. Parker hadn't touched the lock; he'd gone through the wire, and now he stood inside the evidence room.

He hiked his chin. "What?"

She hand-signaled that everything was okay.

Seconds later, footsteps sounded in the hall. She peeked around the corner and saw two cops walking toward her. "Parker," she whispered. "Someone's coming."

She had to do something. If she and Parker went to jail, who'd help Misty?

"A girl, huh?" one officer said to the other. "Well, how about that?"

"Yeah." The other guy was grinning from ear to ear. "I still can't believe it. I'm a father!"

Jeff, Caron thought. He was back from the hospital.

She stepped out into the officer's path. "I just heard the news. A daughter. Jeff, that's terrific." She squeezed his hand. "You must be so proud."

"Yeah, I am."

He was trying to figure out who she was; she couldn't give him time to think, to realize they'd never met. "The sarge is wanting you two at the desk. Right away, he said." She smiled. "Congratulations again on the baby."

"Thanks." Still frowning in confusion, Jeff and the other officer turned and walked back toward the elevator. "Wonder what the sarge wants now?"

The other guy shrugged. "Probably about the baby."

Caron rushed back to the hall outside the evidence room. Parker was standing there with a clear plastic bag in his hands. Flashes of Sarah ripped through her mind. Caron's mouth went dry. She walked to the door on legs she wasn't sure would hold her and reached through the wire. "Just the leash." Her voice was faint, strained and weak.

Parker slid the leash out of the bag. His eyes looked nearly black and turbulent. She sensed his fear of what might happen to her when she touched the leash. She was afraid, too. She might sense Linda's murder; that threat was real. And if she did, in her weakened condition, such a violent image might well be fatal.

Parker seemed to know. "You don't have to do this." Desperation edged his voice. "We'll find another way."

She looked up at him, her heart in her eyes. "We don't have time."

Just in case, once more, she studied his face. A muscle in his cheek twitched. And the hand holding the leash shook. He cared. He hadn't given her the words before, and he wasn't going to give them to her now, but she could read the message in his eyes. She wasn't alone.

He blinked and his expression grew frantic. "No. No, you can't. Caron, you can't do this!"

Cold dread clawed at her stomach. She lunged and grabbed the leash.

She should close her eyes. Seeing Parker looking so stunned, so worried, tore at her concentration and slivered her focus. It was about to happen; the sensations welling in the pit of her stomach warned her that it was, and they were growing stronger. She drank in the sight of him. Those darling black curls that teased his ears and nape, the set of his jaw, his wonderful mouth. It was fixed and hard now, but she pretended it was curled in that tilted half smile she'd first cursed, then coveted. Her heart felt so full; she wanted him to know, but the sensations strengthened. There was no time.

She clutched the leash to her chest and squeezed her eyes shut. The image came instantly. Linda driving across the Greater New Orleans bridge, passing the cutoff to Decker's, going on through a tunnel to Marrero. Then a flash, and she was driving hell-bent-for-leather down a weedy, rutted road. But where was that road? Linda was driving so fast that Caron couldn't see the surroundings. Two lefts, then a sharp right turn, then on to a clapboard house. She ran around to the back—and Caron saw the shed.

Linda fumbled with the lock, finally opened it, and tossed it to the ground. She knelt over Misty. Untied the ropes, then scrambled through her purse and pulled out a bottle of aspirin. She shoved two pills into Misty's mouth and rubbed her neck to make her swallow.

Stretching over Misty's chest, Linda grabbed a red glass. Water sloshed out onto the dirt floor. She poured what was left down Misty's throat, then stood up. "I'm going to lock the door again, Misty," she whispered. "But only for a few minutes. Then I'll come back, and take you home."

Misty didn't answer.

Caron reminded herself that she'd imaged Misty after this time, that after she'd swallowed the pills the child's fever had gone down.

Linda was outside the shed now. Caron heard the lock click closed. Something heavy hit her in the back of the head. Dazed, she saw a shadow fall across the door; arms raised, a thin strap stretched taut between two large hands.

Caron's heart thudded wildly. She wanted to let go of the leash, to not experience Linda's death. But she couldn't make herself do it. If she was strong enough, she might learn who had killed Linda. She had to go on. She had to! Linda had helped Misty!

She felt the wind whip down her face. Felt the leash wrap around her neck. She felt Linda's surprise, her fear. Linda began twisting, fighting her attacker...fighting for breath. Caron struggled along with her, but he was so strong!

And then she was Linda. Her head grew light. Colored spots blinded her eyes. She grabbed at the leash cutting into her throat and tried to tear it loose. She needed air!

The spots grew larger, began drawing her deeper and deeper into a dark cloud. Something hard—a fist-size rock—cracked against her skull. Blinding pain streaked through her head. Fluid, hot and sticky and wet, seeped down the back of her neck. Blood.

She was dying. She could feel her body grinding to halt. Her thoughts numbing, her rushing blood slowing to a trickle. Parker! Caron cried. No, oh God, no! Parker!

She was dying. Caron was *dying!*

Before he realized he'd moved, Parker was on her side of the door, grabbing the leash and scooping Caron up into his arms. Linda Forrester's murder. Jesus God, how could he have let her do this?

"Caron?" He nuzzled her with his nose, shaking so hard he feared he'd drop her. "Honey, for God's sake talk to me!"

No answer.

Her pulse was thready, weak. She lay limp, her face still, her eyes closed. Memories flooded his mind: wrenching flashes of Harlan in the morgue, his cries to Sarah, his begging her to come back to him. Tears blinded his eyes; raw terror burst forth from his soul, and an icy-cold blanket of fear wrapped around his heart. "Damn you, Caron Chalmers! Don't you dare die on me!"

Her lashes fluttered.

They did, didn't they? His heart stopped, as if afraid to beat, as if afraid the feel of it would pull her away. Sweat sprang from his pores, mingled with his silent tears and rolled down his face to his mouth. He licked the salt from his lips and begged, "Caron, honey, *please!* Don't leave me!"

She covered his heart with her hand. "Parker."

Relief washed through him. The fear eased from his throat. Still, he couldn't talk. His nerves and emotions were raw, gaping wounds. He'd almost lost her!

"I'm okay," she whispered.

Her color was coming back. The sparkle of life was returning to her eyes. Never in his life had anything ever looked so beautiful.

"But you look like hell."

Wild relief sang through his veins, and he laughed, straight from the heart.

She gave him a watery smile. "I still don't know where Misty is, don't know how to get there exactly."

Parker looked down at the woman in his arms, and a surge of tenderness enveloped him. "We'll see to Misty right after Dr. Z. sees to you."

"I'm fine." Caron stroked his jaw. "Really."

"You're not fine. You damn near died." The truth of it cut him to the bone, and had him curling her closer.

She wrapped an arm around his neck and pressed her face against his shoulder. "Take me home, Parker. To the apartment. I need food and sleep."

Parker started down the hall, stepped in and mashed the elevator button. Caron had never in all the time he'd known her put her own needs before the girl's—or his, for that matter. That she was seeming to now concerned him. She wasn't as "fine" as she was pretending to be.

When they walked by the sergeant's desk, he called out, "Hey, what's wrong?"

Parker didn't slow a step, or miss a beat. "Pregnant."

Caron smiled against his chest and pinched his neck to punish him. "Married *and* pregnant, Parker?"

"You'd prefer pregnant and unmarried?" Heat seeped through his body. The idea of being married to Caron, of her carrying his child inside her body, excited him. They'd wake up together in the mornings. And they'd make love deep into the night.

He stepped out into the cool night air and looked down at her. Streaks of moonlight shadowed her face. Guilt shadowed his visions of their life together. He'd lied. He wanted to tell Caron the truth. He should have told her long ago. But he hadn't. Now he doubted he had words to give her that wouldn't take her away from him. She'd feel betrayed. And his name would be added to the long list of men in her life who had used her. Her father, Greg Cain, Mike—whoever he was—and Parker Simms. He couldn't do it. Not now. And maybe never. He had too much to lose.

"You sure you're feeling okay?" Parker sat opposite Caron at her kitchen table.

"Yes, I'm sure." Knowing she was closer to knowing where Misty was, Caron could keep mental tabs on her, and relax until dawn. They needed daylight to find the shed. She needed rest; she'd need strength then. And if her second brush with death had taught her nothing else, it had taught her to seize every moment. This one belonged to her and Parker. "I must be too tired. I'm going soft in the head."

Parker dug into the white paper carton and pulled out a forkful of shrimp egg fu young. "All right, Snow White, here you go."

Leaning forward over the table, Caron took a bite. Scraping the fork's tines with her teeth, she leaned back in her chair and chewed.

"Well?" Parker propped his elbow on the table, the fork poised in midair.

"It's good." She scooped up the burger and held it out to him. "Your turn."

Grim-faced, Parker slid the burning candle between them aside. "Don't shove it down my throat. It's been years since I've eaten red meat."

Caron laughed. "I wouldn't do that."

He stretched over, took a healthy bite of burger, then fell back. The chair groaned. Looking pensive, he slowly chewed, then swallowed.

God, but he was a beautiful man. Strong-featured, tender-handed. He gave her that smile, that infamous tilt she'd once vowed she hated, and her insides softened to mush.

"It's okay."

"Okay?" She guffawed and wiggled her bare toes against his thigh under the table. "The world's greatest hamburger, and the best you can say is it's okay?"

"Okay is good." He captured her foot and dragged a fingertip along her arch. "Especially for red meat."

It tickled. She tried to tug her foot back.

Parker wouldn't let go. "Uh-uh. Ransom."

The look in his eyes warmed. The candle's flame flickered a dance in their depths. Her heart began a slow, hard beating, a primal rhythm welling up from somewhere deep inside her. She'd never before felt it, not like this, and its mystique drew her, like a moth to a flame, like her to Parker. "Demands?" Her voice sounded husky.

"Share your bed with me for the next few hours. That sofa of yours is too short, and I'm beat."

Was he asking her to sleep with him, or to *sleep* with him?

"Don't look at me like that, Caron."

"Like what?" She got up and tossed her trash into the bin under the sink.

"Like you're half-afraid I'll jump your bones."

She was, but she was also half-afraid he wouldn't.

"We're just going to sleep a few hours until it's time to try and find Misty. Okay?"

"Okay." Relieved and disappointed, she nodded and walked into her bedroom.

Parker gave her time to shower and put on her flannel nightgown. She climbed into bed, tugged the nightgown down around her ankles and double-checked the top button to make sure it was securely fastened.

After his shower, Parker came in, wearing only his jeans. The lamplight glinted off his much-admired shoulders and on his hair. The man had the broadest chest she'd ever seen. It was sprinkled with thick, dark hair that wound down to a thin line and disappeared beneath the waist of his jeans. Beautiful. She swallowed hard.

He clicked off the lamp, then unzipped his pants. When they hit the floor, she heard the stuff in his pockets jingle and roll out. What was he wearing? It was too dark to see.

He got into bed and shifted his weight. The mattress sank, threatening to roll her over to his side. She gripped her edge, tempted to stretch out a toe to see if he was naked. But, deciding she was better off not knowing, she stayed put.

"Good night, Caron."

"Good night." Her heart was pounding a zillion beats a minute. She'd never actually sleep with him here. They'd slept in the same bed before, but not with him maybe naked. Oh, God, he couldn't be naked!

"Caron?" He sounded woozy already.

What now? Didn't the fool man know that talking was darn near impossible? "Yes?"

"I borrowed your toothbrush. I hope it's okay."

It wasn't okay. Her toothbrush had been closer to him than she had. Jealous of a toothbrush? Caron groaned inwardly. She'd slipped over the edge. "That's fine, Parker."

He rolled onto his side, his back to her. "Did you set the alarm?"

"Yes." He smelled soapy and crisp and fresh and clean. All male. And he was throwing off enough body heat to melt the polar ice caps. Both of them. She'd never sleep a wink. Not a wink.

That was her last coherent thought.

The phone rang.

Parker cranked open a lid and glared at the clock. Four a.m. The room looked . . . strange. Where the hell was he?

Memory flooded back. Caron's. He was at Caron's.

A second ring split the silence.

He untangled their legs and arms, reached over her and grabbed the receiver, then nudged her awake. "Caron."

She grunted a protest and nestled against him again. Even asleep, she wanted to be close. Smiling, Parker nudged her again and put the phone to her ear.

"Hello," she mumbled in a croaky voice.

Parker heard the click. Whoever it was hung up. He moved the receiver to his ear and heard the dial tone, then dropped it back into the cradle. "You usually get calls in the middle of the night?"

"No." She opened her eyes. "No, I don't." She turned over to face him, her eyes wide now, alert and fully awake. "Parker, I sense danger."

He got out of bed and tossed Caron a pair of jeans from the chair, then grabbed his pants. "Come on."

"Where are we going?"

"Out of here." One leg in his pants, he shoved the other through, hiked them up, then zipped the fly. "We're sitting ducks, Caron."

He went to the closet, grabbed the first blouse he saw, then tossed it to her, too. "Would you come on?"

She scooted out of bed and jerked on her jeans. "What's the hurry, Parker? I said I sense danger. I didn't say the apartment is on fire."

Her sweater in his hand, he strode back to her, swept her fingers out of the way and took over buttoning her blouse. "Look, I've learned the hard way to respect your senses. When you image danger, I react. Got it?"

She smiled up at him. "Got it."

He gave her tush a friendly pat. "Good. Let's move."

* * *

"I think you're overreacting, Parker." Caron started across the complex's lawn, toward the row of parked cars. The Porsche looked out of place. Glossy and black and reflecting the yellow light from the sign across the street, it stuck out like a sore thumb. "It was just a hang-up call. The danger might be totally unrelated."

"Or it might not be." He stopped walking at the front of the car. "Whoever left that message on your door damn well knows where you live."

He could have gone all night without reminding her of the message, and she would have been just fine. She stepped off the curb and reached for the door handle.

Tires screeched. Caron looked toward the sound. A black car was speeding toward them.

Parker jerked her half-way over the hood of the car, then shoved her into a crouch and pulled her along the row of cars to a rusted-out pickup.

Loud pops split the air. Louder, staccato ones in a swift barrage sprayed her apartment and jarred Caron's teeth. Glass shattered—windows and windshields. Metallic *pings* sounded in a long series that had her ears ringing. Dust from the bricks on the building flew. They were shooting at *her* home. At *her* car.

Lights snapped on. People in other apartments began screaming. A baby started crying. And across the street a man walked out of the store carrying a bag of groceries, saw what was happening, dropped the bag and darted back inside. Still the firing of bullets rent the air.

Smelling smoke, Caron moved back far enough from Parker's shoulder to see the flames. Her car was on fire.

Then, just as suddenly as it had started, the shooting stopped. The car sped away, its tires squealing. Caron looked up and saw it fishtail, clipping the corner.

When it was gone, she looked at Parker. "Decker?"

"Or Forrester." Parker grimaced. "Or maybe Sandy."

"No, not Sandy." That something that had been niggling at her drew closer, hanging just at the frayed edge of her mind.

"He's in this up to his eyeballs, Caron. I know that hurts you, but that's the way it is."

Understanding dawned. "Oh, God!" Caron jumped to her feet. "Oh, God!"

Parker stood up and grabbed Caron's arms. "What?"

"Misty!"

People began pouring out of the apartments to check the damage, some crying, some cursing. Some dressed in pajamas, some men with bare chests and feet.

"Come on." Parker began moving toward his car.

Caron followed, sidestepping an old woman carrying a baseball bat. That was as futile and illogical as her locking the door to keep Killer out of her car. Caron reached for the door handle.

"Don't!" Parker held up his hand. "Move back."

Caron leaned against the nearest craggy oak and watched Parker check out the car. He walked around it, then lay flat on the ground and looked at its underside. When he stood back up, he popped the hood and inspected the engine.

Seemingly satisfied, he nodded. "Okay, let's go."

Caron got into the car and grabbed the phone. The wire dangled loose from the receiver. She tossed it to the floorboard. "Find a phone. The store. Stop at the store." She raked her hand through her sleep-tossed hair. "God, I knew it. I knew I was missing something basic."

"What?" Parker wheeled in and braked to a stop. Before he shifted into Park, Caron was getting out of the car.

"Mary Beth," Caron shouted back at him, and yanked the receiver from the phone hanging on the store's outer wall. She dropped a coin into the slot and dialed, and seconds later she was talking.

She put in a second quarter, dialed again, then waited. No talking this time. A third quarter hit the slot, and again she said nothing. Then a fourth. She paused a second, then keyed in a series of numbers. What was she doing? She held the receiver for a long time, staring down at the ground, obviously listening, but she didn't say anything. Caron stiffened suddenly, dropped the receiver, and rushed back to the car.

She bumped against the front fender. When she jerked open the door, she shouted, "Gretna!" then launched into telling him what had happened. "Charles Nivens was with Mary Beth. She's getting him to check the Hunt files for a client named Vanessa. We should've done that before, Parker, but I was afraid of his Mafia connections."

"Mafia? Who's Mafia-connected?"

"But he wouldn't dare tell them—"

"He who?"

"Nivens."

She hissed the name in exasperation and slammed the door. "Aren't you listening? Nivens wouldn't tell them, because they'd start watching him. They'd find out about Mary Beth."

"What's Mary Beth got to do with Nivens?"

"They're having an affair, Parker," Caron told him. "Nivens would never risk losing Mary Beth or giving his in-laws a valid reason to kill him."

She twisted around in the seat. "Damn it, if I'd had my mind on work, where it belonged, and not on you, I would have thought that through sooner.

"I tried getting Decker and Forrester, but neither of them answered."

His mind was still reeling from what she'd said. But she'd made four calls, not three. "Did you talk to Sanders?"

"No." She snapped her safety belt; the latch clicked. "Would you drive?"

"Why not?" Somehow Parker had to get her to accept the truth. It wouldn't be easy. Another man had betrayed her trust. Sanders might not have killed Linda Forrester but he had damn well withheld the report of Misty's kidnapping, and more.

"Because he wasn't there. He's out looking for Decker and Forrester and trying to run down the redhead. There's still nothing on her." Caron smacked the dash with the heel of her hand. "Go, Parker!"

"If he wasn't there, how do you know?"

"He left me a message on his answering machine. We've done that for years to keep tabs on each other during an investigation. He buried the missing-child report—for Linda, I know it."

"Did he do it, Caron?" She had that betrayed look. "Did Sanders kill Linda?"

"No!" She buried her head in her hands. Her hair fell like a curtain around her face. She tossed back her head and glared at him. "When Linda was dying, I sensed Misty getting weaker." Caron's lower lip quivered. "She's getting sicker, Parker. I can feel it."

Right before she'd collapsed, Caron had called out Misty's name. Linda was dead, and Misty was without medication to keep her fever down. What was causing the fever, Caron didn't know. But the aspirin Linda had given Misty had reduced the fever...for a while. "That means Misty—" Parker shoved the gearshift into reverse.

"Yes!" Caron cried. "Misty knows who killed Linda Forrester. She saw it happen!"

"Ah, Jesus..." Parker stomped the accelerator.

"They'll go after her."

"We'll find her first." Parker clenched the wheel in a death grip, dodged a white station wagon. Then he realized what Caron had said, and he turned a wary glance on her. "Did you say *they?*"

"Yes!"

Tears coursed down Caron's cheeks. Without a word, Parker pulled her closer and wrapped his arm around her shoulder. His questions could wait. Right now, she needed to concentrate on where the shed was located. Somehow he knew that the tears she was crying were Misty's. And there was no one there to comfort the child.

Chapter 9

Dawn broke just as Parker turned down the third winding dirt road. "Do you recognize anything?"

"What's to recognize?" Caron tried to keep a step ahead of panic. "There's nothing but brush and trees out here."

"Be patient." He gave her thigh a supportive pat. "You'll find the right one."

He was thinking of Sarah, Caron knew, the way she'd confused the signs then. Parker didn't know Sarah's name, of course—Caron hadn't broken that confidence—but he *was* thinking of her.

And so was Caron. In the hum of the tires on the pavement, she heard Sarah's cries for help, those shrill screams that had weakened to whimpers, then to deafening silence. The wind-whipped trees became fire and flame, billowing towers of thick black smoke, cloying and concealing and burning Caron's throat raw. She'd stayed until the walls had fallen and there was nothing left to burn. Until the embers had died and all that could be seen was cold ash. Sarah's torture chamber had fallen. And still Caron had found no peace.

Sandy said Sarah's husband had burned down the building. That didn't feel right, but Caron hoped that he had. For him, there was solace, if not peace, in knowing that no one else would suffer there. For Caron, there was neither. She'd failed, and Sarah had died.

The road curved left for the third time. Caron gripped the door handle, fighting desperation. "This isn't right, either. Turn around." The last road sign she'd imaged when holding the leash had been the one for Lafitte. Now everything depended on instinct, and she was terrified of being wrong.

"You sure?"

"Yes. There were two left curves, then a right."

Parker stopped, turned the Porsche around, then headed back down the road, swerving through the cloud of dust the car had raised.

The dark curl was taunting his ear again. This time, Caron didn't hesitate, she just reached out and smoothed it back.

He looked over, and something hard in his face softened. The pain in his eyes was gone. Odd. Until it had disappeared, she hadn't realized how much pain had shone in his eyes. Worry for Misty filled them now.

"When this is over, we need to talk." His grip on the wheel had his knuckles white. "There are things I need to tell you."

The odd pitch of his voice was telling. She wished she could see his face, but he'd looked away. A lot remained unresolved between them; Parker had as hard a time being open about his feelings as she did. But he did feel. One of them had to take the risk . . . and the plunge. "I care about you, too, Parker."

He reached out to her. "Don't stop."

"I won't." Her heart thundering, Caron clasped her hand in his and laced their fingers together until their palms pressed. It was a gloomy dawn, too cloudy for pretty pinks and golds to show in the sky. But inside her the sun shone warm.

Something flashed black off Parker's left shoulder. A dirt road, nearly hidden by tall weeds. "Stop!"

Parker slammed on the brakes.

Caron slid his way and bumped her chin on his shoulder. "Geez, Parker." She cupped her stinging face in her hand. "I didn't mean on a dime."

"Sorry." He pecked a kiss to the tip of her chin, then just waited.

She hadn't often experienced quiet, undemanding acceptance. Caron loved him for that. The pain in her hands gone, she unbuckled her safety belt, then turned, her knees on the seat, to look out Parker's window.

"I can't see past your shoulders." She stretched over the steering wheel. He steadied her with a hand to her waist, and she saw the tire tracks rutting the road. "That's it."

He set her back to her seat. "Hold on." Parker put the car in reverse and backed up.

She pointed through the windshield. "See how the brush is bent. This is it, Parker!"

Parker reached to the back seat and retrieved a black vest. "Put this on."

She slid it on over her blouse. It was too big, and hung on her shoulders. "A bulletproof vest?"

"Yes."

"What about you?"

"I'm fine."

He did care; more for her, than for himself. The muscles in her chest quivered. She kissed his jaw to tell him how much his caring meant to her.

"Hold that thought," he said, reaching under his seat. He pulled out a nickel-plated Colt, checked the chamber and snapped it shut, then shoved it into the waistband of his jeans. He nodded toward the vest. "That thing fastened?"

"Yes."

"Okay, Snow White." He gave her a heart-stopping smile. "Let's go get Misty."

Caron put a restraining hand on his arm, wanting, needing, to tell him that she loved him . . . just in case. But the words stuck somewhere between her mind and mouth, and, afraid he didn't want to hear them, she played it safe. "I care about you, and I like your kisses, Parker."

"I know, sweetheart." He smiled so tenderly that her heart ached. "Me, too." He jammed the gearshift into first and hit the accelerator.

Weeds and tall grass slashed at the sides of the car. Caron looked back. A cloud of dust trailed behind them. "Slow down. They'll see us coming a mile off."

He braked to a crawl. "How much farther?"

Caron recalled the image. "A curve right, then the fishing camp will be straight ahead."

"No heroics," he said. "When we get there, you stick close, but stay back."

It was impossible to do both, but she nodded anyway. He was remembering her going into Sarah's building when Sandy had told her to stay in the car. She'd wished a thousand times, a million times, in the year since that night that she'd listened to him.

A weedy patch of yellow sunflowers broke the monotony of green and brown to their left. Her stomach curled, and her chest tightened. And relief, precious and sweet, flowed through her veins. This *was* it. This *was* the right place!

Parker stopped at a wide spot in the road, turned the Porsche around, then cut the engine. "We'd better go in on foot."

He grabbed a clanking black bag from the floor of the car. "Ready?"

Caron swallowed hard, fighting images of Sarah, of going into the bar. They were replaying in her mind and she couldn't make them stop. "Ready."

The tall grass was brittle and pricked at her legs and arms. It was waist-high in most places, higher in others, scraping her shoulders and catching in her hair. She knew it was grass, but in her mind it was Sarah's attacker, tormenting, torturing.

Parked stopped and whispered, "Watch for snakes. As hot as it is, they'll be slithering to every mud puddle."

Her attention riveted to his warning. Caron watched the ground. The sun peeked out from behind a heavy black cloud, warming her head. Just as she was putting her foot down, she saw a brown egg and sidestepped. Again she

imaged Sarah, sidestepping the loose stone in the parking
lot. The man grabbing her arm, jerking her into a van.
Gagging her...

Parker reached back, and Caron halted. The gentle
pressure of his fingers on her upper arm warned her to keep
silent. She was so scared she didn't think she could talk if
she wanted to; just her breathing sounded like a foghorn in
the still morning air. What if Misty was dead? What if
Parker got killed? What if she never in her life got to hold
him again?

Parker crouched down. Caron crouched beside him,
more black fear creeping into her heart. Looking past his
shoulder, she saw a clearing. In the middle of it, surrounded by mossy oaks, crepe myrtles and scraggly pines,
was a clapboard house, worn and weathered almost
black—where it wasn't green from tree mold. There were
two wooden rockers on the front porch, and fishing rods
were stacked in the corner by the door. A new Jeep was
parked in the drive. It was the fishing camp she'd imaged!

Parker felt Caron's fingers dig into his shoulder. He
didn't look back; he knew this was the place. His stomach
churned. Everywhere he looked he saw Harlan on his
knees, begging Sarah not to leave him, saw Sarah beaten
and bruised and lifeless, lying on the tray behind that silver door.

He pried Caron's fingers loose from his shoulder and
inched forward to the edge of the clearing. Caron crept up
behind him. "Do you see the shed?"

"It must be around back." He could almost hear her
heart beating, pounding as hard as his own. One slip. One
false move. One mistake. And before they could do anything, Misty could be dead. *She* could be lying on that cold
metal tray.

Inside the house, a TV was blaring; the sound carried out
into the yard. *Wheel of Fortune,* Caron thought, recognizing the music. The innocent tune grated at her ears, annoyed her.

Moving stealthily, Parker crept farther to the left, stop-
ping near the center of the house, still protected by the tall

grass. The crunching of it under their feet sounded like cannons firing. Caron broke into a cold sweat.

"Stay here," Parker whispered.

Caron grabbed his sleeve and held on until he looked back. "What are you going to do?" She inched forward and prayed for her pulse to level out.

"Try to see how many are inside." Parker patted her knee. "Stay down."

He stole out of the tall grass onto the lawn. Behind a giant spike-leafed laropia, he sprang from the crouch to a bend and sprinted from bush to bush toward the house. Flattening himself against the outer wall, he pulled out his gun.

The sun glinted on its shiny barrel.

Caron cringed. He might have to use it. Her pulse was pounding in her ears, and her knees were shaking. Too weak to hold the crouch any longer, she dropped to her knees on the ground—and heard the hiss, and the godawful rattle she'd so feared hearing. *Not now. Oh, God, not now!*

Slowly she turned her head...and saw the snake. About three yards from her, it was already raised, poised to strike. The sweat soaking her body became cold chills. Her every instinct warned her to run. Darting her gaze, she looked for Parker. But he was nowhere in sight.

The snake didn't move. Neither did Caron. She forced her breathing to slow to shallow puffs that barely lifted her chest. Her instincts urged, then insisted that she move. She fought them, and stayed put. Sweat trickled down her back, down her neck and pooled at the front clasp of her bra. Her nerves wire-thin, she stared, terrified. Mesmerized.

The snake dropped down, slithered across a white rock, then on across the bed of mown grass. When Caron saw how large it was, she nearly fainted. Over four feet long.

Something moved to her right. She gasped.

"Shh!" Parker motioned for her to follow.

On hands and knees, they crawled through the prickly brush to the back of the house. Caron saw the shed. The gray slats were as weathered as the rest of the fishing camp, with one exception. A new brass lock hung from a clasp on the door.

A hot rush of tears surged to her eyes. Relief warred with the fear locked in her heart. It was all she could do not to run blindly to it and break down the door.

They inched around to the back wall, and Parker stood up. "Is she in there?"

Caron rose to her feet; her legs were unsteady. Her chest was heaving as if she'd just run fifty miles. "Yes. I know she is. But I can't see her."

He hiked his arm and wiped the sweat from his face. Dirt smudged his cheekbone and streaked from his chin to his ear. "There's only one window, and it's facing the house. I couldn't tell how many people were inside."

Parker lowered his black bag to the ground. "I saw one man cooking something in the kitchen. But the damn TV was so loud, I couldn't hear if there was anyone else in there."

Caron was coming unstrung; her gaze was wild. If she was thinking about Sarah half as much as he was, she couldn't handle any more pressure. Parker didn't dare to tell her about the gun the man had set on the counter. Or about the poison the bastard was sprinkling on a plate of spaghetti.

Until the moment he'd seen that with his own eyes, he hadn't been sure they'd find Misty in the shed. Hell, he hadn't been sure she'd been abducted and was in danger. He'd believed that Caron believed it, but until that moment, Parker himself hadn't been one hundred percent sure.

Now he was coldly certain. The man meant to kill Misty. And if they tried to stop him and gave him half a chance, he would kill them, too.

Caron gasped for air. Sweat was still rolling down between her breasts. It was muggy-hot, humid. Her lungs protested every indrawn breath as if she were asking them to inhale steam. A heavy-duty adrenaline surge multiplied the effect. "Can we break the lock?"

"Can't risk the noise." Parker wiped at the sheen on his brow. "It's too thick. I don't have the right cutting tools for it, or the hasp. I'd have to bust it, and it faces the house. We'd be caught before—"

"How are we going to get in?" Caron touched the wall of the shed. Her strength seemed to flow right out of her body, and she crumpled to her knees in the dirt. "She's here." Breathlessness invaded, that same sensation she'd suffered just after entering the Rue de Bourbon bar. Caron darted a wild look up at Parker. "We have to hurry."

"We can't." Parker grabbed Caron's hand, swinging it away from the wall of the shed. "Damn it, Caron. You're not going to risk getting killed. The guy inside has a gun. We don't know yet what we're up against."

"But Misty—"

"If we die, who'll help Misty then?"

Parker was right. Her belly full of frustration, Caron clenched her jaw. "I want to see her."

"The window faces the house."

When she showed no signs of relenting, he gave in. "Okay, I'll cover you."

Caron inched to the corner of the shed and scanned the area. A butterfly flew from a potted geranium toward the tall grass. A frog croaked. Nothing else moved, and the back of the house was silent. She inched up the wall, hidden from view from the back door and from all but one window in the house. At the front corner, she paused again.

Parker's fingers brushed hers. She looked back, and he nodded. She made the corner and tiptoed at the dusty window to see over the ledge. It was shadowy inside, streaked with light coming from between the slats. Her heart in her throat, Caron cupped her hands to shield her eyes and pressed her nose against the dirty window.

And there, sprawled on the floor, lay Misty. So still. So very still.

Caron whimpered and tapped a fingernail against the glass.

Misty didn't move.

She was too late. Too late. She'd taken too long, made too many mistakes finding the right road. Misty *was* like Sarah; she, too, had paid the ultimate price for Caron's mistakes. Her heart crumbling, Caron let out a guttural moan and screamed silently. *Sarah!*

Her fingernails scraped the glass, making a screeching sound. *Not again! Dear God, please, not again!*

Inside, Misty lifted her head. Her hair dragging on the dirt floor, she looked up at Caron.

She was alive!

Parker jerked Caron's arm.

When she slammed against him, he half tugged, half carried her to the back of the shed, moved on around to the other side, then pinned her behind him.

"She's alive, Parker," Caron whispered raggedly. Tears streaking down her face, dirt smudging her nose, she slumped against him bonelessly. "She's alive."

Parker squeezed her close and, over her shoulder, watched the house. The man he'd seen through the window came to the back door, looked around, then disappeared back into the shadows inside.

"Take this, and keep an eye out." Parker thrust the gun into her hand. "Anybody comes out, shoot. Anybody."

He bent down and tested the strength of the wooden slats. Finding one that suited him, he jerked. The nails holding the wall in place groaned and popped the slat loose. He jerked again to free it.

Caron craned her neck and checked at the corner. A robin flew from one oak to another stirring its branches. Nothing else moved.

A loud crack rent the air, and she spun around. Parker held the ripped-out slat in his hand. Blood trickled from his knuckles. Seeing it, knowing it was his, made her stomach flip. She checked the house. No one was coming.

"It's just a scrape." Parker set the board on the ground. He looked into the shed through the thin hole in the wall, then stepped back and nodded. "You're smaller. Go on. Get Misty."

Caron passed him the gun and wedged herself into the tight hole. The rough wood scraped her back and chest raw. Splinters pushed through her skin like hot spikes. She couldn't move. "Parker," she whispered. "I'm stuck!"

There was a rustling sound, and then his feet were against her hip. He pushed hard, and she broke through, stumbled, and crashed into the far wall.

Lawn tools fell. Metal clanged against metal. Something sharp cut into her shoulder, burning like fire. Shears. Caron swallowed a scream of pain and threw them onto the floor. "A scrape. Just a scrape."

Time had just run out.

A gun shot split the air.

Parker? Caron's heart seemed to stop. No. No, it couldn't be him. They'd come too far, gone through too much. *She needed him!*

Misty whimpered, and twisted on the floor.

Caron scrambled over lawn tools to get to her. "Come on, honey." Praying Parker was all right, she scooped the girl into her arms. "You're going home."

"My leg hurts."

Fighting tears, Caron looked down into the dull eyes looking up at her. Misty's heated body told Caron the child desperately needed a doctor. "I know, honey. Just hang on."

Straightening from a bend, Caron grunted—and saw a long shadow fall across the floor.

She held Misty tighter and looked up. A man she didn't know filled the doorway. And in his hand he held a long black gun that was pointed directly at her face.

The protective vest was useless.

Looking down the empty black hole of the barrel, Caron's thoughts whirled. Staggeringly strong empathy pains for Misty assaulted her. Images of Sarah flashed horror scenes through her mind. And a cold fear that Parker had been shot crushed her heart and turned her blood to ice.

The gun didn't waver. Caron couldn't move, couldn't breathe. She looked into the man's eyes. Cold. Indifferent. Uncaring. He was going to kill them. Stark terror settled over her like a shroud. Where in God's name was Parker?

Parker kept the Colt trained on the center of the man's back. His trigger finger itched, but . . . In the second after he fired, the man could shoot, and he couldn't risk Caron or Misty taking a bullet. When adrenaline was pumping this hard, reaction times were damn fast.

Knowing Caron was inside, that the man held a gun on her, enraged and terrified him. The snapping of a twig, the crunching of dry grass, and the man would hear. And Caron or Misty could die.

The plate of poisoned food lay scattered on the ground in the clearing. Parker eased past it. He was out in the open, an easy target, and Harlan's voice was buzzing so loudly inside his head that he could barely hear his own thoughts. Caron's face kept swimming before his eyes.

Sweat beaded on his brow and dripped down his face. He didn't dare wipe it away, didn't dare make any movement that could distract him, even for a split second. Inching forward, he stepped into a huge red stain on the grass. A fist-size rock lay there, covered with dried blood. Strands of blond hair clung to it and blew in the light wind. His stomach muscles clenched, and bile rose in his throat. In his mind, Harlan screamed Sarah's name.

No, Parker told himself. No, it wasn't Sarah's. It was Linda Forrester's blood. Caron had been right; Misty had seen the killing.

He heard the hammer of the man's gun click, heard his voice. Why didn't Caron scream?

Parker grabbed the rock. He forced himself to mentally count down as he moved. Five, four, three, two—then he threw it at the man.

It clipped his gun arm. The man spun, and his gun went off.

Parker rushed him.

Caron watched Parker barrel into the man's back. The gun flew from his hand. A tangle of legs and arms and flying fists, they blocked her path. Gritting her teeth against the pain in her shoulder, she stepped back, deep into the shed, and shielded Misty against the wall. The noises had her half-crazy—groans and grunts as dizzying punches were thrown and received. Horrible hollow sounds, fists meeting flesh, bone splintering—the sounds of men locked in mortal combat.

She stood dazed, not wanting to watch, but unable to look away. The man was as big as Parker, street-tough and strong-willed. Entangled, the two of them fell to the ground and separated. The other man scrambled to his feet. Growling deep in his throat, he charged, and landed Parker a devastating left hook to the chin that Caron knew would have killed her.

The color drained from Parker's face. Cold rage, as silent and deadly as a heart attack, settled like an aura around him. It terrified her...and the man. He began backing away.

Parker let out a cry that curdled her blood, then rammed his fist into the man's ribs. The man flew back, then crumpled to the ground.

Parker dropped his fist and looked down at him.

It was over. Her heart in her throat, Caron carried Misty out of the shed. Blood soaked Parker's knuckles. His skin was dripping with sweat, and his chest was heaving as he dragged air into his lungs. "Are you all right, Parker?"

He nodded and spit a blade of grass out of his mouth.

Caron looked down. The man's face was distorted; a bruise already discolored his cut jaw, and his left eye was swelling. His chest didn't seem to be moving. "Is he...dead?"

"No. But when he comes to, he'll have a hell of a headache." Parker drew in a deep breath that heaved his shoulders, and looked at Misty's closed eyes. He lifted a blood-encrusted finger to her forehead, then smoothed back her hair. "She's hot."

Awed that hands that had fought so brutally could now be so tender and gentle, Caron nodded. "She needs a doctor." Not wanting to frighten the child, she let Parker see from her eyes that the need was urgent.

Car tires crunched on the gravel in the drive.

"Get her out of here." Parker pulled his keys from his pocket and pressed them into Caron's hand. "Check the car. If I'm not there in three minutes, leave without me."

Her mouth parted in protest. Parker pressed a fleeting kiss to it and turned her by the shoulders. "Three minutes."

* * *

Caron ran across the clearing and into the tall grass. Snakes be damned; bullets were more lethal.

It was so hot, so humid; in scant seconds she was panting hard. By the time she reached the car, she was worried sick about Parker, fighting for breath and damn certain she was going to throw up.

Caron set Misty down a fair distance from the car. Wincing against the pain in her shoulder, she checked the car over, as she'd seen Parker do. On finding nothing wrong, she retrieved Misty, then settled her into the tiny back seat, checked her watch, and visually searched the brush for Parker. No sign.

Stretching, she grabbed the thermos from the front seat and splashed tea into its top. Cradling Misty's head in her hand, Caron put the cup to the child's lips. Her coloring was a pasty white. Bright red splotches stained her cheeks. And her eyes were fever-glazed. She needed medical attention—now. Caron forced her voice to be calm. "Try to drink this."

The child dutifully swallowed, then fell back. Caron gently lowered Misty's head to the seat, then raised up to again check the brush. Still no sign. Where was Parker?

Misty's leg was red and swollen. "What bit you, honey? Do you know?"

"A spider."

"The one that crawled up the shovel?"

The child nodded.

It had been a brown house spider—nonpoisonous—unless ... Caron frowned. "Are you allergic?"

Misty nodded.

"Let's go! Let's go!"

Parker! Caron spun around and twisted into the passenger seat.

Seconds later, they were speeding down the road, a cloud of dust about a mile high trailing behind them.

"She needs a doctor, Parker. Fast."

"Dr. Z.?"

"Yes."

His face was streaked with black soot. How it had gotten that way, Caron didn't know, and she didn't ask.

He smiled back at Misty. "Hi."

Misty was too weak to speak. She lifted a limp finger.

Caron frowned and dragged her damp hair away from her face. "What took you so long?"

His smile faded. "I torched the shed."

"Parker! You deliberately destroyed evidence?"

"Yeah, I did. But I removed everything from the shed first."

"I'm glad it's burning," Misty said.

Caron held Misty's hand and lifted her gaze. Flames licked at the roof of the shed, crept up the walls. Black smoke billowed in towers up to the sky, and in her mind, this fire mingled with Sarah's. This building, too, would burn to the ground.

Parker?

She slid her narrowed gaze to him, but he was watching the road. No, she told herself, Parker couldn't have torched Sarah's building. He hadn't even known Sarah James.

Or did he? Was *that* his dark secret? What he'd been holding back?

Her heart thudded a low, wild beat. The guilt Caron had so often seen and sensed in him, the reaction he'd had to being at the morgue. Had Sarah been the woman he'd identified there?

No. No, he would have told her. She was letting her imagination run away with her. She'd confided Sarah's story to him, and he'd comforted her. He would have told her.

Like Mike and Greg had? Like her father had?

She shoved the ugly thoughts away. But a nagging doubt slithered back and gnawed at her. Wanting to ease her mind, she started to ask Parker, but his grim expression and the jostling and bumping inside the car told her that swerving through sandy dirt at high speed required his full concentration.

The doubt raged. And she looked back. It all fit. His hatred for her at the beginning. His bitterness and lack of faith, his cold disdain for her and her gift. His pulling away every time she'd mentioned imaging.

He'd wanted to tell her the truth on the way to the camp. They needed to talk, he'd said. When this was over... It all fit.   Drowning in a sea of betrayal, she silently cried. *No. No, not him. Not Parker, too. I love him!*

Stop it!

She had to stop this. He wasn't like them. He wasn't! He wouldn't do that to her! She had to trust him. She had to give him the benefit of doubt. She loved him; he deserved at least the benefit of her doubt.

Hearing Misty groan, Caron looked back.

Misty's lips were turning blue.

At 3:00 p.m. Dr. Z. came into the waiting room. Parker grimaced. The good doctor's shoulders were slumped. Not a good sign.

Caron jumped up from the sofa.

"She's fighting," Dr. Z. said, looking at Parker, "but it's rough going. Her temperature is 104, her breathing is labored—we have her on a respirator now—and she's dehydrated. She went so long without treatment that she's having severe difficulty."

The doctor rubbed her temple. "Caron, when did you first feel the pain in your leg?"

Caron licked her lips. "I don't know, exactly."

"It was the eighteenth." Parker put an arm around Caron's shoulders. She looked ready to snap. "We were at Shoney's, remember?"

"That's right, it was."

"Then it's been nearly a week since she was bitten." Dr. Z. shook her head.

Panic edged Caron's voice. "She can't die."

When the doctor didn't deny it, Caron's tremors became full-fledged shakes. Parker tightened his grip on her shoulder. "Dr. Z.'s doing everything she can."

The doctor took Caron's hand. "Parker is right. I am. But I've never lied to you, Caron, and I won't start now." The doctor's eyes looked faded and weary. "Misty is critical. My best may or may not be good enough to save her. Only time will tell.''

Caron slumped against his side. Parker had to do something, or she was going to fall apart at the seams. ''Have you contacted her parents?''

''Misty won't tell us who they are.''

''Caron.'' Parker waited until she looked at him. ''You'd better talk to her.''

Caron nodded, straightened, then crossed the hall and went into Misty's room.

Parker watched her go, damn worried himself. If anything happened to Misty, he wasn't sure Caron could handle it.

Dr. Z. patted Parker's hand. ''I was wrong about you, Mr. Simms.''

He swung his gaze from Misty's door to the doctor.

''Caron loves you.''

''I think you're mistaken.'' That denial had his heart feeling like a cold lump in his chest.

''No, I'm right.'' The doctor cocked her head. ''She isn't suffering the same symptoms as Misty now.''

She wasn't! He wrinkled a perplexed brow.

''Her emotions aren't so focused. They're split between her concern for Misty and you.''

Caron couldn't be in love with him. As much as he wished Dr. Z. was right, she had to be wrong. Reasonable, logical, but wrong.

''And you're worthy of her.''

''I'm not fit to wipe her shoes.'' A knot of emotion caught in Parker's throat. ''She...'' He couldn't make himself go on.

''She doesn't know about you and Sarah. Or about Harlan.'' Dr. Z. gave him a sympathetic nod. ''Yes, I know. Sandy explained.''

Parker stuffed his fisted hands into his pockets. ''Are you going to tell her?''

''No, I'm not.'' The doctor looked up at him through glasses with spot-speckled lenses. ''You are. And I don't envy you the task.''

''She'll be hurt.''

"Yes." Dr. Z. nodded her agreement. "And furious."

She started walking back toward the hallway between the waiting room and Misty's. "Stay close, Mr. Simms. If things go badly, Caron is going to need you."

Parker nodded, outwardly calm. But inside he was splitting in two. If things went badly, Caron wouldn't have him. And, more than anything in the world, he wanted her.

At three o'clock the next morning, Caron was still pacing. Sprawled in an upholstered chair, Parker watched her. "Come on, honey. You need to try to rest."

She walked to a potted ficus, pinched off a brown leaf, then paced back in the other direction to the door. "I can't rest. Misty's fighting for her life in there."

Caron slumped against the doorframe and sent him a searching look. "Why won't she talk to me? Why doesn't she want her father here? She's crazy about him, Parker."

It was task time again. "Have you called Sanders?"

"No." Caron shoved away from the wall and took up where she'd left off pacing. "I'll call him in the morning."

"I think you should call now." Parker sat up, propped his elbows on his knees, then laced his hands. "That man shouldn't be tied up at the camp house too much longer. He was injured, Caron. I cracked his ribs."

"Misty suffered almost nine days. She'll be suffering a lot longer—maybe all her life. For all I care, he can stay there till his ropes rot."

Hearing the venom in her voice, Parker reconsidered disputing her. But he knew she didn't mean it; it was emotion talking, not Caron. "Fine by me. I'll call. I just thought you'd rather have him in jail. Forrester, too."

"I do want them in jail." Caron jerked her hair back from her face.

"Okay, then you call Sandy."

She glared at him. "I don't want to talk to him!"

Parker made the call.

A half hour later, a battle-worn Dr. Z. came into the waiting room. Caron stopped. Parker walked over to her, curled a supportive arm around her waist.

The doctor started to speak. Her voice cracked, and she paused to clear her throat. When she looked up at them, Parker's stomach sank. The news wasn't good.

"Misty's not responding to the medication," the doctor said. "I desperately need to know what treatment has been successful for her in the past. We don't have time to experiment with the various remedies." Dr. Z. touched Caron's arm. "You've got to reach her parents, Caron. Otherwise, Misty is going to die."

Chapter 10

Caron and Parker sat on opposite sides of Misty's bed. It was late, nearly dawn. The room was quiet. Misty was even more so.

Caron met Parker's gaze above Misty's head, read the message in his eyes, and sent one back saying she'd try again. She closed her eyes, focused, strained to see something, anything, that would steer her to Misty's parents. But no image came.

She was too tired, too emotionally drained. Helpless and frustrated and worried sick that even though they'd found Misty she was still going to die, Caron cast Parker a bleak look and mouthed the words. "She's fighting me, and I'm too weak."

The corner of Parker's mouth twitched. He was having to work at it not to frown. "Misty, honey, if you were my daughter, I'd want to know you were safe. I'd be scared. Don't you think your dad is scared?"

The thought that he might be had Misty's eyes clouding. "Can you tell just him?"

Caron brushed her hand over Misty's cheek, fearing she already knew the answer to the question she was about to ask. Were her suspicions about Misty's mom valid? "Why don't you want your mom here, too?"

The clouded eyes shuttered, closing Caron out. "I was bad. She's mad at me."

Caron softly stroked Misty's hair. It'd take a week to get the dirt and tangles out, but until Dr. Z. said it was okay, Misty wouldn't be getting a shampoo.

Her voice and expression deadly serious, Misty looked at Parker. "I didn't mean to be bad."

"Of course you didn't." He lifted her hand in his. It looked so tiny and pale and fragile against his huge palm. "Caron's right, though. Your mom will be too happy to see you to be angry."

Someone rapped on the door. Caron looked at Parker, then at the row of windows beside the door, which gave a clear view into the hallway. They'd asked the staff to show themselves at the windows before knocking, but Caron didn't see anyone. The hairs on her neck lifted.

Parker cracked the door open, looked out, then stepped aside. "Come on in, Sanders."

Caron's heart slowed to a canter. Logically, she knew Misty was safe here. Emotionally, however, she knew nowhere was safe—not until everyone involved in her abduction had been arrested.

"I don't want to disturb the kid." Sandy's voice carried into the room. "Have Caron come out."

The moment Misty heard his voice, she tensed. Perplexed, Caron looked down. "What's wrong, honey?"

Her gaze glued to the door, Misty didn't answer.

Sandy moved in the hall and Caron saw him through the window, chewing on his stubby cigar.

Misty screamed. And, pointing a finger at Sandy through the glass, she kept on screaming.

Taken by surprise, Caron tried to calm her. "Shh, it's okay. That's Sandy. He's my friend."

Her eyes wild, Misty thrashed on the bed, trying to pull away from Caron. "He's bad! He's bad!"

Caron tugged Misty into her arms and cuddled her close, feeling the rapid beating of her heart. A scrap of an image, quickly suppressed, flashed through her mind. Blood. Horror. Misty's horror...

Looking up over Misty's head, Caron locked gazes with Sandy. The shield between them slid away, and in that shattering moment he confirmed her fears. Sandy *had* done something, something very bad.

And Misty had seen it.

It took a full half hour to calm Misty down. Seeing her that way had ripped Parker's heart wide open.

Caron came back into the room, looking as frayed as Parker felt. One glance at her and he knew that Sanders hadn't explained a damn thing.

"Sandy told me it was mistaken identity," she said.

"Right." The look in her eyes held as much doubt and disbelief as his own. Parker dragged his hand through his hair, then sat down on the edge of Misty's bed. "Okay, sweet stuff, it's time to talk straight."

Misty shook her head. Dark circles smudged the skin beneath her eyes.

He took Misty's hand, cradled it in his own, and softened his voice to a whisper. "I know you're scared, Misty. Caron and I have worked hard to help you, but we can't help you anymore unless you let us. You've got to tell us what you know, okay? Do you understand that?"

"Yes."

The soft light from the wall lamp behind the bed pooled amber on the stark white sheets and shadowed Misty's face. Parker hoped he was handling this right. The only little girl he'd ever been around was Megan. And they'd never been through anything like this. How frank should he be?

He recalled a lesson he'd learned on his grandpa's knee. Kids have to learn to lie. They're born honest, and they stay honest—until somebody teaches them to lie.

Caron stepped away from the bed and walked to the window overlooking the parking lot. When she pinched the blinds and looked out, Parker looked back at Misty.

"Your folks are worried, honey. They need to know you're okay. I think if you saw them, you'd feel better."

A huge tear slipped down to her cheek. Parker caught it on his finger. "Are you afraid of them?"

"No."

Parker reached over and picked up the phone on the bedside table and passed it to Misty. "Call them, honey."

She didn't take the receiver. She wanted to; her hand was twitching. But, for some reason Parker didn't understand, she couldn't do it. "I'll dial it for you. Tell me the number, Misty."

"I can't."

"Why?" Parker forced his voice to remain reasonable, his tone gentle. It was difficult. Caron had spoken to Mary Beth. Charles Nivens hadn't found a scrap of information on Vanessa. The mystery woman Caron suspected was Misty's mother was still at large . . . and a real threat to the child.

"Because."

"Misty, I don't know what else to say, but we've got to call. We need your medicine."

Caron let go of the blinds. They snapped shut, and she turned. "Enough," she said through pinched lips. "Now look, Misty, I know you love your dad. I saw you two at the park. You were happy. He was happy." Caron stepped closer to the bed. "But right now, your father isn't happy. Right now, he's scared to death you're lying dead in a ditch somewhere. He's hurt and worried and he misses you. Now you give Parker the number. And you do it right now!"

Her eyes wide, Misty gave Parker the number.

Parker dialed it. The authority in Caron's tone had surprised him. It shouldn't have; she was a teacher. But it did. And he suspected Misty's compliance was more an instinctive reaction than a planned one.

"Misty, what's your dad's name?"

"Collin Phillips."

"And your mom's?"

"Don't talk to her." Misty frowned, and what little color she had left her face. "Talk to my dad." Her voice was reed thin.

Parker nodded and patted her hand. She was slipping away; he could feel it. "All right."

"Promise."

"I promise." Parker looked at Caron. She was shaking and her eyes were uneasy.

A woman answered the phone. "Phillips residence."

"May I speak to Collin Phillips?" Parker asked, a knot forming in his throat. "I'm calling about his daughter, Misty." This Christmas Eve call was going to net one very happy man . . . if Misty survived.

"Who is this?" She sounded panicked.

"Get Collin Phillips, please."

After a pause, a man came on the line. "Hello."

One word. Yet it conveyed so much. Caution. Wariness. Fear. Parker understood why. The man could hang up elated or devastated, and he knew it. "Are you Collin Phillips?"

"Yes. What do you know about Misty?" Terror joined the other emotions in the man's voice.

"Is that my dad?" Misty asked.

Parker winked at her. "My name is Parker Simms. My partner and I have found your daughter."

"Found her! You found Misty? Is she all right?"

Choosing his words carefully, Parker answered, then asked about Misty's medication and passed the information along to Caron, who left the room to relay it to Dr. Z.

"We're at the Zilinger Institute, Mr. Phillips," Parker said. He turned his back and closed his eyes, hating to have to tell the man this. He whispered, to be sure Misty wouldn't hear. "She's critical."

"Daddy." Misty tried to reach for the phone, but she was too weak to lift her hand.

Tears burning his eyes, and the back of his throat, Parker propped the phone at her ear on the pillow.

"Misty? Misty, is that you?"

"Daddy," she whispered. It was a faint breath sound.

"Oh, God! Oh, God! Are you all right, honey?"

"Don't cry, Daddy." Misty sniffled. Fat tears rolled down her cheeks. "Please don't cry."

Parker turned away and swiped at his face. His chest felt as if someone were standing on it. Caron was leaning against the window, looking out. When had she come back into the room?

The need to go to her, to touch her and be touched, ached in him like a raw wound. He lifted a hand to touch her shoulder, then hesitated; she would see his tears.

Trust her.

Yes. Yes. He lowered his hand to her shoulder. She turned and looked up; she was crying, too, but she gave him a liquid smile. Parker smiled back and pulled her tight against his chest in a hug. He wanted to tell her what he was feeling, all of the things that were welling up in his heart, but he could only manage her name. "Caron."

It was enough. She pressed hard against his chest and held him tighter. They stayed that way for a long moment, locked together in an embrace that no words could have explained. Then he eased back, curled his arm around her waist, and felt her arm circle his. Together they turned toward Misty.

Dr. Z. was at the bed, injecting medicine into Misty's IV. The worry in her eyes was still there. They weren't out of the woods yet. But they were moving in the right direction.

A discreet tap sounded at the door.

Parker answered it, talked softly with someone for a moment, then motioned Caron into the hall. When she stepped outside, she saw Sandy.

"Parker tells me you're calling her folks."

Caron nodded bitterly.

Sandy didn't meet her gaze. "I thought you'd want to know…" His voice faded, and he looked at Parker. "We're still groping in the dark on Vanessa."

"I think she's Misty's mother," Caron said. "We'll confirm that with her father as soon as he arrives."

Sandy looked at Parker, and if Caron hadn't been looking directly at him, she would have missed his nearly imperceptible nod. "We can't find a trace of Decker or Forrester, either, Caron."

"What?" Caron gasped.

"We've checked the airport, train station, bus terminals—they've vanished."

"Credit card slips?" Parker asked in a level tone.

"We're working on it." Sandy took the cigar stub out of his mouth. "Lot of roads lead out of New Orleans. We're looking at a few days."

Parker stiffened, opening a door he wasn't sure wasn't better off closed. "Your murder scene is the fishing camp where you met with Linda."

"I got your call, Parker." Sandy studied his cigar. His hand was trembling. "The man you left tied up in the house is at Charity Hospital. Three broken ribs and a sprained wrist." He looked at Parker's chin. "Our guys are on-scene at the camp now."

Caron frowned. This didn't make sense. "What about the people we heard drive up?"

"I told you, honey. They never got out of the car." Parker narrowed his eyes, demanding Sandy tell Caron *he'd* been the "they" who hadn't gotten out.

Sandy clamped his teeth around his cigar. "I've got to go. I just wanted to let you know what we're up against."

Parker looked at Caron. She'd caught it, he realized.

"Keep us posted." Parker had to bury his emotions deep to keep a calm face and a civil voice. Anger boiled in his gut. Sandy wasn't going to tell her, and Parker *couldn't*. It was bad enough that he hadn't yet told her his own sins. He couldn't tell her about Sanders's.

Parker glared at the man's back, willing him to turn around and face the music. He didn't. He headed down the hall, and stopped at the elevator. When he stepped inside and the door closed behind him, Parker knew Sanders had decided not to tell her. Not now, not ever.

And the proverbial knife slid in, right between Parker's shoulder blades. He had no choice.

"Caron?" he began uncertainly, staring at the floor.

"It's okay, Parker. I know. It was Sandy."

He looked up and something inside him died. Caron's eyes held the same betrayed look they had when she'd told him about her father. "I, um, need some air."

"I'm going with you." He reached for her hand, but she curled it to her chest and stepped back.

"No, Parker." Her eyes were rimmed with red, and her chin was quivering. "I'm better off alone."

Her words slammed into him like a hard right. She was trying so hard not to cry. His heart felt as if it had been squeezed and hung out to dry. He couldn't let her shut him out. He couldn't let her just walk away. The words rushed unbidden out of his mouth. "I need you, Caron."

She stopped, but she didn't turn around. He went to her, taking the longest three steps he'd taken in his life. "I've wanted to tell you so many times. But I couldn't."

Her eyes shone her doubt. He was holding back, and she knew it. And for the thousandth time since he'd seen Sanders leave the fishing camp, he cursed the man. Sanders would never give his confession to Caron. And Parker's Caron would never hear.

The bleak look in her eyes, the ramrod stiffness in her shoulders, proved that Caron had made up her mind. She'd trusted a man for the last time.

God help him.

Caron swallowed the sob that was threatening her throat. She loved Parker so much, and still he was lying to her. He didn't need her; he just didn't want her alone with her fears. Didn't he think she'd know the difference?

He'd told her he needed her for the same reason that he'd torched the shed. He wanted Misty to know that what had happened to her couldn't happen to her again. He wanted Caron to know that what had happened to her again had happened for the last time.

"Caron, I wish I had the right words. I wish I could take the hurt..."

He was sincere. And, touched by his concern, Caron leaned against the wall next to him and pressed her forehead against his arm. "I understand." The strange thing was, she really did. He cared. He didn't love her, but he cared. She wanted love.

"Do you?" His eyes burned black with stormy emotions.

The shield hiding his thoughts melted away. He was torn, afraid of hurting her, afraid of losing her. He *wasn't* like Sandy, like her father or like any of the others. He was going to tell her the truth; she sensed it!

"Not now." She pressed a fingertip over his lips. "Not here." A hospital corridor was no place for soul-baring confessions. They deserved privacy and uninterrupted time; and they'd have it, just as soon as they wrapped up this case. They needed to laugh together and make silly jokes, and to enjoy each other. When they'd had those things, the good that could come between two people who cared about each other, then it would be time to share their dreams and desires . . . and their secrets.

"I don't know how to thank you. . . ."

Caron looked into the soft eyes she'd so often imaged and saw gratitude. Inexpressible gratitude.

Collin Phillips sat on Misty's bed, cradling her in his arms, and his smile lit up his whole face. He didn't look homely anymore, Caron realized. His bulbous nose was still red, but his long, lean face was too full of love for his daughter to be anything but handsome.

He stroked Misty's shoulder with a bony hand that bordered on gaunt and spoke to Caron and Parker. "I wish I could tell you how much having Misty back means to me. I—I—" Choking up, he paused, then smiled. "Thank you."

Parker stepped forward. "We'd like a moment, Mr. Phillips." Parker looked pointedly toward the hallway.

Phillips unfolded his lanky body, dropped a kiss on Misty's forehead and followed Caron and Parker into the hall.

"We have a few questions," Parker said.

"So do I. Are you with the police?"

"No." Caron ignored Parker's grimace. This time she was playing it straight. "I'm a psychic, Mr. Phillips. I imaged Misty. That's how we knew she was in trouble."

"I see."

He didn't. But he was a kind man and a grateful one, and he wasn't about to insult Misty's rescuers. "When your daughter went missing, why didn't you file a kidnapping report?"

"I did!" Phillips wrinkled his nose and shoved his glasses back on his face. "The kidnappers said they'd . . . kill—"

he stumbled over the word ""—Misty if I went to the police. But a man in my position knows the odds. Getting my daughter back unharmed was more likely with the police than without them, so I went down to headquarters and talked to Detective Sanders. He took the report and said he'd keep the record off the wire. I assumed that meant the other officers would know, but that the information wouldn't be available to outsiders.""

"When exactly was Misty kidnapped?" Caron said. A sick feeling had her stomach queasy. Sandy *had* been into this up to his cigar stub.

"On the fifteenth. We lunched at the park, and I left to go back to work. The next thing I knew, I was getting a call at the office telling me she'd been abducted."

"Did they ask for a ransom?"

"Yes."

Parker grimaced. "How much?"

"Five million."

It fit. Caron's heart knocked against her ribs. All the pieces fit.

"Where's your wife, Mr. Phillips?"

"I'm not sure, Mr. Simms." Phillips's face and neck splotched red, and he lowered his gaze. "I haven't seen her for days. The pressure was too much. She said she had to get away." Bitterness threaded into his voice.

"When did she leave?"

"I'm not sure." He gave Parker a sad smile. "The days have been running together, you know? Tuesday, I think."

The images that had whirled in Caron's mind time and again returned. The park. The woman binding Misty's hands. The hatred . . .

"What's your wife's name, Mr. Phillips?"

He frowned and shoved at his glasses. "Vanessa."

Caron looked at Parker, and at the same time he looked at her. "I'll call Sanders," Parker said.

Caron frowned and looked at Phillips. "We know who kidnapped your daughter." Shoving open the door, she went back into the room and over to Misty.

The child was still a pasty white, but her eyes were more alert. She was getting stronger.

Parker came back, and he and Phillips stood behind her. Caron edged up onto the bed. "Your mom took you to the man, didn't she, Misty?"

She looked past Caron's shoulder to her father.

"Misty, look at me." Caron touched her chin. The room was quiet, the only sound the steady beeping of the heart monitor connected to Misty's chest. "You've got to tell us."

Phillips stepped to Caron's side and took his daughter's hand. "I need to know, honey. Just tell the truth, okay?"

Her tiny face twisted in pain. "My bike wasn't broken, Daddy. Mom said my tire was flat, but it wasn't. We stopped behind the store. The man scared me. But Mom said he was going to fix my bike, that I had to go with him. I told her I didn't want to, but she said he was a good stranger. She made me go."

His face a blind mask of pain, Collin looked down...and saw the rope burns on Misty's wrists. "She tied you up?"

Misty blinked, then blinked again. Tears splashed down to her cheeks. "Mom didn't mean to lie!" she cried on a choking sob. "She didn't mean to hurt me!"

Misty gasped and clutched her chest. And the intermittent beep of the heart monitor became a shrill, steady blast.

In the waiting room, the hours crept by. How many, Caron wasn't sure; it seemed a lifetime. Parker and Collin Phillips were sitting together, talking quietly. Caron stood at the window, looking outside. They'd pushed Misty too hard, forcing her to admit her mother's wrongs. Why hadn't she sensed it? Why hadn't she known that Misty couldn't handle it? It was her fault. If Misty died, Caron was to blame. She'd made a mistake. Just as she had with Sarah.

Two nurses all in white walked across the parking lot, laughing. A brown car screeched to a stop at the emergency entrance. A man got out and rushed to help his pregnant wife inside. They were coming to have a baby. It was a boy.

A palpable tension clouded the room, but suddenly it elevated, thickened enough to slice. A second later, Caron heard footsteps behind her, stiffened, turned, and saw Dr. Z.

"Misty's fever broke and her breathing is improving," the doctor said, her eyes shining overly bright. "She's going to make it."

Tears sprang to her eyes, and Caron ran into Parker's arms. "We weren't too late." Deep sobs rattled her chest. "Oh, Parker, we weren't too late...."

Parker squeezed his eyes shut. How could he have doubted her? How had he been so blinded by Harlan's rage and despair that he hadn't seen her for the woman she was?

He forced his eyes open, refusing to run. He wasn't hiding his feelings—not anymore. He wept openly, unashamed. "No, love." His voice gruff, raw and ragged, he pressed his cheek to her shoulder. "We weren't too late."

"Take her home, Parker." Dr. Z. examined Caron with a motherly look. "You're both exhausted, and there's nothing more you can do here."

"But I don't want—" Caron began.

"To collapse on my floor, I hope." Dr. Z. clucked her tongue. "Your job is finished. You found Misty, and she's going to be fine. Her father is here, the guard is right outside the door, and Detective Sanders will be coming back momentarily. He *did* want you to find her. She's safe now. Her needs have been met, Caron. Yours, however, have not. You need rest."

Parker agreed with a healthy nod and rubbed his two days' growth of beard. "While you're at it, could you mention something doctorly here about her diet? The lady lives on Butterfingers."

"No candy." She wagged a finger. "Now go home."

"All right," Caron muttered, primed to blister their ears for ganging up on her. But Misty was watching avidly. She smiled at the girl, then gave the good doctor and her cat-that-swallowed-the-canary sidekick a glare to let them know they weren't getting away with a thing.

"See you in a little while, sweet stuff." She pecked a kiss to Misty's cheek, then stood. Her legs wobbled.

"Come on, jelly knees." Parker slid an arm around her shoulder. "Let's go home."

Parker adjusted the heat on the stove, then cut the omelet in two and slid it onto plates. He arranged wedges of buttered toast around the edges, and put a plate in front of Caron. "Eat."

She grunted at him and dutifully picked up her fork. "I don't like the way this is working out."

He slid onto a chair opposite her. "We're done, Caron. It's up to the police now."

She swallowed a bite of the eggs. Spicy tomato sauce and melted cheese tingled her taste buds. "Hey, this is almost as good as pizza."

Parker grinned. "Thanks—I think."

"I love pizza." She took another bite and crunched down on a piece of toast. "What I hate is the way this case is working out."

"Caron, we're done, honey. Let it go."

She sighed and stared off.

"Okay." He put down his fork. "Let's have it."

Caron smiled. He really was such a nice man. "Okay. Logic tells me Forrester killed Linda. I *know* the man's as guilty as sin. So why doesn't it feel right?"

Parker pushed his food around on his plate. "Because you've omitted Sandy's part in this."

"Yes." Suffering again the sting of his betrayal, she shoved a bite of omelet into her mouth and slowly chewed. "But Sandy isn't capable of murder, Parker. He— Oh God."

"What?"

"Sandy *knew* where Misty was! He *knew* she'd been abducted right from the start!"

Parker winced. She was fast on the uptake. Within minutes she'd have it all worked out. "I don't think he did. He asked me to help you find her. Remember?"

"Yes," she admitted, some of the excitement fading from her voice. She swept back her hair and gave him a pleading look. It was still damp from the shower. "You still haven't told me why you agreed."

Parker looked her right in the eye and did what he'd vowed he'd never do again: He lied. "I told you. He and Charley were friends."

"Right."

"Right," he insisted, damning his voice for its wimpy tone. But it was hard for a man to work up much righteous indignation when he was dead wrong.

Caron saw despair in Parker's eyes, and the truth hit her like a sledge. She loved him, yes. She'd known that since...well, she didn't know exactly how long she'd known it. It had crept up on her while she wasn't looking. But love was there. And sitting here at this table, seeing him look at her with his heart in his eyes, she felt new stirrings join the others. She loved him, and she was in love with him. That truth scared her to death.

The unwelcome voice of reason intruded, telling her she was crazy even to consider what she was considering. He knew she'd figured it out, and still he hadn't told her the truth. He *was* like her father. He was a slick charmer who wouldn't blink at using her love for him as a weapon against her. He was no different from the rest. He'd want her to "see" something, be it racing forms or—or whatever.

Her head listened to the logical whisper of reason and agreed completely.

But her heart ignored it.

As full as a swollen stream, it promised that Parker was exactly the man he seemed—warm, loving, caring. He'd proven time after time that he was *not* like her father. The night someone had left that god-awful message on her door, Parker had arrived shirtless, frantic and terrified for her. He'd begged her *not* to image, *not* to return to Decker's to touch Misty's bike, *not* to touch the leash. He'd acted on gut level instinct, on raw emotion, because he cared about her. That was the real Parker Simms. His methods at times were sinfully shaky, but weren't there times when a man had to follow his heart, and damn his conscience?

Of course there were. And there were times when a woman did, too. This was one of them. "You know kids lie about being beaten and abused, because in their hearts they can't believe their parents really meant them harm.''

She paused, and when he didn't say anything she went on. "I'm not abused, or a child, Parker, but I can be hurt. I know you've never meant me harm.''

"Never," he said on a rushed breath. "I swear it.''

The room stilled as if it were in the eye of a storm. Caron stood and went around to his side of the table. He scooted back in his chair and looked up at her, his gaze burning. The cool gray she'd seen there the day they'd met, and so many times since, was gone. Warmth and care and so much more were in his eyes now.

Feeling powerful and humble, she just stared at him and let the feelings soak in. Parker Simms was gorgeous and gentle and the most virile-looking man she'd ever seen, and she loved him with all her heart. Now she had to trust him.

"One day you'll tell me, Parker.'' She dropped a kiss to his lips and brazenly settled on his lap. "Until then, I can wait.''

He brushed her lips with his, drew back, then brushed them again. He lifted a strand of hair from her cheek and smoothed it back with his big, rough hand. "You scare the hell out of me, lady. You give so much.''

"Kiss me.'' She parted her lips and pressed them to his. The words were hard for him, but Parker could reassure her without words. He could show her that the want and need and desire she was feeling were there in him, too.

His mouth hot and hard on hers, he bore down, melding their lips, tangling their tongues. Desire flamed, grew stronger, consumed....

He let his mouth slide over her cheek and whispered raggedly against her ear. "Caron?''

"Yes, Parker.'' She understood his question. "Yes.''

The muscles in his legs and arms bunched and grew thick. He held her tighter and stood. She nuzzled his neck, placed tiny kisses along his collarbone, knowing this was right.

He walked through the lit hall to her bedroom, then let her slide down his hard length to the floor. "Are you sure, honey?''

One more chance to reconsider. More nervous than she'd ever been in her life, she clasped her hands and wet her lips. A flicker of doubt lit in her mind. Taking risks that involved her heart was still so hard. She gripped his waist and looked up. "I've never invited a man to my bed, Parker. There've been a few sexual experiences, but they've been rare." That was true. They'd been heated encounters borne from deep-seated cries for approval and acceptance. Acceptance that had faded as soon as the flush of desire had passed. Never before had she been the initiator, the one who desired, the one whose body craved mating as it craved food. And never before had she been the one left vulnerable to being refused and rejected.

"I need to know it's *me* you want." She forced herself to look up from his chest and into his eyes. "Not just any woman."

He blinked, and the frown wrinkling the skin between his brows smoothed. "I only want you, Caron." He softened his voice and that darling curl tilted his lip. "You."

A warm glow started deep in the pit of her stomach and fanned through her chest. She was in love. She wanted and needed this man. And she was going to be open about her feelings. If he didn't love her back, if she suffered for taking the risk later . . . well, she'd suffer. But she wasn't going to run.

Her hand trembling, she fingered the hair on his chest, unable to meet his eyes. "I've been hurt, Parker. And the truth is, I'm afraid of you."

"Why?" He cupped her face in his hands. "Don't you know how much I want you? Can't you see that I'm crazy about you?" He sank his teeth into his lip.

"I'm afraid because they only hurt me." The single light burning in the hallway cast a stream of light across the bed and his chest. His expression was hidden in the shadows. "But you—you can devastate me."

Parker dropped his hands to his sides. He stood rigid, his hands balled into fists. There was nothing charming, no resemblance to a womanizer, in him now; his expression was darker than a moonless night. "Caron."

He didn't move, and she knew that until she looked at him he wasn't going to move. For them, it was now or never. She lifted her chin and met his gaze.

"You're not alone in this." He stroked her cheek with the pad of his thumb. "My heart's right here."

He kissed her tenderly, gently, lovingly, caressing her back, her sides, her face. She lifted her hands, curled them around his neck and felt a tiny explosion of desire deep inside. This was right. So right. "I need you," she whispered, stepping closer into his arms.

"I need you, too, Caron. More than I've needed anyone in my life."

He cupped her face, caressing it with tiny kisses that soon became long, lingering ones. He whispered tender longings, gentle love words that she needed to hear, longings and words she deciphered not with her ears, but with her heart. In his arms she felt cherished, wanted, adored, the way only a woman in love can feel. And the need to touch nothing but him, to let her hands and body tell him all she was feeling in her heart grew urgent.

She swept his neck with lazy strokes, let her fingertips explore the dips in his clavicle and, hampered by unwanted fabric, she began working at the buttons of his shirt with eager, fumbling fingers.

His deep, hot kisses had her straining to him, urging him for more, probing his mouth with wide sweeps of her tongue. He grazed her ribs with his palm and unknotted the belt to her robe, then eased the suddenly rough fabric down. Skimming her shoulders, it fell to the floor.

He drew back and took his time looking at her, head to heel, with a lazy gaze. She forced herself to stand still, to let him look his fill without shame or embarrassment. She wasn't running, and she wasn't pushing him away. His gaze lingered lovingly on her breasts, on the vee at her thighs, and the heat in his eyes enraged her senses; it was a rich reward.

He again met her gaze, his eyes heavy-lidded, his lips softly parted, his chest rising and falling more rapidly now. "It was inevitable, Caron," he whispered shakily, in a voice as smooth and seductive as velvet. "Inevitable."

He dipped his tongue deep into her mouth, rolled with her onto the bed, then turned onto his side and stretched out beside her.

Warm and fluid, they touched; breast to chest, thigh to thigh, mouth to mouth, their gratified sighs mingling. He told her she was beautiful, whispered all the things he wanted to do to pay homage to her, making her feel beautiful and warm and wonderful. He rubbed her nose with his, swept her side from rib to hip, fanning the fires burning low in her belly. Her hand under his shirt, she touched him. His bare flesh quivered; skin over hard-packed muscle, feeling like heated silken steel. She reveled in his strength, in his gentleness, in the tremor in the rough hands that grazed her skin. So telling, his touch. Uncertain, longing, aching to please. And care. Such . . . care.

She sighed her pleasure and eased the shirt from his shoulders. He shifted free, and she tossed it to the floor. Running her fingers through the hair on his chest, she skimmed his hard nipples. Her palms tingled, and the need in her burned deeper, stronger. Gently squeezing his sides, she followed a path over his abdomen to the clasp of his jeans, needing to feel him with nothing between them—naked skin to naked skin, naked soul to naked soul.

She let her fingers drift on the hard placket, then twisted the metal button. The backs of her fingers brushed against his stomach. He sucked in a sharp gasp and shivered. His chest swelled from the strong breath. Suddenly afraid she'd pushed too far too fast, that his need didn't match her own, she sought his permission to go further. "Parker?"

"Yes," he rasped brokenly against her neck, his fingers caressing her shoulders, his teeth lightly scraping the skin at her throat. "Oh, yes."

The button gave way. He grunted his pleasure and sought her lips. Their tongues, hot and wet, swirled magic, and she worked her fingers until his zipper spread its metal teeth.

"Ah, Caron.... The things you make me feel." His breath fanned across her breasts, warming them, infusing her with a sense of power, of prowess. Humble, grateful, she flattened her hands on his hips and slid the rough fabric, and the softer fabric beneath it, down over his muscular thighs.

Dazed by his kisses, she lifted her hand to his chest. Parker captured it and dragged it down to that swollen part of him that was hungering for her touch. The soft hair there curled around her fingertips, clinging, and her breathing grew more rapid, more shallow and ragged.

He lifted to his knees on the mattress, and began burning a slow trail of heated kisses to the rise of her breasts, raking the swells with his teeth, tugging, then blowing hot breaths that raised her nipples to nubs. "You don't know how many times I've imaged this. I want it to be so right."

Imaged. She smiled and circled his broad back with her arms, let them explore the tense muscles dancing under her fingertips. "I know," she whispered, arching her neck. "I know...."

He tugged at her breast, then freed it to the chill night air; touched her with gentle hands and loving lips, with tender murmurings that arrowed magic straight to her heart, then continued on a languorous journey of exploring her body, of adoring and praising her. His hands trembled, revered; and when the fire inside her raged, she rejoiced in it, delighted by the sounds of their heated breaths mingling, the nubby feel of the sheets at her back, of her fingertips tingling, gliding along his spine; the warm, woodsy smell of his skin. "Parker." She needed more. She needed him inside her. She nipped at his shoulder.

"A little longer. Just a little longer." His breath, hot and moist, fanned her stomach.

"Now." She let out a soft moan from deep in her throat and dragged her fingers along his scalp.

He lifted his head, positioned himself on his knees between her thighs and reached past her to the side of the bed. "I want you now, Caron." He reared back, resting his buttocks on his heels, then slid a condom down over his swollen shaft. "I'll always want you."

She reached for him, pulled him down and guided him into her body. Shuddering his pleasure at their joining, he bowed his back and buried himself inside her. She felt gloriously full, content just to hold him, to squeeze him tight. Making love had never been like this. Breasts-to-chest, thigh-to-thigh and heart-to-heart with Parker, she discovered the magic.

He nuzzled her temple, whorled his tongue in the shell of her ear and nibbled at the soft skin behind the lobe, whispering that she was beautiful, that he loved her body, that he loved the way she made him feel.

Loving gazes and warm caresses soon grew urgent. The demands of their flesh grew more insistent, no longer content with teasing and taunting and arousing. She took his mouth in a searing kiss and arched her hips.

Needing no more urging, Parker began to thrust, long, lush strokes into her heated flesh, long, fevered groans of inexpressible pleasure.

Hands that had been tender, groped. Lips that had been gentle, crushed. And hips that had melded so smoothly, so sweetly, ground and meshed, hungering to get even closer. The pressure inside her mounted, swirled tighter; Parker thrust hard, then harder. The pressure built, peaked, then shattered.

"Caron," he ground out from between clenched teeth. His body slick with sweat and strain, he pumped hard, still seeking release.

Awash in sensation, Caron fitted his male orbs in her hand and gently squeezed. He growled her name on a sharp indrawn breath, then bowed his back in a final thrust that hollowed his buttocks and drove her up on the bed.

She watched him come, watched the strain in his face change to ecstasy, and a soul-deep joy flooded her.

Still shuddering, he lowered himself to her chest and took her lips in a long, loving kiss. She wrapped her arms around him, and when he started to move away she flexed them to hold him in place. "No, don't leave me. Not yet."

"Not yet." He opened his eyes. Understanding burned bright in their depths. "I'm not running, Caron. And I'm not leaving." He kissed her firmly. "I still need you."

They nuzzled, and cuddled and whispered lovers' secrets for long, luxurious minutes, and then he rolled onto his side, bringing her with him.

She lifted a fingertip to his lips, then pulled back to focus. Her heart was so full it threatened to burst, and when she told him, she wanted to see his face. "Parker," she whispered, her gaze sweeping his mouth, his hair, his twinkling eyes, "I love you."

Parker stiffened. He didn't know what to say. Guilt swarmed in, invading him. And more than he wanted to make love with her again, he wanted to tell her the truth. He'd had no right to make love with her. He'd lied to her, spied on her and deceived her. He'd had no right to take from her.

Yet he had taken. He had . . . taken.

Angry with himself, he set her away, then hauled his body into the bath and discarded the condom. His image in the bathroom mirror taunted him. He couldn't meet his own eyes. He had to tell her. Right now.

Resolved, he crawled back into her bed. She stroked his hair. He swore he'd never tire of the feel of her hands in his hair. It was the most nurturing gesture he'd ever felt, yet the most arousing one. She'd given him so much, and was still giving to him. He raised her hand from his chest and pressed it firmly against his mouth. "Caron, you know I—"

"Shh . . ." She pressed a fingertip to his lips. "You don't have to say anything. I don't expect it. I just wanted you to know how I feel, Parker. I just wanted you to know that I love you. That's all."

He had a lot to say to her. But before he could respond, she yawned and turned onto her side, then nestled back against him. If he told her tonight, she'd be awake cursing him and crying. She was exhausted. And so was he.

He pulled her closer, cupping her breast in his hand. She was perfect. Everything he'd ever wanted in a woman, and more. He wanted to give her the words, but first he had to give her the truth. It had waited this long; it could wait a few more hours.

No, it couldn't wait. Not another minute. Caron had laid her heart and soul on the line for him, and he wouldn't diminish the importance of that to him by letting his lies remain between them. "Caron, I have to tell you—" She went board stiff in his arms. "Honey, what is it?"

"It's Misty!" Caron scrambled from the bed, started tossing on her clothes. "Hurry, Parker! Oh, God, hurry! They're going to kill her!"

Chapter 11

The hospital corridor was deceptively quiet.

Sandy wasn't there, and the guard wasn't outside Misty's door. Caron scanned the hall, ceiling to floor. Nothing but the change from white paint to white tile broke the monotony, yet she felt the same sense of violation she'd felt in her apartment, the same sense of rage that she'd felt the night someone had left the message on her door.

At her side, Parker whispered. "You were right. Something is going down."

Caron nodded her agreement, not surprised that his investigative instincts mirrored her intuitive ones. They stopped outside Misty's door. Caron pressed the palm of her hand against it. A flash of fear had her jerking back.

Parker didn't so much as lift a brow. He just reached into his shoulder holster and pulled out his gun. "Find a nurse. Have her call Security."

Caron nodded, ducked down so that she couldn't be seen through the window, then made her way down the hall.

Two nurses were talking at the nurses' station. "Call Security and get the police," Caron said, without explaining.

The women just gaped.

"Do it now!" When they started grabbing phones, Caron rushed back to Parker.

He motioned for Caron to stay where she was, then moved to the row of windows and risked looking in through a crack in the drawn drapes.

"Oh, Jesus," he whispered, dropping into a crouch.

"What is it?" Caron whispered back. Memories of Sarah, of the night she'd died, rushed back, clouding Caron's thoughts and perceptions. Again she saw Sarah's battered body. Again she saw the flames licking at the building, consuming it. No one else would ever suffer there.

Parker whispered. "It's Vanessa and Forrester. He's armed."

"Misty!" Panic, fear, bombarded Caron, clawed at her stomach and chest. Not again. Not Misty. Damn it, she was supposed to be safe! It was supposed to be over!

"Vanessa's beside her on the bed."

"Where are Collin and Sandy? They were supposed to be here!"

"They are. Tied up on the floor, against the far wall."

An image of some sharp object flashed through Caron's mind. "We've got to go in. Vanessa knows."

Parker looked worried. "Can you handle her?"

"Yes!" Where in God's name was the hospital staff? Where was security? The police?

Parker moved to the door. His eyes changed. The softness faded, and something cold and hard settled in its place. He shoved hard. The door swung open, slammed back. They rushed in.

Metal struck metal and Forrester's gun clanged against an IV pole, then slid across the floor. Vanessa turned, a syringe in her hand. Caron lunged, clipping the woman's shoulder with a momentum that knocked her off the bed. The syringe flew through the air, then bounced harmlessly on the tile. Its plastic cracked.

Caron went over the foot of the bed, throwing her weight, and landed with a *swoosh* of breath on top of Vanessa, pinning her to the floor.

Vanessa fought back, fought hard, as though her life depended on her breaking free. Caron dodged angry fists arcing toward her in wide swings, deflected sharp nails attempting to claw at her face, and suffered jabs from feet and thrashing knees trying to dislodge her. She held hard and fast...and she fought back.

Behind her, something crashed. She glanced back. Parker landed a hard right to Forrester's stomach that doubled him over. He lifted a foot and aimed it at Parker's groin. Parker shifted on the balls of his feet, grabbed Forrester's ankle and twisted.

Forrester hit the floor.

Vanessa wrangled free and clipped Caron a dizzying blow. Pain ripped through her chest. Raw terror grew to black rage. Caron raised her fist, saw fear in Vanessa's eyes, and paused. Memories of what the woman had done to her daughter, memories of Sarah, gushed into Caron's mind. "Your daughter? Your own flesh and blood?" And with a guttural cry of outrage, Caron slammed her fist into Vanessa Phillips's perfect face.

The woman crumpled and went limp. Caron looked and saw Forrester dive for his gun. Parker was quicker, kicking it out of reach. He whipped around, planted his foot firmly on Forrester's chest—and leveled the Colt, targeting Forrester's heart.

"Don't shoot!" Forrester yelled. "Christ, don't shoot!"

Her limbs leaden, her arm throbbing from the blows she'd taken from and landed on Vanessa, Caron moved to untie Sandy and Collin. Then she went to Misty.

The child's face was pasty and white, but she was unharmed. Caron cuddled Misty, trying to soothe her. "You saw a lady at the camp the day before Parker and I came, didn't you?"

Misty nodded, her eyes brimming with tears. She pointed to Vanessa. "Mom and the lady that untied me."

Caron nearly cried. "You saw a man choke that lady."

Again Misty nodded. "He cut her neck with a knife."

"I know, honey." Caron tightened her hold, tried with all her might to absorb the horror of what Misty had seen into her own body. The pain of losing Sarah didn't lessen, just as Misty's pain wouldn't lessen. She'd always remember seeing Linda Forrester murdered. But with the right kind of help, Misty could learn to cope. And she'd be alive to cope. She'd survived.

Caron found comfort in that. "We don't have to talk about it anymore now." Remembering how confusing what she'd imaged as a child had been, she cupped a finger under Misty's chin and lifted until they saw eye-to-eye. "But you can't keep your feelings inside about this. You have to talk about it until it doesn't scare you anymore. Okay?"

"Okay."

Caron released Misty and stood up.

Nursing her jaw, Vanessa scooted across the floor to the wall, then slid up it to sit.

Caron pointed at her. "That's far enough."

"I'm going to kill him." Collin started toward Forrester.

"Collin, no!" Grabbing his sleeve, Caron looked up at him. "He's not worth it."

Collin tried to brush off her arm, but she held tight. "Misty can't lose you, too. She needs you!"

He looked at his daughter, saw the fat tears tumbling down her face, and the fury drained from his. He rushed over, scooped her up in his long arms and held her while she cried.

"Sanders, get your guys and get these people out of here." Parker kept the gun trained on Forrester. "Then start explaining."

Sandy moved to the hall. The officers were arriving.

Caron looked down at Vanessa. How could anyone so beautiful on the outside be so ugly within? She'd had everything. "I want to know why."

Vanessa grunted and motioned at Collin and Misty. "Look at them." She dragged a hand through her red hair. "It's been that way since she was born. He doesn't give a damn about *me*. It's *her*. He's always loved *her!*"

Caron looked down at the woman in pity and disgust. She was jealous of Misty. So jealous she would have killed her own daughter. "He's her father. He's *supposed* to love her."

Before Vanessa could say any more, Caron walked closer to Parker, careful to avoid Forrester's reach. "You okay?"

"Fine." He looked up at her. "You?"

She started to disclose what she'd learned from Misty, then decided against it, nodded, and walked toward the hall. After Forrester and Vanessa had been taken into custody, there would be plenty of time to let Parker know that this wasn't over. Caron glanced at Sandy. He was talking to Parker. She remembered back, how it had been between her and the detective through the years. Since she was seven, she had respected and admired him. He had been her friend and confidant, her partner in helping others. Something good inside her died. Her heart ached, mourning the loss, and she fought tears.

Vanessa had been willing to kill Misty. But she hadn't killed Linda Forrester.

Neither had Linda's husband.

Her shoulders slumped, Caron walked on into the hallway and slumped back against the wall. That left two suspects: Sandy and Decker. One of them was guilty of Linda Forrester's murder.

And Caron knew which one.

Following Sandy in the Porsche, Parker looked over at Caron. "I thought you'd be happy. Misty's okay."

"She's still not safe." Caron swept her hair back and stared straight ahead. "She saw the killing, Parker." Caron's voice cracked.

"We thought she had, but I was hoping…" He couldn't look at her; the pain that had haunted her since Sarah's death would be there in her eyes. But a scrap of conversation replayed in his mind, and it gave him no alternative. He wouldn't play ostrich like her mother. He wouldn't bury his head in the sand and let Caron go through this alone. "You saw the killing, too."

"Yes." She reached for his hand. "When I held Misty."

He laced their fingers and gave her a reassuring squeeze. Sanders made the turn onto Belle Chase Highway. Parker followed. "I know it was Decker, Caron."

"How?" She sounded surprised.

"Because of the leash. Because Linda had told him if Keith Forrester didn't, she would release Misty. Mary Beth

had heard her swear it in the diner, remember? Thank God
he didn't know where she was; he hadn't lied about that. If
he had known she was in the shed, he would have killed her,
too. I believe Linda had gone to the camp to meet Sandy,
but she'd found out Misty was there and intended to return her to her father. Decker couldn't have had Misty
live—she could have identified him.''

''How do you know that? I imaged Linda telling Misty,
but—''

''Sanders told me.''

''And you believe him?''

Parker glanced at her. ''Yes, I do. He's a bitter man,
Caron. Bitter about his demotion at work. Bitter at Linda
for duping him. Bitter at letting his heart rule his head. But
he didn't kill her.''

Caron thought about that. Sandy had withheld information, and more, but Parker was right; Sandy hadn't
killed Linda.

Something Ina had said came back. *''He knows I've
called the police. But he ain't stomped my irises yet. . . .''*

Ina.

''Parker, I know where Decker is.''

''Where?''

''Ina's. He's at Ina's. He knows she called the police.
He'll know Sandy heard about it.''

''And he'll want to keep her from talking.'' Parker
stomped the accelerator and motioned for Sanders to follow.

Creeping from hedge to hedge in the dark, Caron inched
her way across Ina's shell drive and up to the window where
she'd seen Ina the night she'd escaped from Decker's house.

Though it wasn't quite dawn, the curtains were open.
Looking inside, Caron saw Ina, sitting in a wooden rocker,
her rosary in her hand, her fingers curling around a bead,
and her lips moving silently.

Caron shifted to see farther. Ina looked up and saw her,
then jerked her head, motioning back toward the kitchen.

Caron nodded to let Ina know she'd understood, then
moved back to where Parker and Sandy had gathered.

Her heart pounded a hundred beats a minute. "She knows we're here. He's in the kitchen."

Parker checked the Colt's chamber. "You take the front, I'll take the back."

Sandy nodded. "Right."

"You're going to trust him?" Caron didn't want to say it, but this was Parker. *Parker!*

What if Sandy and Decker were working together? What if—?

"He didn't kill her, Caron. Sandy brought me in on this to see to it you remained safe, and he told us about the leash so that we *could* find Misty."

Sandy looked straight into her eyes for the first time since all of this had started. "I didn't do it, Caron. I was at the camp. We argued, and I slapped her, Caron—that's what Misty saw—but I did not kill Linda. I loved her. I've always loved her."

"*You* left the message on my door."

"Yes. Linda asked for time, so I didn't file the report. Then you came back. I knew Linda. I knew she'd do the right thing and turn Misty loose. She didn't know about the kidnapping until after it happened, Caron. I swear it."

The shield between them melted, and Caron sensed his feelings in a rush, sensed that he was only telling her the truth. "You were protecting her."

"Yes." He rubbed his ruddy jaw. "She needed time. And you were closing in too fast." He held up a hand. "I wrote the message, but I'd never have hurt you, Caron. I asked Parker to help you to keep you safe. I swear to God, I just wanted to slow you down."

"Where'd you get the blood?" Parker asked.

"Charity Hospital. I lifted a tube on its way to the lab." Sandy looked down at his shoes. "It's all in my report. A full confession of everything is on my desk. As soon as this is over I'm turning myself in."

"We'd better go," Parker said, looking guilty as hell.

Sandy had betrayed her. Worse, he'd betrayed himself. He'd go on paying during the lifetime he'd spend in prison.

Caron stood at the edge of the drive and watched them split up, Parker moving toward the back door, Sandy toward the front.

Moments later, she heard the back door split and give way. She started toward the back of the house. Before she reached the corner, the front door banged open.

Scuffling sounds had her hurrying her steps, but at the back door she stopped abruptly. It hung from one hinge.

Parker had Decker pinned in a chair at the kitchen table. A plate of food was in front of him.

Caron walked inside. Parker was no worse for wear. Sandy came through from the front, Ina following him.

"Are you okay?" Caron asked her.

She smiled, bobbing her purple-turbaned head and adjusting her pink robe. "Fine, child. Just fine."

Decker glared at Sandy. "She was a slut. You loved a slut, Sanders. Keith was loaded. He gave her a ticket out. But do you think Miss Rich Bitch did anything for me? Nothing. She gave me nothing but a hard time. And when I asked her for help, she refused. 'Keith's lost everything,' she said. But she was lying. I knew she was lying, and I made her pay."

Nauseous, Caron walked outside and inhaled great gulps of clean air. Too much, too fast. Too much to absorb.

Tires screeched to a halt on the street. She saw the red lights atop the car, heard the radio static coming from inside it, and sat down.

Leaning back against a magnolia, she looked up through its naked limbs. The sky was getting lighter. Dawn had broken. She closed her eyes and thought about Misty, about her students at Midtown, and then about Sarah.

"I'm sorry," Caron said to the woman she'd failed. "I'm not perfect." Plucking a blade of grass between her finger and thumb, Caron sighed. "I never said I was perfect. And I haven't forgotten. But I can't go on hating myself for making a mistake."

"Caron?"

Parker stood in front of her, his legs spread, his hands dangling at his sides. She looked up at him and saw desolation in his eyes.

"You're crying." He dropped down to sit beside her. "I heard you mention Sarah."

She heard the catch in his voice, felt the tremble in his hand on hers, and a dark shiver coursed up her spine. She'd been right, after all. "How do you know her name?"

He didn't answer.

"I never told you her name, Parker."

Parker was dying a thousand deaths. He loved Caron. Loved her more than he'd thought he could ever love any woman, especially after he'd seen in Harlan what loving could cost a man. And now he was going to lose her.

"Answer me."

She tried to free her hand. He held on for dear life, willing her to feel all the love he had for her. He'd wanted to tell her privately—he'd started to tell her twice—but the time had come now.

"I knew Sarah for years, Caron."

"What?" She tried to scramble to her feet.

"No, don't go. Let me explain. Please, Caron, don't run out on me."

The words slapped her like a splash of cold water. She *had* been going to run. She dropped back down onto the grass.

"Her husband, Harlan, and I were partners. We started the business right after college. I was best man at their wedding."

Parker wanted to see how she was taking this, but didn't dare to look at her. If he did, he knew he'd never get through the telling. "I went with Harlan to the morgue that night—to identify Sarah's body. When you and I went there, you asked what woman I was seeing—"

"And you told me she was someone special. She was the reason you got involved," Caron said. "I remember when we first met, I sensed someone you loved had been abducted."

"That's true." He forced himself to meet her gaze. "But that isn't why I got involved."

She frowned. She could stop him now. She knew he'd torched the building Sarah had died in, but Parker needed this; his conscience needed soothing.

"For a year, I've been on a case. Trying to prove a woman committed fraud. Harlan had a sixth sense about people. He was sure this woman was guilty. And he was sure that her interference had cost Sarah her life."

Parker sighed. "I wasn't sure. Not at first. But the longer I watched her, the more convinced I became...for a while. Then I got to know her. And the more I learned about her, the more certain I became that she wasn't a fraud."

He looked at Caron.

"You're talking about me? You thought I was the fraud? You— Oh, God, no! Not you, too! Parker, not you, too!"

"Please, just listen. Please, Caron."

"I don't want to hear this. Please!" She cupped her hands over her ears. "I don't want to hear this!"

"I learned that you weren't, Caron. I learned that you're warm and loving and beautiful. That you'd never do anything to hurt anyone."

He hated the hurt he saw in her, the way she clenched her hand into a fist and pressed it against her chest.

"Caron, please... I watched you in Midtown. I never saw any sign that you were psychic. If you'd been me, what would you have thought?"

She grew still. So still that it frightened him. He wanted to reach for her, to beg for forgiveness, to do whatever he had to do to get them through this together. "Scream at me, Caron. Hit me. Do anything and everything that you need to do to get rid of the hurt. Just don't leave me."

"You said," she began, then paused and swallowed. "You said that you didn't believe it. Harlan did. Why didn't he investigate?"

Parker hated telling her this most of all. He knew Caron. She'd feel responsible, which was why, he imagined, Sanders hadn't told her before now.

But for this truth, too, the time had come. "Harlan called me one morning," Parker said, feeling no desire to tell her that Harlan had called last Christmas. "He was reaching out for help, only I didn't realize it. He loved Sarah very much. I thought the things he was saying were part of the normal grieving process. I thought it was the grief, Caron. I never thought..."

The last of the police cars pulled away from the curb. Guilt swirling in his stomach, Parker pressed their linked hands against his mouth. "Harlan committed suicide that day."

She moved her hand to his face. Tears coursed down her cheeks. "It wasn't your fault."

"I know that now. But I felt it was then. That's why I starting checking on you. That's why—"

"I understand. It hurts, Parker, and I won't lie and say it doesn't. But you didn't know me. All you knew was that your partner had lost his wife—a woman you loved. And then you lost your partner." Caron gave him a watery smile. "You didn't want anyone else to lose."

A lump of emotion lodged in his throat. "You forgive me?"

"I'm not Peggy Shores, Parker." She sniffled and stroked his jaw. "I love you."

He pulled her into his arms, planted fast and furious kisses on her lips, her eyes, on the tears on her cheeks.

"Ahem."

They both looked toward the sound and saw Mr. Mud Boots, who lived around the corner. "Ina says you two should come inside. She's got breakfast ready."

Her arms wrapped around Parker's neck, Caron cocked her head. "Are you Mr. Klein?"

"Sure am." He lifted a bushy gray brow. "Jasper." He scratched his head. "My wife don't know you two were the ones necking in the car out front of the house, though. And I told Ina not to tell her." He winked and walked back toward the house. "That'll be our secret."

Caron smiled and predicted, "He'll tell her."

"Yep."

"Parker," she said, rubbing that darling curl at his ear around her finger. "I've been thinking."

"Oh?" He sounded wary.

"We make a good team."

"Oh, no. No more partners for me, Caron."

"Why not?" She gave the curl an indignant little flip. "We solved the case."

"Yeah, we did." He dropped a kiss on the tip of her nose. "But I don't want you to be my partner."

Her heart shattered. He didn't love her. He really didn't love her.

"I want you to be my wife."

She snapped her head up. "You do?"

He nodded.

Her spirit soared. She bit the smile from her lip. "I don't know about marriage, Parker. You bust a lot of doors."

"Only when they're locked."

"Closed," she said. "My bedroom door was closed, not locked."

"Okay, closed." He gave her a sheepish look that was totally fake. "But you were on the other side of it."

"True." She nipped at his chin. "Still, you're awfully impulsive."

"Impulsive?" He looked genuinely surprised. "Me?"

"You." He was darling. So very darling. "Didn't you charge over the night Sandy left that message on my door?"

"You were in danger. What would you have me do?"

"You forgot your shirt."

"Geez, Caron." He raked his hand through his hair, stopped midway, and slid her a suspicious look. "What are you doing?"

She laughed. "I'm giving you time, you big oaf, to remember the one thing you've forgotten to say."

He cast her a blank look.

She rolled her gaze heavenward. "You love me, Parker."

He shrugged. "Of course."

"Fine." She stood and dusted the grass from her rear.

"What did I do wrong now?"

"Nothing."

"You're tight-jawed."

"Of course I am." She kept walking.

He grabbed her arm and swung her around. "I want to settle this," he said. "What's it going to take?"

Satisfied, she poked him in the chest. "We're getting married." Caron snorted. "Somebody's got to keep you straight. You do have a knack for rationalizing deceptions, Parker. Stealing books and breaking into evidence rooms.'' She grunted her disapproval. "I'm the only woman I know who can make you toe the line. Besides, your mother's been great, letting me borrow her clothes and everything. The least I can do is to give her the grandchildren *you've* neglected to give her.''

"Another haranguing woman, nagging me for babies. Just what I need." He scowled. "How many?''

"Two, I think—after we've practiced for a while. We've mastered kissing, but we still have a long way to go.''

His eyes softened to that warm and wonderful dove gray. Melting inside, Caron plucked a dead leaf from his sleeve. "And we'll work together, too. No, don't glare. It won't change my mind. We *will* work together, Parker. But only when I image.''

"Okay.'' The scowl he clung tenaciously to faded.

"No other women. Not ever.''

He let out a frustrated sigh. "I love *you*, Caron.''

She smiled and wrapped her arms around his neck. "That's all I've been waiting to hear.''

He dipped his head toward hers. "You've been waiting for convincing.''

"True. Trust is a fragile thing, Parker.'' She lifted her face for his kiss. "But I trust you.''

Ina called out from the back door. "Parker, Caron, you children come on in now, you hear? These eggs is getting cold and tough as shoe leather. I ain't being blamed for no leathery eggs this morning, and I ain't redoing 'em. I got a Christmas dinner to get on the stove.''

"She recovers fast,'' Parker muttered under his breath.

"She's got a thing for Fred.'' Caron fingered Parker's lapel. "Where's Fred spending Christmas?''

"Oh, no. No matchmaking, Caron, and I mean it.''

"Honey.'' Caron wrapped her arm around Parker's waist and slunk against him. "I want everyone happy today.''

Ina ducked out again. "Seeing's how you're the one what knocked it down, you'd best get this door fixed before dark, Parker Simms. Dang thing wasn't even locked. Didn't Charley teach you nothing about turning knobs, boy?''

"All right, Ina." Parker laughed. "Just let me kiss my fiancée one more time. It's Christmas, you know."

"Fiancée?" Ina stuck her head back through the doorway. "Well, I'll be switched. If that don't make me as happy as a dead pig in the sunshine." She cupped her hands to her mouth and shouted over the fence. "Did you hear that, Lily Mae? The smoochers are getting married!"

"She heard," Parker told her. "Everyone in a five-block radius heard."

"How happy is a dead pig, do you think?" Caron waggled her brows at him.

Ina stopped, then wagged the dishtowel in their direction. "I'm old, not senile, and I ain't deaf, either. I know good and well what day it is. It's Christmas."

"I'll call Fred," Parker whispered. "He'll mellow her."

"You're a soft touch, Simms."

"Yeah, I have my moments." Parker rubbed her nose with his. "Merry Christmas, honey."

It would be merry. Together, they'd moved out of the past and beyond the misty shadow. Caron smiled. "Merry Christmas, Parker." And she kissed his lips.

*   *   *   *   *